Wonder a
Chance's ey

Kyndal wanted to touch him the way she had the first time they'd made love. A lover's touch. One last time.

The stubble along his jaw deepened in the hazy light. She drew the back of her fingers through it a couple of times, enjoying the way the scratchy texture left a tingle on her skin.

Their gazes locked and she answered the question in his eyes. "You had some dust in your whiskers."

She read the almost imperceptible movement in his body. The slight bend of his torso toward her in invitation. He was going to try to kiss her, but she couldn't let that happen.

She'd loved him, and he'd left her. She wouldn't travel that road again.

Dear Reader,

Perhaps you've heard of Mammoth Cave? Kentucky, my native state, is littered with caves. Mammoth Cave is the most famous, but smaller ones honeycomb beneath the surface of much of the land area.

Some of my high school friends happened upon a cave near Kentucky Lake, and four of us set out one day to explore it. Armed with only two flashlights and the mindset of teenage invincibility, we were totally naive to the dangers that might lurk there. We thought it was a cool thing to do. And it was! Stepping into the total blackness of those new surroundings was like stepping into another world. We squeezed through crevices and crawled through passages like giant earthworms, somehow managing to find our way back to the entrance at day's end.

My memories of that day are vivid and still wildly exciting even these many years later, so when I started pondering a unique setting for a novel, the idea of the cave took over my imagination and wouldn't let go. Former high school sweethearts Kyndal Rawlings and Chance Brennan needed to get reacquainted. The cave was the perfect place for their reunion.

Whether your preferences lean toward the outdoor recreation region of Kentucky Lake or the rolling hills around Lexington, the Bluegrass State is an enchanting place you'll want to visit—along with my website, www.pamelahearon.com.

Until next time,

Pamela Hearon

Out of the Depths

PAMELA HEARON

Recycling programs for this product may not exist in your area.

ISBN-13: 978-0-373-71799-6

OUT OF THE DEPTHS

This edition published by arrangement with Harlequin Books S.A.

For questions and comments about the quality of this book please contact us at Customer_eCare@Harlequin.ca.

www.Harlequin.com

Printed in U.S.A.

ABOUT THE AUTHOR

Pamela Hearon lived thirty-one years in western Kentucky before love with a handsome Yankee lured her away. She and her husband raised their family of three children and several cats while she taught English to quirky eighth-graders. Life has taught her that, no matter the location, small-town America has a charm all its own—a place where down-to-earth people and heartwarming stories abound. And, although the Midwest is now home, Kentucky still holds a generous piece of Pamela's heart. When it's time to tell her stories, the voice in her head has a decidedly Southern drawl.

To my parents,
Arnold and Jo Hearon, with love.

CHAPTER ONE

THE INTERCOM BUZZED like a trapped insect, and Chance's mind immediately shot to items he could use to put the old thing out of its misery. When he became a judge, his gavel would top the list.

"Sorry to bother you again, Mr. Brennan. Sheriff Blaine on line three." Despite having fielded hundreds of calls during the day, Alice sounded as fresh as she had at eight that morning.

Chance took the opportunity to stretch his back and shoulders as he swallowed the last bite of a turkey club. "Thanks, Alice. Now, please, go on home. It's late." Before she could hang up, he added, "I hope your dad's surgery goes well Monday. If you need anything, just let me know."

"I will, Mr. Brennan, and thanks again for all your help. Good night."

"Night, Alice. See you Wednesday." Chance punched the button to line three, leaving the phone on speaker. "Hey, Buck. What's going on?"

A frustrated sigh exploded in his ear.

"Caught kids at the cave again, Chance."

Chance bit back the expletives on the tip of his tongue. He didn't have time to deal with the teenagers and their nonsense. "How many?"

"Five. These was having an orgy and smokin' pot. Probably got a stash hidden in there somewhere."

"Which means they'll be back. Or somebody'll be

back." Chance massaged his eyelids with his thumb and forefinger. The constant hassle with kids and the cave was making him doubt his sanity about buying that property, even if it was a prime lakeshore piece. One girl already had stitches from cracking her head on a low overhang. How many more of them getting hurt was it going to take?

"That's what I figure, too. I'll have a look-see tomorrow. Maybe I'll find it or find whoever comes after it."

The sheriff's easy manner didn't fool Chance. If a stash was there, Buck Blaine would find it. His redneck mannerisms conned a lot of people, but underneath the hick exterior beat the heart of a criminal investigator.

"You need me to come to the office?" Chance offered halfheartedly. "I'm still in Paducah, so it'll take a half hour or so, but if you need me…"

Buck's customary chewing gum smacked across the phone line. "Nah, no need. Trespassin's gonna be the least of these kids' problems. We can hold off on the paperwork till tomorrow."

Chance rubbed his hand down his face, relieved he wouldn't have to add a stop at the sheriff's office to his already late night. "Sounds good to me."

"We've got most of their parents on the way, so I'm gonna make sure these young'uns have had a bad night." Chance could almost feel Buck's laugh vibrating the receiver. "They'll think twice before they visit your place again."

"I don't know, Buck. These kids don't even think about things the first time." With all the secluded areas around Kentucky Lake, it was beyond Chance's comprehension why the damn kids insisted on partying on his property. "Can we keep this out of the paper? If the cave gets any media coverage, kids will likely swarm it again."

"Can do."

"If that state-of-the-art, handy-dandy security system I've ordered ever gets installed, you may be out of a job."

The sheriff gave a gritty chuckle. "I can only wish, but I doubt it. The Bible promises the ignorant are with us always, you know. Or somethin' like that."

"Amen, brother." Chance raised his soda in a toast. "I've seen enough frivolous lawsuits to know ignorance is a certainty."

"You got that right. See you tomorrow?"

"I'll be there. Night, Sheriff."

"Good evenin', Chance."

Chance hung up and looked at all the piles of paper covering his desk. The call had broken his concentration. Getting back into the wearisome Davenport case seemed unlikely now, even if his dad did expect the finished briefs by Sunday. He'd have to wait until he could see it with fresh eyes. Tomorrow.

He glanced at his watch, noting it was after nine. Friday night and still in the office. "Brennan, you need a life." He wadded up the sandwich wrapper and pitched it into the trash.

His mom had tried to warn him what it would be like, tried to make him see joining his dad's practice wasn't a good idea. Bill Brennan had never accepted anything but perfection from his sons. Perfection had come easily for Hank but seemed always just out of Chance's reach.

"'Ah, but a man's reach should exceed his grasp, or what's a heaven for?'" Chance read the plaque on his office wall, a gift from his dad.

Those kids at the cave needed such a parent. One who cared enough to kick their asses if they acted stupid.

Then again, those kids at the cave would probably kick back. Kids were different now. He smiled at the memory of Old Man Turner showing up with a gun and running

Kyndal and him off of his property. One look down the barrel of that shotgun made sure they wouldn't be back.

If Old Man Turner were still alive, Chance would hire him as a guard for a month or two. But he doubted that tactic would work on these kids. They weren't nearly as naive as he and Kyndal had been.

Kyndal Rawlings. At one time, he'd thought the two of them would be together forever. Now *that* was naive. Their separate ways had turned out to be in entirely different directions. She hadn't gone to law school the way she'd always planned…had become a photographer, of all things—working for some damn liberal environmentalist website. Of course, she did stage that sit-in against hot dogs in the high school cafeteria claiming they were made from throwaway parts, so maybe the clues were there all along, and he was just too smitten to see them.

He hadn't thought about Kyndal in a while. In fact, he'd pretty much refused to let himself think about her since they'd split. When he did, guilt still gnawed at him. Breaking up with her had been almost as hard as losing Hank, but it was the right thing to do, damn it. That was obvious now. He would never have made it through college and law school if they'd stayed joined at the hip. Every class together was unhealthy, but Kyn couldn't loosen her hold. She demanded his total attention.

Just as his career did now.

If he wanted a judgeship by the time he turned forty, there was little room for dating.

But someday, the right woman would come along. Someone goal-oriented. Career focused. Someone with an impeccable reputation and a drive to match his own. A few connections to sweeten the deal wouldn't be a bad thing, either.

He'd straightened the scattered papers and had switched

off the desk lamp when the intercom buzzed again, startling him, ratcheting up his wish to sledgehammer the damn thing.

"Chance?" His dad's voice boomed over the line.

"Yeah, Dad?"

"Good. I was afraid you'd left already. Your mom just called. The travel agent got us on an earlier flight Sunday morning. Can you get those briefs to me tomorrow?"

"Okay. I'll finish them up tonight." As if he had a choice. His parents' first trip away together in years. Only three days, but it was a start. He switched the lamp back on.

"And I want you to take this new Farley case. Look over it. We'll discuss it first thing Wednesday morning."

"I'll be ready."

"Seeing Denise this weekend?"

"No."

"You're a fool. Someone's going to snatch her up."

"If I'm lucky." Denise Macomb was the flavor-of-the-month his dad was trying to cram down his throat. She met all the criteria, but her voice sounded like a violin badly played.

"Get those briefs done," his dad said by way of parting.

Chance watched the intercom light switch off. "You have a life, Brennan." He sighed and ran his hand through his hair. "And this is it."

SNAP...SNAP...SNAP. Three good shots before the tiny bottom lip started to pucker again.

Thank you, Lord, for digital cameras and comfortable shoes. Kyndal's third straight day of twelve-hour shifts was almost over.

"I think we got her." She smiled at the young couple hovering nearby, only now truly noticing them.

The young man's shirt had Ted's Car Wash stamped

on the pocket. His zit-covered face suggested he couldn't be much more than seventeen. A chunky high school ring hung from a chain around the girl's neck.

Kyndal sized them up, knew immediately they were here for the free 8x10 and wouldn't be able to afford any of the great package deals Shop-a-Lot offered at a bargain price of $29.95.

She watched the way they handled the infant so carefully, saw the pride shining in the boy's eyes as he kissed his baby girl and his baby girlfriend on their foreheads. How long before he'd be out of this picture?

"Come over here and you can see the shots." Kyndal swiveled the freestanding monitor to face the couple.

The best part of this job was getting to see the parents' eyes when the portraits clicked on. Without exception, they all softened instantly. If only she could capture that moment on film, those images would be priceless.

The shots were better than good, and Kyndal watched the parental expressions turn fretful when they realized they had to choose.

"They're all so precious. Can we get all three, Danny?" The young mother's voice held little hope, but the blue of her eyes shone intensely like the stone in the ring around her neck.

The young man's head dropped, and he lowered his voice. "We can't afford 'em, Lisa. We can only get the free one."

Kyndal remembered the glow on her own mom's face when friends admired the free 8x10 of Kyndal at twenty-eight months. She would go on and on about Kyndal's smile looking "just like her daddy's."

Mason Rawlings had walked out of their lives a month after that portrait was taken, but her mom still talked about his smile to this day.

I might have his smile, but that's the only thing I ever got from him. She couldn't help wondering if he had any regrets.

Life wasn't easy for teen parents—nor was growing up as the child of one as Kyndal knew firsthand.

She sighed in resignation, aware she was about to give these kids a break and forfeit her last three hours' commission in the process. "Which one would you like? I'll print it for you." She allowed her mouth to droop into a pout of feigned preoccupation, tried to sound bored, glanced at her watch to let them know it was closing time.

The girl chewed her bottom lip until the young man prodded her with his elbow. "Number three."

Kyndal pressed a key and pretended to be busy as she fumbled with some order forms. She turned back as the paper slipped from the printer. "Oh, shoot! I've printed billfolds of the wrong one. Here, you can have these." She held the prints out to the young man, but he hesitated. "No charge," she assured him. "I'll just have to throw them away."

"Now." She hit another key, queuing up number two to print as two 4x6's. "You said number two, right?"

"No, we said number three." The young man gave her a look that could have indicated she'd sprouted an extra nose.

"Crap. I've done it again." She watched their guarded looks of amusement as she thrust the second sheet toward them and sighed dramatically. "Third time's a charm, right?"

Another keystroke sent the correct command, and the 8x10 slid from the printer. "She really is a doll." Kyndal checked the finished product before handing it over. "Sorry for the inconvenience."

The lights blinked, indicating five minutes until closing

time. The couple moved toward the exit, the young mother clutching the photographs to her chest.

Kyndal watched until they were out of earshot. "And that's why I have to get back to a job where I can shoot golden eagles instead of golden-haired toddlers." The hope that tomorrow would bring that dream job back was never far from the surface. She let it rise to the top as she disassembled the gear and lugged everything to her car.

Tomorrow will bring the perfect shot that will make me somebody. Tomorrow will bring the perfect shot that will make me somebody. The mantra couldn't block out the sluggish start of the old Jeep's engine, but if she said it often enough, it had to come true. That's what affirmations were for.

When she reached her apartment, fatigue convinced her to leave everything in the car except her laptop. Dover, Tennessee, wasn't a hot spot for crime. In fact, Dover, Tennessee, wasn't a hot spot for anything. But it was centrally located between the other two towns where she took family portraits on Wednesdays and Thursdays, and the apartment she rented was clean. And cheap.

She'd tossed a package of ramen noodles into some water before she saw the message light blinking on the phone.

The light always brought the same thought to her mind. *This could be the big one.* Her hand shook as she pressed the voice mail button.

"Kyn. It's Mom. Going on a little road trip with Lloyd for a few days. Talk to you later."

Lloyd who? When did a Lloyd come into the picture? And "a few days" meant she'd quit her job at the dog kennel. Or gotten fired. Kyndal swallowed her frustration and sent a mental warning to the little girl she had photographed at closing time: *Being a parent to your forty-four-year-old mother is not an easy row to hoe.*

She deleted the message, but the light blinked again, indicating a second message.

"Hey, Kyndal." Mike Sloan's southern drawl oozed from the handset. "Heard about a tourism magazine startin' up in your hometown. Sounds like a good fit for you. Gimme a call."

A job opportunity? In Paducah? She grabbed the phone and had half of Mike's number punched in before logic reared its head. Would it be wise to trust the man whose dumb-ass moves had caused her to be blacklisted for the past six months? He and his shady contacts ultimately caused the lawsuit that became the demise of the True Tennessee website—and her own reputation by association.

But his intentions had been good. She punched another button. He was trying to make things up to her.

Four years of eye-opening, truth-seeking public awareness of pollution in the Cumberland River brought down by an asinine lawsuit over a totally unnecessary hack job. Her stomach tightened at the memory.

But it turned completely over at the thought of many more ramen noodle suppers. The ten-cent price had made them a staple when she was growing up, but she'd always dreamed adulthood would bring better fare. And it had for a few short years. Then it was back to ramen noodles—just like Mom used to fix.

But someday her luck would change when she found that perfect shot.

The lure of landing a magazine job and splurging on a carry-out pizza won out over the anxiety of talking with Mike. She dialed the rest of his number, keeping one eye on the pot on the stove.

"Hel-lo?" he drawled.

"Hey, Mike. It's Kyndal. Got your message." She hurried on, trying to move the conversation directly to the point. "So, you've heard about a new magazine starting up?"

"Hey, Kyndal darlin'. How you been?"

"I'm still getting by. Not getting rich, but paying the bills." Thanks to the savings she'd put away during the four good years at True Tennessee. "A tourism magazine out of Paducah, huh?"

"Yep. Outdoor magazine about your beloved old Kentucky home."

Her heart beat faster. Four years of Nashville had been exciting and fun, but city life wasn't her thing, and it was way too expensive after the website went under. Dover was too far at the other end of the spectrum, though. Moving back to Paducah and Kentucky Lake…now *that* was a dream worth having.

"You still shootin' brats at the five-and-dime?" His words came out slightly garbled by the cigar he inevitably kept in his mouth.

"Well, I've wanted to shoot a few, but so far, all I've done is photograph them. You still smoking those cheap-ass cigars?"

Mike's laughed turned into a vicious cough. She waited for it to subside then launched her next tactic to get him on the subject.

"Tell me about the magazine quick before those things kill you."

"Okay, darlin', don't go gittin' your bowels in an uproar. Here's the deal. You remember Charlie Short?"

Kyndal dredged up a memory of a squatty fellow with a bad toupee. "Yeah, I remember him."

"The state's contracted with him for a quarterly tourism deal showin' the natural wonders of Kentucky. Now, while *I* think that means its women, the guys callin' the shots are looking more for landscape. Seasonal photos and whatnot. I thought of you. On both accounts."

"I'm sure you did, you old codger." Sixty-eight years old with four divorces under his belt and a huge beer belly over it, Mike Sloan would forever be a player in his own mind. "Quit flirting and stick to business. What's Charlie Short wanting? Anything particular I can impress him with?" She stirred the flavor powder into the noodles.

"Caves."

She stopped stirring. Had she heard him right? "Caves?" She moved the pot away from the heat and turned off the burner.

"Yep. Apparently, Kentucky's loaded with them. Not well-known ones like Mammoth Cave. Small caves. Ones that might have had historical significance or are just interesting in formation. Know of any you could shoot, like quick? He's wantin' to make a decision pretty soon. Maybe the next week or so."

Kyndal's chest tightened, and she took a deep breath, letting it out slow and controlled. "Yeah." Her voice cracked, and she cleared her throat. "I know of one. I can go shoot it tomorrow."

"You're not workin' tomorrow?"

She responded to the sadness in his voice with enthusiasm in her own. "Five to nine, Tuesday. Nine to nine, Wednesday, Thursday and Friday. A forty-hour week with time left for freelance work. Or days at other Shop-a-Lots if I can find some that want me."

Mike sighed, which led into a loud cough followed by a wheeze that probably saved her from further comments. "Here's his email address."

She took down the information. "Does Charlie know about…"

"Yes, darlin', he knows about the lawsuit and that you had nothing to do with any of the shenanigans…just got caught in the cross fire. Says he doesn't give a damn as long as your shots are good. So this may be the chance to get your good name back."

"Your lips to God's ears, Mike." Hope flickered at his words. "Thanks. I owe you one"

"No." He gave another long, remorseful sigh. "I owe *you* one, and I hope this is it. See ya."

"Bye." He was already gone.

She poured the noodles into a colander to drain and checked the fridge for nonexistent butter.

So the cave was drawing her back. Chance's special place. Their special place. The place he'd taken her after his brother Hank's funeral. The place where they cried out all their anguish, clung to each other for hours and finally lost their virginity. Tears stung her eyes at the bittersweet memory.

Could she face the cave now?

It might be good for her. Give her closure. Let her put the Chance Brennan chapter of her life behind her for good.

Chance Brennan. She closed her eyes and gave in to a minute of nostalgia. Black, curly hair. Eyes like rich espresso. Full lips that made her lick her own just thinking about them.

Theirs was one of the great love legends of Paducah Tilghman High School those two years. Most-Likely-to-Succeed and the varsity quarterback. Poor girl, rich boy. Government-subsidized housing versus country club estates. An unlikely yet somehow compatible pairing—to everyone except Chance's dad.

She could still see the relief in his dad's eyes when Chance got his acceptance letter from Harvard and she didn't. Bill Brennan never thought she was quite good enough for his son. If he'd known how serious things had gotten between them, he probably would have sent Chance to a military school his senior year.

An involuntary shudder shook her. How careless they'd been about unprotected sex that day in the cave. Jaci had her convinced she couldn't get pregnant the first time. Some best friend. It was a miracle they didn't end up like her mom and Mason. Or those kids in the store tonight. Where would they be but for a little bit of luck?

Probably back in Paducah, eating at Max's Café instead of having ramen noodles. She scanned her spice rack for nothing particular.

Chance was back in Paducah, practicing law with his dad, according to Jaci. That news came as no surprise.

What would it be like to have a life like that? Being somebody from the day you were born? Having money for everything you needed? A ready-made career? Parents who were around?

There was the rub, of course. Repayment for Chance came in the form of having to put up with Bill Brennan's constant presence.

Kyndal took a bite, but the noodles had lost their flavor. She gave the mixture a heavy dousing of pepper and took another bite.

Tomorrow will bring the perfect shot....

A warm tingle ran up her spine. She wasn't sure if the cause was the pepper or the thought of going back to the cave. No way would she let it be because of Chance Brennan.

She would show him…and his dad…show them all.

She was going to be somebody.

CHAPTER TWO

"WHERE YOU HEADED SO early on a Saturday morning? The LBL?" Mrs. Crain set the large to-go cup on the counter.

Kyndal nodded as she counted out the exact change, feeling guilty she'd forgotten to include coffee on her grocery list. "I'm gonna take The Trace through the Land Between the Lakes and try to get some shots of the bison or elk. Then I'm going around to the Kentucky Lake side to a cave."

Mrs. Crain's eyebrows knitted in disapproval. "You taking anybody with you?"

"No, ma'am." Kyndal shrugged sheepishly. She'd given up trying to make people understand that a photographer had to take chances sometimes. A male photographer was considered brave or adventuresome. A woman was just dumb.

"Caves can be dangerous, you know. Couple of boys disappeared in one around Carlisle a few years back. They was never seen again." Mrs. Crain popped open a sack and slid a quiche-filled puff pastry inside. "A tiny thing like you hadn't got any business traipsing alone around some cave." She rolled the top down tightly and held it out. "Here. Take this."

"Mrs. Crain, I don't want you to—" Kyndal protested.

"Stick it in your knapsack. If you get lost in that cave, least you'll have some sustenance."

The hair on Kyndal's neck prickled at the words. She

hadn't considered the cave would bring on anything more dangerous than a severe bout of oversentimentality. She gave a nervous laugh. "Don't you be worrying about me. I'm not going exploring. Just getting some shots for my portfolio."

She took the sack and held it to her nose, catching the warm scent of the rosemary Mrs. Crain used in her pastry. "Mmm. Thanks, Mrs. C., but this won't make it to my backpack. I'll have to gobble it up while it's hot." She lifted her coffee in salute as she backed out the door of the little bakery.

"White beans and corn bread if you're back in time for lunch," Mrs. Crain called as the door closed.

Kyndal climbed in the Jeep that was still running and flipped the heater off. She'd just wanted to take the chill off the October morning, but the coffee coupled with the down vest and thermal top left her toasty.

She shrugged out of the vest as she pulled from the parking lot onto The Trace, the road which cut through the heart of the Land Between the Lakes. The sleepy little Tennessee burg of Dover was ideally located five miles east of the southern entrance to the LBL. What better location for a photographer than a two-hundred-and-sixty-square-mile stretch of government wildlife preserve almost literally at her back door? With Kentucky and Barkley Lakes as its western and eastern boundaries, the LBL was an outdoorsman's paradise.

She munched on the free quiche as she debated whether or not to spend the five bucks to drive through the Elk and Bison Prairie. Twenty-three dollars was all she had left of this week's budget, but that should be enough if Mom didn't call again needing to borrow some.

Twenty miles into the LBL, she threw a kiss at the sign telling her she was in Kentucky. By the time she reached the entrance of the prairie, she'd convinced herself it was not only worth the price but a necessity. How many photographers east of the Mississippi got a chance to shoot elk—and the chance to visit with her favorite ranger—for the bargain price of five dollars?

Rick Warren's tall form, silhouetted against the early morning sun, brought a smile to her lips. A former marine, he still had that military look: straight posture, broad squared shoulders, blond crew cut…and a gentleman in every way.

Jaci saw it as an omen her husband's friend from college had taken a job in western Kentucky. She was convinced Rick and Kyndal were a perfect match and had been relentlessly trying to hook them up.

Not that Kyndal would mind a hook-up with the handsome ranger. Under the guise of photographer, she'd become a regular on the hikes he led—The Snake Crawl, The Night Prowl, The Eagle Watch—but it wasn't until The Owl Outing two weeks ago that she'd been certain he was interested in her…or anything other than deer droppings.

As the only person to show up in the drizzle, she'd shared two hours alone with the hot, but *very* mannerly, ranger. The evening had been quite chaste, but she and Jaci held out hope. Rick Warren definitely had potential—if she could break through that reserved exterior.

Rick's smile spread as she approached the guardhouse and rolled her window down. The cool air brought a rosy glow to his cheeks, lending him an additional boyish charm.

"Morning, Ms. Rawlings." His strong drawl warmed her twice as fast as the coffee had.

"Morning, Ranger Rick." She watched his dimples deepen at the nickname.

He glanced at his watch. "You're out early on a Saturday morning."

"Living in Dover doesn't give much reason to be out late on Friday night." She shrugged and gave an overly dramatic sigh. "Getting up early on Saturday's not too difficult."

"I know what you mean. In Camden, they roll the sidewalks up at nine."

Kyndal laughed. "At least Camden's got sidewalks."

Rick wiggled his eyebrows a couple of times as his blue-green eyes held hers. "I hear Clarksville leaves its sidewalks out all night on Saturday. Maybe we should have dinner together and check it out."

"Why, Ranger Rick." Kyndal tilted her head in question. "That sounds like you're asking me out on a date."

"Well, it's only a date if you accept. If you decline, it was a humiliating attempt at humor." He coughed, an awkward little sound that sent white puffs of breath into the morning air, and the color of his cheeks intensified.

Kyndal squinted, trying to look serious. "You know, Rick. In spite of our mutual friends and all those hikes we've been on, I hardly know you. You're not an axe murderer, are you?"

"No, ma'am." He shook his head.

"In that case, I accept. And it's about time."

His shoulders dropped into a more relaxed position. When he tipped his broad-brimmed hat back, she noticed the faint wisp of sweat on his brow. "The department's got two more weeks of Saturday night Ghosts and Goblins Tours, so I won't be free until November. Can I call you then?"

Kyndal fished her wallet out of her purse and found the stash of business cards tucked in the side pocket. "I didn't make it into the phone book, so here's my number." She handed it to him, along with the five-dollar entrance fee. "I'll look forward to dinner."

He tucked the card into his shirt pocket but shook his head at the money. "Accepting a date with a ranger should have some perks." He motioned toward the stretch of road leading into the prairie. "Now be careful in there. It's mating season, you know."

His wink sent a surge into areas of her body that had lain dormant far too long. She gave him a flirty wave as she pulled away.

The drive through the prairie turned out to be a lucrative venture. Within forty-five minutes, she photographed two bull elk with their antlers intertwined in a struggle for supremacy, an eagle perched on a massive stump, bison in various stages of leisure and another bull elk nuzzling a female about the ears and neck. He tried to mount her once, but she moved away.

"You're gonna have to give her more foreplay, big guy," Kyndal murmured as she clicked off her shots.

On her way out, she stopped at the guardhouse to show Rick the scenes she'd caught on her digital camera.

He gave a low whistle of approval. "You have that artist's eye. My pictures always turn out terrible. Heads cut off or out of focus."

"Well, maybe I can give you some lessons sometime."

Rick handed the camera back through the window. "I'd like that." A subtle nuance in his tone made her think he wasn't talking about photography. The idea caused her hand to quiver under the weight of the camera. "So where you headed now?"

"I'm going to shoot a cave on the western side of the lake."

A crease formed on Rick's forehead. "You're going spelunking? By yourself?"

"Not spelunking." Kyndal kept her voice light. "No crawling around through narrow passages. Just going through some rooms near the entrance and taking a few shots."

A car turned into the reserve and headed toward the security gate.

"Well, I know caves, and they can be dangerous. You be careful," he said.

She nodded and waved a quick goodbye as she pulled away. Jaci would be thrilled!

Pleasant daydreams of Rick occupied her mind through the drive to the northern exit of The Trace. It wasn't until she crossed Kentucky Dam to the western shore of Kentucky Lake that she realized she didn't know exactly where she was going.

She was relatively sure she could hike to the cave through the woods from the nearby boat ramp, the way Chance had taken her the first time. She still remembered her awe at the size of the cave. A network of small caverns connected by narrow passageways, some so low, crawling was the only way through. She'd felt as if she was roaming through a gigantic block of Swiss cheese. They'd gone back a second time, taking a road that dead-ended close to the mouth of the cave.

Try as she might, she couldn't get her brain to remember enough details to know where that turnoff would be. She'd have to take her chances with the hike through the woods.

When she pulled into the parking lot for the boat ramp, littered with trucks pulling trailers, her heart crawled into her throat.

This cove had been Chance's favorite fishing hole, and he always swore someday he'd own the piece of property flanking the southern rim. They'd spent so many days out on Kentucky Lake in his little rowboat—fishing, picnicking, occasionally sneaking one of his dad's beers into the cooler, making out on the beach. Fishing became her favorite sport that summer although she never picked up a pole.

During one of Chance's fishing trips without her, he'd found the cave. His plan had been to show it to Hank, but he never got the opportunity.

Kyndal took in the small cove, surrounded on three sides by the reds and oranges of fall foliage and the dark blue of the lake beyond. She breathed a deep, contented sigh. Some things in her life had changed greatly over the past nine years, but this site hadn't changed one bit.

With that assurance, she armed herself with her camera bag and backpack and headed through the woods. Her heart pumped fast. She loved being outdoors on a mission, a world of possibilities before her.

Dew still clung to the leaves underfoot, and she made the passage almost in silence. Even if she hadn't been able to see the lake as she climbed the hill toward the gray limestone bluff, she would've known it was there. Mist lay low in places where the sun hadn't yet reached, and a pungent fishy odor hung in the air.

She'd often heard people complain about the stench. Not her. To her, it smelled like home. The lakes. The rivers. Any time she was in Paducah, she drove to the foot of Broadway below the flood wall for a glimpse of the Ohio and Tennessee Rivers that converged there. If she was down or feeling low, she only needed that sight to feel soothed. As long as the rivers were still there, everything would be okay.

The thought put a spring in her step as she mounted the steep incline to the bluff. Coming to the cave this morning was the right thing to do. She could feel it. She would get her photos and get this job. The date with Rick was a sign.

Kyndal crossed the ridge to the plateau that held the

entrance to the cave and stopped dead in her tracks, reading the large signs posted to nearby trees. No Trespassing! Violators Will Be Prosecuted.

Evidently Mr. Turner, the old codger, was still around. Should she try to find his house and get permission?

She didn't remember seeing a house anywhere in the vicinity. Even if she found it, there was no guarantee he wouldn't turn down her request.

The only chance she had at this job was photographs of a cave.

She edged toward the entrance, half expecting an alarm to trigger, yet feeling pretty certain that fear was absurd. Who ever heard of an alarm on a cave?

She checked the trees for surveillance cameras. Unless they were hidden in squirrel or bird nests, she was unobserved.

She stepped closer. It wasn't as if she was going to hurt anything. She was there out of appreciation for the beauty, not to mar it in any way. Freedom of the press should bring nature's delights to everyone, not just those who could afford to be landowners.

Her indignation pushed her to the mouth of the cave. She could feel the cool dampness of its interior as she leaned her head inside.

She looked at her watch. Twelve after eight. Forty-five minutes would get her all the shots she wanted. She'd be in, out and gone.

Allowing no further debate of the matter, she made her way to the edge of the meager sunlight. She turned the flashlight on and moved through an open crevice from the first cavern into an adjacent one.

Nothing looked familiar, but the primordial green, earthy scent catapulted her back in time. Closing her eyes, she could almost hear echoes of the sobs and sighs and cries of ecstasy she and Chance had left behind nine years ago.

A surge of warmth rushed through her despite the chilly surroundings and a sentimental breath caught in her throat. She scanned the area with her flashlight. So many openings, all probably leading to other rooms. No time for nostalgia.

“Today will bring the perfect shot that will make me somebody.” Her voice slid around the smooth bowl of the cavern and returned to her.

She ducked through an opening into another area, not sure what she was looking for but confident she would know it when she saw it.

Before moving another step, she pulled the masking tape from her backpack and hung a strip from the opening she’d passed through. The afternoon in the cave with Chance taught her more than lessons in life. If he hadn’t unwound a ball of twine to follow back, they might still be here. She chuckled, remembering how pleased he was that Mrs. Cooper’s mythology class had rendered information worth remembering.

Several caverns later, she found what she was looking for. A natural column of sandstone in the middle of the room gave it an interesting feel. She arranged the portable lights from her backpack on each side, in precisely the right spots for dramatic shadows, and clicked away.

When she adjusted one of the lights, her foot knocked it over. As it fell, a brilliant spark of light reflected from the opposite wall. She picked up the lamp and moved it about, tracing the trajectory it took as it fell. There it was again! The light glinted from a horizontal crack in the wall roughly fifteen inches tall, maybe two or three feet wide. The crevice narrowed and turned down at each end, causing her to shudder. It looked like a frown in the face of the wall.

She walked over to examine it more closely. The hole had formed a couple of feet above her head, but even her limited view brought a gasp. The ceiling on the other side appeared to be solid quartz, glittering like millions of diamonds.

The pounding of her heartbeat thudded in her ears. The shot from this angle through the gap was intriguing but from inside that next cavern, aiming up directly at it… She could barely breathe at the thought.

The crevice was large enough to fit through, but reaching it was the problem. Her fingers just bent at the opening if she stretched. Augh! Why did she have to be so short?

She walked around the area, tracing the wall with the beam from her flashlight. The light showed no other way to reach the other side, so she returned to the crack with new determination.

If she jumped, she could get her palms flat onto the facing of the hole. Her arms were strong from lugging around equipment, but the wall was so smooth, she couldn't get any purchase with her boot. After four or five tries, she noticed a bit of scraping left from her feet, though.

She jumped again, trying to suspend herself long enough to batter the soft wall. It worked. Her toe sank in a tad, enough to give her leverage to move an arm deeper through the opening.

Her arms burned and threatened to rip out of their sockets, but she held on and heaved, scrabbling her toes against the wall for any hold she might find.

The rim of the hole was only five or six inches thick, and her fingers soon clasped the inner side. Giving a scream that could have landed her a role in a horror film, she hauled her torso onto the ledge, balancing precariously like a human teeter-totter.

She eased the flashlight out of her pocket and focused the beam into the small room. Her position didn't allow much air into her lungs, and what little was there rushed out at the sight that met her eyes. She'd been wrong. The ceiling wasn't the focal point. The entire room was floor-to-ceiling, wall-to-wall crystals.

The room reminded her of the geodes she'd gathered at the LBL's Geology Station as a kid. On the outside, they looked like lumpy dirt clods, but inside, they were solid crystal. This one was big enough to hold her rather than the other way around.

She'd never imagined a find like this. Shots from inside that cavern were once-in-a-lifetime occurrences and the opportunity she'd waited for her whole life…the one that would make her somebody. Her head whirled with possibilities.

First, she'd have to find a way in and out of there that wouldn't make her dizzy. She lowered herself back to her starting point. Having both feet on the ground helped her think more clearly.

The obvious solution would be a ladder. Nothing too tall. A stepladder would work. But she'd also need a partner. Someone who could pass it through the opening so she could climb out and keep all her equipment safe.

Jaci.

Oh, she'd pitch a fit and whine a lot but eventually she'd agree. Cajoling her would take some time. Kyndal needed to get started right away so they could make it back by early afternoon.

She stuffed her camera and lights into the bag, grabbed her backpack and made a mad dash for the entrance, following the strips of masking tape like beacons.

Once outside, she halted, blinded momentarily by the bright sunlight. She squinted and swallowed great gulps of fresh air.

"Hold it right there, young lady." The voice was male and gruff.

Kyndal let out a frightened yelp and swung around to face a burly man in a sheriff's uniform. She supposed she should be relieved that she wasn't looking down the barrel of a gun, the way she and Chance had years before. Still, the sheriff's presence was nothing to celebrate, not with all the signs posted.

"You got permission to be here?" His tone implied he already knew the answer.

Kyndal's clenched gut warned her not to lie, but it didn't seem prudent to confess that she'd deliberately chosen not to ask for it, either. "Well, no, but—"

"No buts about it. It's clearly posted there's no trespassing." His eyes narrowed suspiciously as he took in her appearance. "What's in the bags?"

"My camera and equipment." Kyndal went for an innocent look, opening her eyes wide. She slid the camera bag into the crook of her arm and started to unzip it.

The sheriff moved quickly for a man his size. In one smooth move he stepped back and drew his gun. "Drop the bags!"

Kyndal's heartbeat shot into overdrive. She released the bags with a thud beside each foot.

The sheriff spoke in a low, no-nonsense tone. "Now put your hands 'hind your head and turn around real slowlike. I'm placing you under arrest."

Kyndal willed her legs to do as he commanded. A violent shiver made the rounds through her body. Under arrest? She'd never been arrested! This was all a mistake. Surely he'd listen to reason. "I'm sorry." She fought to keep the vibration out of her voice. “Really. I was just trying to get some photographs of a cave. I didn’t think the owner would mind.”

A strong grip held her wrist and brought it down to the small of her back. She gasped as cold metal encircled one hand. The same grip on her other arm caused a surge of panic, but the sound of the closing handcuffs brought out sheer anger. Restraints were clearly uncalled for. “I can’t believe this!” Her ears burned with humiliation. “This is all a misunderstanding.”

The sheriff took her bags with one hand and her arm with the other and steered her toward his car. “Well, Miss Unbeliever, let’s get to the office so you can start explaining how you misunderstood all these signs.” A sarcastic chuckle curled his lips into a sneer. “Your English sounds pretty good to me. Now then, you have the right to remain silent. Anything you say can and will be used against you…”

CHAPTER THREE

THE GRAY BRICKS OF THE holding cell reflected Kyndal's mood. Leaning back against the bars allowed a visual escape from *that* part of the reality, and she refused to make contact with the thin mattress on the cot that took up one wall. The only other fixture was a stainless-steel toilet stuck in the back corner. The thought of having to use the odious thing brought bile to her throat. She gripped the sheriff's telephone tighter, trying to bring her nerves under control before she made the call.

When they'd first arrived at the Marshall County Sheriff's Department, a teenage girl had been in the first cell. She was crying softly when the sheriff opened the door leading from his office into the narrow corridor that gave access to the cells. He stopped Kyndal in front of the girl.

"Melody," he barked like a drill sergeant. "You know this woman?"

The girl shook her head and started to bawl. "N-No, sir. Isn't my mom here yet? My stepdad's gonna kill me."

Sheriff Blaine's grip tightened on Kyndal's arm. He marched her past the empty second cell and into the last.

The girl's incessant wailing had frayed Kyndal's nerves to the point where she'd wanted to cry, too, but she'd fought the urge. Tears wouldn't help. From what she'd seen, showing any sign of weakness to Sheriff Blaine was like waving a red flag in front of a bull.

Later, after the sheriff came and removed Melody,

things got eerily quiet for a few short moments. Suddenly, a burst of shouting ensued from the next room, and a man's voice bellowed obscenities Kyndal never knew existed along with "smart-ass bitch," "slut" and "little whore."

Kyndal cringed at the abusive verbal attack. It reminded her of her second stepdad, Hal. Melody's fears of her stepfather's reaction were obviously well-grounded.

A couple of other male voices—Sheriff Blaine's and a deeper one, perhaps a deputy's—tried to calm him down.

Nothing had any effect until the sheriff threatened him with arrest. "We'll be seeing a lot of Melody, and don't think I won't be checking out her condition." Sheriff Blaine's voice had an edge that would slide through metal. "So don't go thinking you're safe to tie into her when you get home. Now go on out front and let's get these papers signed. I'm ready to get the hell finished with you."

The door to the cell block opened. Sheriff Blaine's heavy breathing preceded him down the narrow passage to Kyndal's cell. He glared at her, red-faced, through the bars. "Made that phone call yet?"

She shook her head, momentarily losing her voice.

"Make it quick."

He turned and stalked back down the hall, slamming the door behind him so hard it bounced back open a sliver. Kyndal heard the shuffle of papers and the sound of another door opening and closing. Then silence.

She took a deep breath and dialed Jaci's number. She'd need a ride back to her car. With Mom who-knows-where with the jerk-of-the-month, it would have to be Jaci. If Jaci wasn't home, she'd take her chance walking before she'd get back in the car with Sheriff Blaine. One ride in the sheriff's car was enough for a lifetime.

"Hello?" Thank God.

"Jaci, it's Kyn."

"Hey, Kyn. Bart and I were just talking about you. Thought we'd give you a call and see if you wanted—"

"Jaci, listen." In his present mood, Sheriff Blaine might come jerk the phone out of her hand if she took too long. "I'm at the Marshall County Sheriff's Office in Benton. I've been arrested."

Jaci's voice exploded over the line. "You've what? What in the corn bread hell happened? What'd you do to get arrested?"

"I trespassed." Kyndal kept her voice level, not giving in to her emotions now that she heard a sympathizing voice. "I needed some shots of a cave, so I went to the one…you know. There were no-trespassing signs, but I thought—" Her voice broke, and she stopped to gain control. "Can you come pick me up?"

"I'm on my way." The phone went dead.

The drive from Paducah to Benton would take thirty to forty-five minutes. Kyndal paced the cell and waited, the minutes creeping by.

Twelve forty-three. Seven hours ago, she'd gotten up with the hope of a new job and a world of possibilities. Now she sat in a jail cell, facing a huge fine, at best.

She wouldn't allow herself to ponder the worst-case scenario. What if it hit the newspapers and her name got linked back to the True Tennessee debacle? She might end up photographing kids the rest of her life.

And how much would a fine cost her? Probably more than the fifty-seven dollars left in her checking account. She was loath to dip into the savings she'd put back while working for the website. She'd already had to do it a few times to help out her mom. But a fine—or bail—wouldn't leave her with any choice.

She lambasted herself. How could she have even considered such a prank? Now Old Man Turner—*Mr.* Turner, she corrected herself—would never allow her to go back to shoot the amazing crystal cavern, and she couldn't bring herself to ask about the shots she'd already taken. She'd have to kiss this job goodbye.

As if the money part wasn't bad enough, facing the old codger and confessing her crime still lay ahead of her. They wouldn't let him bring the shotgun, would they? Her face burned, remembering the baleful look in the old guy's eyes.

Would Sheriff Blaine consider a plea bargain? Maybe she could work off the fine in family photographs. Or staff pictures. A holiday calendar, maybe. With the office number to call in case of emergency. The knot in her stomach loosened a smidgen.

Or would he consider the suggestion a bribe and run the cost up even higher? The knot yanked tighter than ever.

While she debated the wisdom of this tactic, male voices and chuckles filtered through the cracked door. Sheriff Blaine and the deputy came back into the office. Evidently, Melody was on her way home.

Kyndal brushed at the dirt on her jeans, trying to make herself as presentable as possible. Climbing the cave wall had left streaks down the front and sides of her clothes. Running her hands down her hair, she could feel how the humidity had wreaked havoc on it.

Maybe the sheriff would feel sorry for her or think her slightly deranged.

The voices moved closer to the door.

"We questioned the kids. They swear they don't know her. The bags turned up nothing. No pot. Not even a trace. She's not who we're looking for."

Kyndal's breath came out in a rush. They thought she'd been making a drug drop!

"Even so, she *was* trespassing in a clearly marked area."

The voice was smooth and deep, and Kyndal's stomach fluttered at the sound of it. She imagined the tall, dark and handsome deputy it might belong to. "Professional photographers know better than to go on someone's property without permission. I mean, she's not the paparazzi, right?"

The words stung.

They laughed together, and Kyndal's eyes burned with indignation. She'd always prided herself on her professionalism. They knew nothing about her or her work. Hadn't they ever had an occasional lapse in judgment for an exciting opportunity? Everybody did. It wasn't a crime. It was part of being human.

Of course, trespassing *was* a crime.

Anger came on the heels of the other emotions. Anger at the sheriff who had the audacity to think she might be connected with drugs.

Anger at the deputy who obviously considered her an amateur.

But mostly, anger at herself, for getting into this asinine situation.

The door to the office opened wide. The sheriff took his time, stopping to peer into the vacant cells before he finally unlocked hers.

"Go on out into my office. We have some questions we want to ask you. Made your call yet?"

Kyndal nodded and handed him the telephone. She took deep, calming breaths as she made her way down the narrow hall and through the door into the sun-brightened office. She squinted at the figure standing by the window.

Not a deputy, unless he was dressed for undercover work. Jeans and a cashmere crewneck? Expensive taste. Her eyes moved up his frame. Tall. Dark. And, from what she could see of his profile, handsome, indeed.

She blinked.

He turned and her eyes met the steeliness of his rock-hard gaze. Her heart made a quick jaunt into her throat and then plummeted to the bottom of her stomach. The face was a bit fuller. The jaw a tad firmer. The hair several inches shorter. But the eyes hadn't changed at all.

"Chance?" Had the sheriff called her a lawyer? Was her situation that serious? She locked her knees to keep them from buckling. "Why are you here?" The words came out startled and clipped—harsher than she would have used in more congenial circumstances.

A number of emotions crossed his features and she read them as easily as she always had. Confusion. Understanding. Amusement.

So he found her predicament amusing? She held back the smile of recognition and greeting that had been on the edges of her lips, keeping her face neutral and composed.

Chance gave a chuckle, and her mind flashed to the deep voice she'd been hearing—the one she thought belonged to a deputy. Chance's. How could she not have recognized it?

His dark eyes danced, and his full mouth turned up slightly at one end as he walked over to her and extended his hand. "It's good to see you, too, Kyndal."

She clasped his hand. "Did they call you to be my attorney?" A tremor moved up her arm when she spoke the last word. His grip tightened and he covered her hand with his other one. The touch was warm and familiar; it should have been comforting, but it wasn't. It made her want to curl up in a fetal ball.

The three worst moments in her life—when Chance broke up with her, when the website got closed and now this. She cringed. The website was the only one that had nothing to do with him.

He gave her a questioning look as his smile broadened. "No, I'm not here to represent you."

His eyes held hers and she was back in Mrs. Cooper's junior English class, meeting his gaze. She pulled her hand free, not wanting to give him the opportunity to feel it tremble again.

Kyndal's mind raced. Why would Chance Brennan be standing there in front of her? He was a lawyer…but he wasn't there to be *her* lawyer. Was he the prosecuting attorney here to press charges? *Oh. My. God!* "Chance, I can explain all this. I wanted to get some shots of a cave and the only one I knew of was the one where we, um…" *Don't bring that up!* Her mouth was moving too fast. She paused to let her brain catch up. "The one we…we went to—on the lake. There were signs posted about trespassing, but I wasn't going to hurt anything." Chance's eyes danced with amusement. Inside, he was laughing at her! "I'm not stupid, like you're thinking."

"Kyndal, I—"

"I know I shouldn't have trespassed." She talked faster to explain before he went into his prosecuting spiel. "I could read the signs. But sometimes *professional* photographers like *me*—" she emphasized the words "—have to take chances to get the shot we need. As long as nobody gets hurt and property doesn't get damaged, it's usually not a problem." She swallowed hard. "My boots might have done a little damage to one of the walls, but tell Mr. Turner I'll be glad to pay for the damage." What if he was unreasonable and tried to make her pay a bunch of money she didn't have? "As long as it's within reason. I mean, is he even approachable?" She bit her bottom lip to keep it from trembling.

"It's okay, Kyn. It's me." Chance reached out. His finger brushed her cheek in a gesture that shook her to her core.

She turned away quickly, not letting him finish. "I know it's you, but you're working for *him*."

A movement caught her attention. The sheriff crossed his arms and leaned against a file cabinet, silently taking this all in. She'd forgotten about him. "Can you get *me* a lawyer?"

His eyebrows shot up at her sudden address, and he shrugged.

"Kyndal." Chance's voice was right behind her and then his hands were on her shoulders, turning her around to face him. "You don't need a lawyer. I won't be pressing charges." The mature take-charge tone of his deeper-than-she-remembered voice screamed the changes in him. He was a man now. With very large, warm hands.

He was studying her, no doubt weighing the girl he had known against the woman before him.

Much as she hated to admit it, she hoped a few years had added more character and wisdom. And she found herself hoping he found those traits attractive. Not that it made any difference, of course. But she did hope he didn't sigh with relief at his lucky escape.

No sigh. An appreciative smile instead. "I'm the owner, Kyn. I own that land, cave and all."

His hands dropped to his sides, and her temperature dropped a few degrees at the loss of his touch. But the cooling-off period lasted only until his words sank in. He was the owner! He should've told her that first thing. Instead, he'd been having fun at her expense. Her cheeks burned with humiliation. "You've been enjoying this, haven't you?" She lit into him full force. "Seeing me squirm. Why didn't you tell me as soon as you came in?"

"I tried. You wouldn't—"

"You should've tried harder."

"Apparently." He ran his hand down his face, and turned

his attention to the sheriff. "Buck, Kyndal and I are...old friends."

The dismissive wave of his hand when he said those words hit Kyndal as soundly as a slap in the face. The derisive snort shot from her before she could control of anger. "Yeah. We sort of lost contact in college."

Chance's eyes darkened. "I'm sorry you went through this, Kyndal. I've had some trouble with teenagers."

"Apparently." She mimicked his previous tone.

"Did you see anything?"

She jumped at the sound of Sheriff Blaine's voice behind her. "Did I see anything that looked like somebody had been there?" She moved mentally through the areas she had seen this morning. "No. But there are a lot of different ways to go from that first room."

A blast of voice and static came over the sheriff's two-way radio. "Sheriff, there's been a wreck in front of the bank in Draffenville. No one's hurt, but one of the drivers is drunk."

Sheriff Blaine pulled the radio from his belt. "I'll be right there." He zipped up his leather jacket, which stretched tight over his paunch. "Hate to break up the reunion, but, Ms. Rawlings, we need to get you back to your car. I'll stop in Draffenville and send you the rest of the way with Deputy Howard."

Before Kyndal could answer, Chance waved away the suggestion. "I'll take her back to her car."

"Your stuff's at the front desk." The sheriff nodded his head toward the front room. "Hope I don't see you again." He smiled, and Kyndal heard a pleasant tone to his voice for the first time. "Unless it's social." He winked and clapped Chance on the back as he passed.

The sheriff's exit cut her humiliation in half. If only

Chance would leave, she could wallow in what must be a ten-ton vat of self-recrimination hanging in her stomach.

Instead, the weight increased when he crossed his arms and frowned. "Now, what were you really doing at my cave? I'm not aware of any problem it might be creating for Kentucky Lake. No pollution, no chemical dumping—unless it's pot from the kids, which I'm trying to get stopped."

So he'd heard about True Tennessee. She squared her shoulders, determined not to shrink from his tense look. "I told you why I was there. I need photos of a cave. A tourism magazine is starting up."

"Tourism, eh?" He smiled then, but a smirk seemed to hang around the edges of his lips. "Does that mean you've left the dark side?"

"I was never on the dark side," she huffed.

"Liberal environmentalists who stir the shit that closes companies and causes good people to lose their jobs are the dark side personified."

"On the contrary, *Counselor,* liberal environmentalists save lives by *enlightening* the public about the way these companies ravage our natural resources."

"Damn, Kyndal." He wiped a hand down his face in a gesture she'd seen him make thousands of time. "Have you forgotten completely about who you are and where you're from?" He bent toward her, bringing his eyes level with hers. "You're a Paducah girl, and Paducah's a river town. The Ohio means industry. Jobs—"

"Birth defects…cancer." She raised on her tiptoes, causing him to straighten. "And death if we sit back idly and allow the dumping of poisons into our rivers to continue."

He peered closely at her. "You've changed," he said, making it sound like an accusation.

"And you haven't." She allowed a smirk of her own. "I hear you're working for your dad."

His jaw tightened. "With, not for. I'm a partner in the firm."

"Well…good for you."

The small office was getting awfully warm and the conversation had moved into a sparring phase she wasn't up to at the moment. Pretty soon, he would start questioning her again about the new magazine and figure out how far she'd actually fallen. What category ranked below "Total Loser?" Oh, yeah, that would be "My Dad Was Right about You." She couldn't face that on top of everything else today.

She moved toward the door the sheriff had closed behind him. Escape seemed to be the best plan. "By the way, thanks for offering the ride, but Jaci's on her way to pick me up."

Chance moved more quickly and claimed the doorknob. He didn't turn it immediately, pausing momentarily as if weighing his next comment. "I'm sorry, Kyn. This is no way for us to act. Are you in town long?" His free hand touched her casually below the shoulder blade.

There was nothing casual about her body's reaction to his touch. Her nipples tightened as though they had no memory of his walking out of her life without a backward glance. A thin line of perspiration popped out along her upper lip and made her cringe. Before answering, she camouflaged a quick wipe of the area with a cough. "No, I'm going back to Tennessee this afternoon." He removed his hand, and she immediately felt the loss.

"Ah. Well, I was hoping I could make this up to you somehow."

This he wanted to make up for. Not for breaking up with

her and breaking her heart. Not for his major role in the whole men-as-deserters drama of her life.

"*This* isn't something you need to make up for," she snapped.

He smiled. Nothing forced this time. A genuine, tender, gorgeous, all-the-way-into-his-eyes smile that indicated he took her at her word instead of reading the nuance in her voice.

She considered another comment. Something more pointed than the last. Something that would wipe the smile from those yummy lips. But he opened the door, and a welcome rush of air cooled her face. This would all be over soon. She let her comment drop.

The lady working the outer office placed Kyndal's bags on the counter with a curt "Here's your stuff" then went back to typing without giving them a second look.

"We need to get together sometime, and you know… catch up."

Yeah, sometime when I'm gainfully employed...in an awesome job...and married to an awesome guy. Kyndal unzipped her bags and made a cursory check of their contents. She didn't expect to find anything awry, but it was a good way to avoid eye contact. "Um, yeah. That'd be nice. Sometime."

Chance's cell phone rang before he could follow up, and Kyndal sighed her relief when the yellow of Jaci's VW Beetle flashed through the window blinds.

"It's all in the file on Alice's desk, Dad. I finished it last night."

Hearing Chance address his father stirred up memories, but Kyndal had no intention of allowing them to surface, considering how the rest of her day had gone. She inclined her head toward the window to indicate Jaci's arrival, gathered her bags and hurried out the door.

Chance was close behind her, still talking, with obvious irritation. “I told you I’d be there before two, and I’m on my way.”

Jaci’s eyes widened when Kyndal and Chance exited the sheriff’s office together, and Kyndal answered her unspoken question with a don’t-you-dare-ask-any-questions-yet glare.

JACI GAVE A TIGHT SMILE TO indicate the message had been received although her brain was spinning at the sight.

Kyndal and Chance Brennan? Had hell frozen over?

She popped the trunk open and rolled her window down as Chance shoved his phone into his pocket. “Hey, Chance.” She forced a smile. “Haven’t seen you in forever. How are ya?”

“I’m doing well, Jaci. How are you and Bart?”

“We’re fine.” *But what have you done to my best friend? If you’ve hurt her again, so help me, I’ll—*

“I’ve been hearing good things about Décor and More.”

“That’s music to my ears.” She grabbed a few business cards from the stash in the sun visor and handed them to him. “Keep spreading the word.”

A worried look crossed his face, and he seemed about to say something else when Kyndal slammed the trunk. He hurried around to the passenger side, but not before Kyndal had herself safely tucked into the seat. She closed the door and stuck her hand out the window. “Thanks, Chance. You always said you’d buy that cave someday. I’m relieved that you own it today.”

Chance owned the cave? Wow, this should be some story.

Chance’s dark eyes softened as he leaned down to peer in the window. “It was good to see you again. It’s been way too long." He shifted his eyes to Jaci. "Um, Jaci, I heard something about Julia recently…"

Her throat tightened at the mention of her business partner. Chance was Julia's attorney, and if he'd already heard, her bad news must be out. She nodded. "It's true. Breast cancer. Bilateral mastectomy. But they caught it early, so no chemo or radiation."

Sadness shadowed his face. "That's good news, at least. Do you think she'd mind if I called? I'd like to let her know I'm thinking about her."

His words dissolved some of the anger she'd been allowing to surface toward him in regard to Kyndal. "I think she'd like that."

"I'll give her a call, then." He straightened up and pulled out a business card, scribbled something on the back, and handed it to Kyndal. "If you ever need anything, Kyn, here's my card. My cell number's on the back."

Kyndal nodded. "Thanks."

She waved goodbye, and Jaci could see the strain as Kyndal forced her lips in a smile.

When they got onto the street, Jaci reached into the backseat, grabbed a box of tissues and tossed it into Kyndal's lap. "I can see you're in no condition to drive. We're going to my house, and we'll get your car later. Now tell me everything."

Kyndal told her long, dramatic story all the way to Paducah, pain evident in her voice, though nothing like it had been those weeks after Chance broke up with her. Thinking about that time still made Jaci want to castrate him.

She and Chance were the only two people in the world Kyndal had ever fully trusted. When he betrayed that trust, Jaci had watched her best friend fall apart…and she'd been the one left to pick up the pieces.

She pulled the car into the garage and turned it off. They sat in silence while the garage door closed behind them.

She couldn't bear to think about Kyndal going home to that sad little apartment tonight. Meeting up with Chance again had been bad enough, but doing it when she was out of a job went beyond rotten luck. Classic Kyndal. "You're gonna stay here tonight." She held up a hand to silence Kyndal's protest. "And we're gonna go out and end this day on a happy note."

Kyndal shook her head. "I can't afford it, Jaci. I have to keep an eye on everything I spend right now. I'm sure Mom's going to want to leave this new jerk she's with, and she'll need gas money or bus fare to get home from wherever."

Jaci had tired years ago of this person Kyndal called "mom" who was no mother at all, but always referred to herself as Mrs. Rawlings no matter who she was married to "to keep a strong connection to my baby girl." *Pffft!* The only connection that woman cared about was the one that provided her public aid…and now Kyndal's banking account, which was dwindling because of her.

"We're not gonna argue about this, and we're not gonna talk about your mom right now. Tonight's my treat." She turned to face Kyndal squarely, leaning against the driver's door. "What we *are* gonna talk about is this job you're letting pass. You need this job, Kyn, and you need those pictures of the cave."

She snatched Chance's business card from the cup holder in the console and waved it in front of Kyndal's face. "Meeting up with Chance again hurt your pride, I know, but the worst part's over. It's happened for a reason, and maybe that reason is to get you this job." She laid the card on Kyndal's lap where it nestled among the wadded mass of used tissues. "An opportunity has landed right in your lap. Call him."

CHAPTER FOUR

CHANCE RUBBED HIS THUMBS across his brow, noticing the tenderness underneath. Sinus pressure? Tension? Maybe both.

Saturday night. Eight thirty-seven. He'd hoped to be done with work by now. A normal day would've found him finished an hour or two ago. But this was no normal day. Kyndal Rawlings stepped back into his life for less than an hour, and he'd been unable to concentrate on anything else since.

"Dad, you were so right," he mumbled to himself. "Tree hugger or not, that woman drives me to distraction."

But, man! She'd looked good. A little on the thin side even for her tiny frame, but the tight thermal top and jeans she'd worn showed she still had curves in all the right places.

Her green, catlike eyes had been alarmed when she first recognized him. What was that about?

Fear wasn't an emotion he associated with Kyn. She'd always shown so much spunk. Taking care of herself when her mother would leave and stay gone for days. Never missing school. Graduating as valedictorian. Kyndal was a fighter and a survivor.

He'd only seen her truly afraid twice. Once when Amos Turner showed up with his gun to run them away from the cave. And the day he'd broken up with her. The terror of losing him had radiated from her eyes. God, he could still feel her arms around him in that death grip as she pleaded for him to change his mind. These nine years later, the guilt and regret still ate at him. Guilt that he couldn't make what they had gel with what he needed. Regret that he had to end it the way he did because he'd had no other option.

"Damn it! I'm doing it again."

This was crazy. Yes, for a couple of years, he and Kyndal spent every possible minute together, but that finished long ago. They went their separate ways, became different people, grew up, grew apart. End of story.

He snatched up the notes he'd made on the Farley case, determined to divert his attention. It was clear why his dad had passed the case to him. The Farleys' son, Morton, had been killed in a car accident so similar to Hank's it made him nauseous to read.

College kids on summer vacation. Drinking to excess. Driving too fast. Crossing the center line and meeting a semi head-on.

No civil suit would ever bring their son back. Couldn't they see that? Their lives would never be the same. But if they didn't let go of the grief eating them alive, they'd soon be consumed by it, and it would destroy anything they'd ever had together.

The judge who'd presided over his family's case had been a showboat, working hard toward reelection. He hadn't demonstrated a true sense of right and wrong, or given a damn about fairness. He'd turned the whole fiasco into a venue to generate publicity with no regard of the pain he caused. That the idiot ruled in their favor against the tired truck driver was a travesty of justice.

Not a day went by that Chance didn't remind himself how Hank's civil suit ripped apart the last vestiges of family life for them and brought only heartache instead of closure. And it left him with a relentless drive to become a judge who would treat people with fairness and dignity no matter what their circumstances.

He stood and walked away from the desk, trying to leave behind the haunting image of his parents as they'd been since his brother's death.

To this day, they'd never really dealt with Hank's death. Never let their grief out like he had the day of the funeral with Kyndal. Thank God, he'd had somebody like her back then.

Damn it! Back to Kyndal. This round-robin thinking was getting him nowhere and getting nothing taken care of…but he couldn't get her off his mind.

He sat back down and typed *Kyndal Rawlings* into the search engine on his computer and clicked on the first link that appeared—an interesting and eye-opening account of a lawsuit that shut down the True Tennessee website. She hadn't mentioned any of that during their short visit. Not that he blamed her. The article indicated quite a scandal.

If it had been anybody but Kyndal, he would've thought it served her right. But it *was* Kyn, and damn liberal or not, she deserved better. She would survive, though. She always had.

His stomach growled as he closed his laptop, reminding him he'd skipped lunch. Only a wood-fired oven pizza and a cold beer from Max's Café would satisfy the craving.

MAX'S WAS CROWDED, but that was expected. Everybody came to Max's. Getting a seat would take at least an hour, even as a single, but Chance thought he could hold off starvation with a couple of beers. Axel put his name on the list and said he'd find him in the bar when something opened up.

Tripp, the bartender, saw him making his way through

the throng and had a cold one waiting for him by the time he got to the bar.

"You look like you need this." Tripp handed him the frosted mug.

"Tripp, have I ever told you you're my favorite person?" Chance swigged the beer, relishing the biting chill on his tongue and down his throat. "Wanna marry me? Have one of these waiting for me when I get home, and I'll never ask any more of you."

"Never knew you swung that way, Chance." The high-pitched voice by his shoulder could only belong to one person.

"Jaci." Chance turned toward her with a shake of his head. "Are you stalking me today?"

"Nope, but I thought maybe you were stalking Kyndal." Jaci tilted her head toward the door.

Through the opening, he could see the fire pit blazing in the middle of the beer garden. Kyndal sat close enough for the fire to lend a rosy glow to her skin.

Her head fell back as she and Bart laughed together, unaware they were being watched. The firelight sparkled on her silky, black hair cascading down her back. Relaxed and carefree, she looked even better than she had earlier in the day.

Chance's mouth went dry. He took another gulp and shook his head in answer to Jaci's remark. "She told me she was going back to Tennessee this afternoon."

Jaci wrinkled her nose as she smiled. "We talked her into staying the night. Why don't you join us—unless you're waiting for someone?"

Much as he'd like to visit some more with Kyndal—maybe on a friendlier note this time—she hadn't seemed to share those sentiments this morning. She'd been shaken at first, then she'd almost seemed pissed. He shook his head.

"I'd better not. I don't want to make Kyn uncomfortable." He leaned his elbow on the bar and set his beer down.

Jaci snatched it and looped her arm through his, giving him a tug. "Actually, she said she might give you a call. She wants to talk to you about something she found in that cave of yours."

She'd found something in the cave? She'd denied it when Buck asked. Chance's interest was piqued. And if she was going to call him, anyway… "But I haven't eaten yet."

"Neither have we. We've just ordered appetizers and pizza. C'mon."

Chance allowed Jaci to pull him through the door. If Kyndal seemed distraught about seeing him again, he could blame her friend for dragging him over.

"Lookee here who I found in the bar." Jaci's words drew Kyndal's attention.

Chance read the shock that registered in her eyes, followed by daggers aimed at Jaci. A flush spread across her face so quickly it couldn't have been from the fire's proximity. Whether that was a good sign or a bad one, he couldn't be sure. Finally, a cool smile settled on her lips.

"Chance. How weird is this?" Her eyebrows drew together in question when she returned her gaze to Jaci. Probably thinking she'd been set up.

"I never expected to see you here, either." Chance waved away the conspiracy theory. "You told me you were going home." He shook hands with Bart, who was smiling as if he was thoroughly enjoying the drama. "How's the uranium enrichment business, Bart?"

Bart laughed. "When we let go, check your palm. If it's not glowing, I'll make it to my shift Monday."

Jaci wore her cat-who-ate-the-canary smile as she sat down next to her husband, leaving the chair next to Kyndal available. Chance made no move to sit. If Kyndal wanted him there, she'd have to invite him. And, if she didn't, he'd make an excuse and mosey back to the bar.

Jaci handed over his beer, and he took another sip to cover the awkward silence.

"So I guess that time to catch up came sooner than we thought." Kyndal's smile was tight as she pulled out the chair and patted the seat. "Here. Sit down." Her tone wasn't ecstatic about seeing him again—but certainly friendlier than at Buck's office. But then people weren't usually at their best in Buck's office.

Chance took the only relaxed gulp of beer he'd had since leaving the bar, but the downtime didn't last long. When he sat, he found the space tighter than it looked. His right arm pressed against Kyndal's left from shoulder to elbow. He started to scoot over some, but the contact felt pretty good—damn good, really. He'd just have to enjoy the friction that sent little bursts of heat through his sweater every time he raised his arm for a sip—and he'd make it a point to sip often.

"Wow, y'all. This is just like old times." Jaci was almost squealing. The saucy redhead looked and sounded the part of mischievous imp. If nothing exciting was happening, she'd make it happen.

Chance was sure there was more to the comment, and he braced himself for what would come next.

"Except, when we leave, Bart and I will be together, and y'all will go off and be with other people. Seems weird, huh?"

So Kyndal had "other people." Chance's mouthful of beer tasted rather flat.

Kyndal's arm flinched against his, and he felt her stiffen. "Jaci…" Her tone held a warning.

"Yeah, let's not talk about that now." Jaci signaled the waitress for another round of beer. "Private lives, politics and religion are officially off-limits tonight. Let's just enjoy the moment."

Damn. Staying away from politics was a good idea if he and Kyn were going to try to remain civil, but he'd like to hear about this relationship just to satisfy his curiosity. Maybe he could ease into it from a different angle. "How's your mom, Kyn?"

"She's fine." She picked the corner of the label loose from her bottle. "Your parents?"

"They're okay. In fact, they leave in the morning for the first trip they've taken together since Hank—" He stopped and an emotional silence fell over the group.

Kyndal cleared her throat and raised her beer over the middle of the table, but her eyes fixed on his. "Here's to letting go of old hurts."

He doubted total forgiveness was a toast away, but maybe this was a start. As they clinked their bottles together, everybody seemed to relax.

"You know, Chance, you're lucky I showed up when I did." Jaci pointed at the bartender as she let Bart and Kyndal in on the joke. "Tripp was seriously considering Chance's marriage proposal."

"Don't sell your soul for liquor." Bart nuzzled Jaci's hair playfully. "Hold out for home-cooked meals and wild sex—in that order."

They all laughed together, and for the first time since he'd sat down, Chance felt as if it really was like old times.

A plate of cheese-stuffed potato cakes showed up and gave everybody an opportunity to focus on food rather than conversation. Chance glanced at Kyndal's hand as she passed the plate. No ring, so she wasn't engaged. Chance relaxed even more and gave himself permission not to analyze why.

"Hey, Kyn." Jaci's wide-eyed expression was the picture of innocence. "I told Chance you were going to call him about what you found in the cave."

Kyndal choked on her potato cake.

Chance patted her between the shoulder blades. "You okay?"

She coughed a couple of times, cleared her throat and nodded. "Yeah." She smiled, and for a brief moment he was lost in the watery depths of those green eyes. She cleared her throat again. "Really. I'm okay."

She gave a tug that made him realize he had a firm grasp on her arm with his left hand, and the pats on her back had morphed into soft rubs. His grasp nearly circumvented her arm. Though not very big around, he could feel the taut muscles underneath and the strength in them. Reluctantly, he let go and shifted his attention from the feel of her under his hands to what she found in the cave.

She chewed her lip before speaking. "I found a small room made completely of crystals."

"Crystals?" It wasn't the type of news he'd expected, and he had to let the information sink in.

"Yeah, crystals. Walls, floor, ceiling. Everything was white, shiny crystals."

Chance stared into his beer, searching his memory. "I've heard of that before. What's it called?" He waved his hand, trying to reel the word out of his memory. "It's a bubble left over after volcanic activity…a vot…a vut…no, a vug! That's what it's called. A vug. It's sort of like a big geode."

"That's exactly what it looked like!" Kyndal's excitement drew his gaze. The firelight danced in her eyes, made them emeralds.

The bottle was at his lips, but his breath caught. He set it down without taking a sip. "Where is it? I can't believe I've never seen it."

Between bites, Kyndal explained she'd been looking

for interesting shots when a sandstone column caught her attention.

Chance nodded, picturing which room she was in. He'd seen the column. Bats were in that room sometimes, so he generally avoided it, but right then he wished he were there. With Kyndal.

A bit of cheese from her last bite of potato cake clung to her bottom lip. He controlled the urge to brush it off with his thumb. Or nibble it off.

Luckily the pizza arrived, giving him something to think about other than being alone in the cave with the mesmerizing woman sitting next to him…the liberal environmentalist who'd recently been involved in a scandal sitting next to him.

"Well, the opening is about seven feet up." Kyndal helped herself to a slice of pizza, which remained untouched as she continued her story. "It's on the right-hand side when you first enter that room. I wouldn't even have noticed it if I hadn't knocked my lamp over. The crystal wall caught the light."

"Serendipity at work, eh?" Chance chuckled. "Did you see any bats?"

"Bats? Ewww!" Jaci's squeal made Chance aware there were two other people at the table. He'd been enthralled in Kyndal's story, or at least in watching her tell it. All breathless and excited. The same way she used to be when they made love.

The memory shot straight to his groin and left him with a raging hard-on. That kind of urgency hadn't happened lately. It was a bit of a relief to know it could still happen. He shifted in his seat to relieve some of the pressure.

Kyndal was explaining to Jaci and Bart about the beauty of bats and photographing all aspects of nature. God, she was gorgeous with her conviction shining in her eyes. Too bad that conviction wasn't focused in a more productive direction.

Reaching for another piece of pizza, his gaze tangled with Kyndal's for a moment, and he watched her eyes harden as if she'd read his thoughts. Or maybe she'd covered it well until that moment but obviously still harbored resentment toward him. He lowered his eyes and took a bite. Guilt didn't mix well with pepperoni.

Yeah, he probably deserved her anger. Breaking up without ever calling to check on her was a chicken-shit thing to do. Especially after all they'd been to each other. But, damn it, the women he'd encountered at Harvard had been so sophisticated and ambitious. None of them would've given up their dream of being a lawyer to pursue photography.

He chewed slowly, an idea forming in his mind. A way to help her out now and make up for the heartache he'd brought her…maybe even rid himself of the guilt he'd carried for nine years.

He waited for a pause in the conversation. "Would you like to go back to the cave tomorrow?"

Kyndal's look went from startled to something unreadable.

The issue suddenly became important to him, and he pressed for an answer. "Jaci said you're staying over, right? It wouldn't take long. You could show me the vug and get some more shots. We could all go." He waved his hand to include the four of them.

"Don't count us in." Jaci shook her head at Bart, whose mouth was pursed to comment. "I've got to work tomorrow after church."

"On Sunday?" Doubt was evident in Kyndal's voice.

Jaci's face tightened as she shrugged. "We're behind because of Julia's—" she hesitated "—um, surgery."

The mention again of Julia Reinholt's condition nipped at Chance's heart. Had Jaci heard the other rumors—the ones that linked Julia's husband, Stuart, with a young waitress in town? The son of a bitch. Chance kept his thoughts to himself.

Remembering what had veered the conversation in this direction, though, and trying to lighten the mood, he turned back to Kyndal. "So Jaci and Bart are out, but what do you say, Kyn? Do we have a date?"

CHAPTER FIVE

KYNDAL CHECKED THE MAP Chance had drawn for her the night before. His driveway should be coming up around the next bend. For the gazillionth time that morning, she told herself going back to the cave with Chance was not tempting fate—it was shaping destiny. The shots of that crystal room would get her the job with the magazine, give her back her good name and prove to Chance Brennan she really was somebody, after all. So those shots were worth whatever the cost. An hour or two of emotional discomfort seemed reasonable enough.

She'd survived last night, hadn't she?

Seeing the success he'd become juxtaposed with her failures dredged up old insecurities with a vengeance, and pushed this job higher on her necessity scale than just a means to a steady paycheck.

Adding to that misery was her realization that, in spite of the animosity between them, Chance Brennan still had an effect on her mentally and physically—an over-the-top effect.

Yesterday in the sheriff's office, she'd had some freedom to move around. But, last night at Max's, she'd been trapped for three hours in the torture of his occasional touch. Keeping a safe distance today was her only hope of coming out of this with pride and dignity intact.

Jaci had been adamant the strategy-of-choice today was to be an outrageous flirt, talk incessantly about Rick Warren and make it sound like they were a hot item, then leave without a backward glance. And Jaci could probably pull that off. Flirting came as natural as eating for her.

Kyndal, on the other hand, had been unable to finish a piece of pizza or a breakfast roll since Chance made his suggestion to go back to the cave. If eating didn't come naturally, where did that leave flirting?

She unclenched her jaw. Decision made. Strategy set. No flirting. No Rick discussion. No way. No how. Friendly—but distant. All business. Casual business. And above all, no touching.

Two reflectors and a mailbox with the numbers 343 stenciled on the side signaled Chance's driveway. She quelled the trembling in her hands by gripping the steering wheel. The long gravel path meandered uphill through the woods, which were ablaze in the fiery reds and yellows of maples and wild dogwoods. In the spring, it would be a fairyland of creamy-white blooms—a stunning shot she quickly pushed from her mind. No returning to this place after today. Blooming dogwoods could be found anywhere in Kentucky come spring.

The chimney, followed by a roof and the second story of a charming old farmhouse rose into sight as she approached the summit of the hill. Its fresh coat of white paint stood out against the fall colors, yet it didn't look at all out of place. The trees surrounding the house had grown tall, and their branches spread shade across it like protective arms. They'd obviously been there a long time—living proof some things were meant to be together.

A porch wrapped around the front and side of the house, inviting with its cushioned wicker chairs and couches and a swing at one end.

She squeezed the steering wheel a bit more tightly when she spotted Chance waving a folded newspaper in welcome. No doubt about it—he looked as good in person as he had last night in her dreams.

Idiotic dreams!

A chocolate Lab jumped from the front porch and ran to meet her, carrying a Frisbee and wagging its tail.

Kyndal brought the car to a slower-than-necessary stop, hoping it appeared she was careful rather than stalling. "Today will bring the perfect shot that will make me somebody. No flirting. No touching," she whispered, plastering on her most confident smile.

As soon as she stepped from the car, the Frisbee was offered at her feet. She laughed and picked it up, much to the delight of the dog whose tail wagged vehement approval. The Lab shot after the spinning disc the second it left her hand, stretching and jumping to bring it down from midflight.

Kyndal clapped in praise.

"You'll be sorry you did that." Chance's voice startled her with its nearness. She turned to find him only a foot away, a cup of coffee poised at his lips.

She shifted her weight and took a step back, holding her palms out to check them for mud. "Why will I be sorry?" The gesture gave her a couple of seconds to examine the striking form in front of her—something she hadn't really had the opportunity to do the day before.

The day was warm enough that they'd both chosen T-shirts. His black one stretched across his chest, showing the outline of very pronounced pectorals, hidden the day before under his sweater. He'd been put together nicely during high school, but he'd never had biceps like these, threatening to burst the seams of his sleeves.

As she put her hands down, her eyes drifted up to his face. Boyish charm had been replaced by rugged sensuousness. Coarse stubble filled the lower half of his face—

another change since high school. Back then, he'd fretted he'd never be able to grow a beard. Didn't seem to be an issue now.

In answer to her question, he nodded to her feet where the Frisbee lay again and a pair of hopeful eyes beamed from a chocolate snout. "Because Chesney doesn't know when to stop. She'll chase and fetch as long as you'll throw."

Chance's closeness brought the tangy smell of Irish Spring soap to her nose. The scent chased her memory across nine years to a morning when his parents left early, and she'd gone to his house before school. They'd showered together, making love standing up, enveloped in warm water and Irish Spring-scented steam.

She grabbed the Frisbee and tossed the memory away with it. "One more and that'll have to hold us."

"I was afraid you'd stand me up." The corners of Chance's mouth lifted as he took another sip of his coffee.

He wouldn't be grinning if he knew how many times that thought had crossed her mind since last night.

"Wouldn't think of it," she lied. She covered her guilt by a quick look around. "You have a beautiful place. How long have you lived here?"

"Just over a year. I've still got a lot to do." He motioned toward the three-car, detached garage where a row of window shutters leaned against the side in various stages of being painted forest-green. "But it's coming. Would you like to see the inside?"

The eagerness in his voice made Kyndal swallow the refusal on her tongue and nod an okay instead. She'd have a home of her own someday to show off, so it was easy to understand his pride.

He led the way up the side steps into a spacious country

kitchen with glossy hardwood floors, white marble countertops and black cabinetry.

"This is gorgeous." Kyndal nodded her approval at the stainless appliances and hardware brushed to look like pewter. "You're quite a decorator."

"Thanks, but I can't take much credit. When I first began looking at the place, I started buying designing magazines and clipping pictures. Luckily, I found a contractor with some vision."

The smell of fresh coffee against a backdrop of cinnamon made Kyndal's stomach growl fiercely.

His eyebrows drew in with concern. "Are you hungry?"

She didn't think her stomach would agree to food yet although the smell was tempting. She shook her head.

"How about some coffee?"

"Mmm. It smells wonderful, but I'd better not unless you've had a bathroom installed in that cave." She laughed, letting go of some nervousness but reminding herself not to tilt her head sideways because that might be construed as flirting.

The tour went quickly since most of the walls had been knocked down, forming an enormous great room with strategically placed columns where support was needed. The room was warm with leather furniture the color of molasses and a fireplace crackling at one end. Chance silenced it with a remote. "Gas," he explained to her surprised expression. "It felt good early this morning before I went outside, but we sure don't need it now."

Upstairs was still under construction with plastic sheeting hung across doorways. Two of the bedrooms were being combined into a large master suite. One was full of boxes from his move, and the last held only a bed, dresser and bedside table.

Kyndal took a peek and then hurriedly turned away as

her heartbeat rose to a pounding in her ears. Chance's old mahogany bedroom suite. She was so not going to let herself think about times spent in that bed.

A couple of inconspicuous deep breaths brought her heartbeat under control as she moved to the railing. She gripped it and focused on the fireplace below. "Everything is really lovely." Her voice came out high and strained like an old beagle's howl.

"Sorry about the dust." Chance mercifully closed the door to her nostalgia. "It's more house than I need right now." He leaned his elbows on the banister, his arm and leg brushing hers. "But I hope to fill it up with a family someday."

She glanced at him and found his espresso gaze locked on her. "Oh?" She scooted over a couple of inches and coughed, hoping the knot in her chest would shake loose. "Is Chesney pregnant?"

Chance rubbed his hand down his face. "Lord, I hope not. She's just a baby herself." He gave a low, meaningful chuckle. "Besides, someday means years from now—when my practice is built and I'm well on my way to being a judge."

"So you plan on getting involved in politics." *Obviously since judges are elected officials.*

He shrugged. "Nonpartisan…but yeah."

She wouldn't allow herself to analyze why his words squeezed at her heart. She just wanted to go to the cave, get her shots, then hightail it back to Dover, Tennessee, and dreams of a new job—with a few fantasies of Ranger Rick thrown in for good measure.

She turned her back to Chance. "Do you have a stepladder?" She threw the question over her shoulder as they made their way down the stairs. "We may need it to reach the opening to the vug."

"Yeah, I have one, but we don't want to lug that with us for a half mile." Chance waved away the idea. "If the opening's no higher than you said, I can boost you up and then make the jump myself."

His hands were going to have to touch her body in various places. Her mouth went dry at the thought. She'd have to steel herself not to react. It had been a while since anybody had touched her anyplace interesting.

Chance grabbed the backpack by the kitchen door as they headed out.

The temperature had risen even higher, and the sky had darkened appreciably since they went inside. Humidity hung heavy in the air with a cloying stickiness.

"It's so warm, they're calling for a chance of hail. Better put your car in the garage." Not giving her time to argue, Chance went to the keyless entry by the garage door and punched in a code.

Kyndal pulled her Jeep in, allowing only a brief comparison of her car to the black SUV and the sleek, silver Porsche Boxster occupying the other two spots. She was careful not to crowd the corner obviously set up for Chesney with a doggie door, blankets, and food and water dispensers.

She pulled her backpack out of the backseat and slung it over her shoulder. "Will Chesney follow us?"

Chance shook his head as he punched the button to let the garage door down. "She wears an electric collar that gives her the run of about two acres. She'll know when to turn back." He motioned toward a well-worn path through the trees behind the garage. "Follow the yellow brick road."

The Munchkin voice coming from such a body was too incongruous, and Kyndal laughed in spite of herself.

"Well, it's about time." Chance's arm went around her shoulder in a quick hug as they walked. "I've been waiting to hear a real laugh from you for almost twenty-four hours."

The hug felt nice. Not flirtatious. Almost like the one this morning from Bart.

Maybe she was being too sensitive. Maybe it was time to let go of her hurt and embarrassment. Loosen up. Count her blessings. She had a night out with her best friends, a photo-worthy cave and an old friend to share it with, a promising hope of a new job—not bad for someone who'd been facing jail time the day before.

All right, it didn't have to be just business. She threw her arm around Chance's waist and hugged back. "Sorry I've been so uptight. The whole experience yesterday messed with my mind, you know? Too many shocks to the system for one day."

Thunder rumbled through the trees, sending Chesney scurrying back toward the garage. "Well, don't let your guard down just yet. There are some surprises still in store." His arm tightened briefly around her, then he let go and quickened his pace.

As if to punctuate his words, a raindrop plopped onto the end of her nose.

She broke into a jog to keep up.

THEY MADE IT INSIDE THE CAVE just before the storm broke. Chance watched Kyndal shiver as the coolness dropped over them like a wet blanket.

He rubbed the back of his fingers against her arm. "Cold?" It was a lame excuse to touch her again, but touching her was all he'd been able to think of since she'd gotten out of her car. The pink T-shirt hung loose from her shoulders, giving no hint of the curves that had been so obvious yesterday. He wanted to touch them, feel for himself they were still there and ignore the voice of reason telling him that would be a mistake

She shook her head as two hard buds poked through the cotton, contradicting her answer but enhancing the appeal of the T.

"I've got a couple of things to show you if you've got the time." He watched the debate play across her face when she checked her watch. Her "other person" was probably expecting her. He threw out additional enticement. "Some interesting things about the cave…if the kids haven't vandalized them since I was here last."

"Are vandals a problem?" Kyndal's brows knitted.

"You decide for yourself." He pulled a battery-operated lantern from his backpack.

"Whoa!" Kyndal leaned back, squinting against the light shining in her face. "You're packing a big one!"

"Well, you ought to know."

Kyndal snorted at his innuendo. Her eyes darted away before coming back to meet his. "I remember reading somewhere that alcohol shrinks the male genitals." She let her eyes drift downward, stop to squint at his crotch, then brought them back up to lock with his. "Sooo, how much drinking did you *do* at Hah-vahd?"

The last word dripped with sarcasm, more biting than funny, and it wasn't difficult to read the tension in her posture. The merest mention of their past and she'd gone from friendly to pissed in thirty seconds. He would heed the warning and watch what he said. No use getting her riled for the short time they were going to be together.

He turned the lantern so the beam illuminated the dark end of the entry room, bringing to life the neon paint graffiti from the past two months that marred the beauty of the past ten thousand years. Beer cans and liquor bottles littered the floor.

Kyndal's gasp spoke her horror at the sight.

"My feelings exactly." His stomach turned at every name scrawled across the limestone. Levi. Mattie. Rachel. Brant. "'Fools' names like fools' faces—'"

"'Always seen in public places.'" Kyndal shook her head slowly. "This is awful. How can they do this? *Why* do they do this?" Anger and sadness flashed in her eyes, which deepened to emerald in the dim light.

"They're just young." He shrugged, not really having an answer. "They don't realize how special it is."

"We were young, too, but we knew exactly how special it was." Her eyes widened. The words hadn't meant to be spoken, but had somehow escaped. She bit her lip and turned away, moving closer toward the wall of names. "Will anything take it off?" She skimmed the wall with her fingertips, a mother soothing a wounded child.

"Time."

"Time." She heaved a sigh. "Heals all wounds." She pulled her camera from the pack and made a few shots of the names.

Her back was toward him, and the light caught in her black hair, which hung loose and sleek. He itched to touch it, to run his hand down it and into it, to turn her around and look into those emerald eyes, to run his fingers from her temples to the tips of those strands of black silk.

He raised his arm, stretched his fingers hesitantly.

Don't be stupid.

He dropped his hand back to his side and breathed. "C'mon."

They stopped for a few minutes to survey the damage in the next room. No permanent damage, but clear indications of what the teens had been up to. A couple of air mattresses surrounded by handfuls of condom wrappers, empty liquor bottles, some roach clips and meth pipes.

When Buck had used the term *orgy,* Chance thought he was exaggerating.

Kyndal cleared her throat self-consciously, but remained silent. Did the leftover sexual litter remind her of their time there, the way it did him? Talking about it felt too edgy, so he kept quiet, as well.

Leading the way through passages long familiar to him, he pulled her into the adjoining cavern and then deeper into another one.

"You know where you're going?" Her voice held an edge of skepticism.

"Yep." He turned the beam of light onto a slab of limestone that looked slightly out of place—as if it had fallen from the ceiling and had been propped against the wall. He let go of her hand and pushed the slab to one side revealing a narrow tunnel. "We have to crawl through, but it's not very far."

Kyndal bent down for a look. When she raised back up, her eyes were hooded with doubt.

"If you want your backpack, you'll have to take it off and shift it through ahead of you. It might be easier to hang your camera around your neck, but push it around to your back."

Her derisive sigh let him know he'd better not be wasting her precious time, but she shrugged out of her backpack. "I hope you know what you're doing, Brennan." She gave him a push. "You first."

"I know what I'm doing," he assured her. "I'm going to show you one reason I think Old Man Turner ran us away that day."

CHAPTER SIX

CHANCE SLID HIS ARMS out of his pack and dropped it on the ground beside hers. As he squeezed his way through the opening, he realized it had been a while since he'd been through this tunnel. Too much time sitting behind a desk. Not enough time doing fun things like this.

Nothing in the tunnel indicated the teenagers had found it, but he dreaded what he might find at the other end. He shimmied the last few feet and came out into the small dead-end room, sighing his relief. Nothing had changed since the last time he was there, but he'd forgotten the ceiling was so low. He had to keep his neck bent so as not to bump his head.

Kyndal scooted out of the tunnel effortlessly. Her tiny frame probably hadn't even touched the sides. He helped her into a standing position, which proved to be no trouble. She even had a foot to spare. He watched her expression as she scanned the strange contents of the room.

Mounds and indentations—nine of them all together—circled the outside perimeter of the cavern, and each had a leather collar lying at its center.

Kyndal knelt by the nearest one and picked up the collar, reading the name inscribed on the small metal tag. "Ajax?" Her bottom lip protruded in a thoughtful pout. "His dog?"

Chance nodded and knelt beside her. "All of Mr. Turner's dogs, I think. This is where he buried them." He focused the light on a collar about three feet away. "That collar is really old. No name on it. And the depression is the deepest, so it's probably the first grave. Maybe a childhood pet."

"Oh." Kyndal's hand spread across her chest. "That is so sweet." The light glistened in her eyes as she blinked back tears. "All these years, I've thought he was a mean old man. But he had a soft side behind that gun-toting exterior, didn't he?"

A wild urge to kiss away those tears came over him and he stood up abruptly, whacking his head against the low ceiling. He let loose a string of expletives, which did nothing for the pain but eased his frustration somewhat.

Kyndal snickered—enjoying his suffering—and began taking shots of the curious room's contents.

"Well, don't go making Turner into a saint just yet." He rubbed the ache with his fingers until he was satisfied there was no blood. "I also found the remnants of a small still and a lot of empty bottles. I don't think Turner's tenacious guarding of the place was strictly because of his dog cemetery."

At the mention of the still, Kyndal sprang to her feet, shooting a smug smile toward the ceiling. "Ooooo. A still. That would make some good shots."

"It's gone. I was afraid somebody might get cut on the rusty metal." He winced as another pain shot through his head. "But I have something in another room I think you'll find photo-worthy."

Kyndal nodded toward the tunnel. "Let's go, then."

That she was in a hurry to be finished with this excursion caused another echo of pain, this time through the middle of his chest. He quickly reminded himself that the sooner they got back into the glaring light of day the better off they'd both be. These depths held too many memories.

Kyndal was on all fours before he could offer to go first. Her backside wiggling its way through the shadowy tunnel just a foot in front of him made him wish he'd given her a longer head start.

Once through to the other side, they swatted the dust from their legs and shouldered their backpacks once again.

Chance led the way through a series of caverns, taking them deeper into the cave. The cooler temperature pulled the hair on his neck to attention.

"I'm getting a little chilly." Kyndal tugged on his shirt to hold him back. She dropped to one knee and unzipped her pack, pulling out the thermal top from yesterday. Her breasts bobbed under the T as she slipped the extra layer over her head. The cotton underneath caused it to catch, and she struggled to get it over the soft mounds, twisting and turning her body in a dance of oblivious erotic gyrations.

Chance stood hypnotized by the movements, not daring to breathe. How many times had he watched her dress after they'd made love, helped her with a button or a zipper that was difficult to reach? The extra air from his lungs seemed to shoot straight to his groin, blowing into a rock-hard erection.

He cleared his throat to cover the groan that threatened and reached out to lend a hand, jerking the top down with more force than was needed.

"Thanks." Her voice sounded tighter than the shirt.

He strode past her without a word, his purpose finally clear in his mind. Let her get the shots she needed and get the hell out of there. Let her go back to her life and he would go back to his, and let another nine years of somewhat Kyndal-free thoughts begin. Then he'd get some work done this afternoon on that new case.

He heard her scurrying to keep up, so he slowed his pace to accommodate her shorter legs. He ducked through one last passage and found the opening he had been looking for.

Shutting the light off threw the room into utter darkness. Kyndal stumbled hard against him with a small cry of alarm.

"Shhh," he warned, mentally chiding himself for not stopping before they got this close.

"What is it?" A note of fear edged her whisper.

He found her face with his hands and covered her mouth lightly as a warning. Leaning in close, his lips brushed the edge of her ear. "Shhh."

She shivered, a spontaneous and involuntary response, and he smiled at the confirmation that he could still do that to her. A flick of the tongue against her ear would send her into sexual overdrive. Or at least it used to.

In spite of their ideologies—and what he'd said yesterday—she really hadn't changed that much. Neither of them had. Which made being here together even more threatening.

He nudged away the thought, pronouncing the words in a barely audible whisper, careful to keep his tongue safely in the confines of his mouth. "Bats. Lots of them."

Her quick intake of breath sucked his hand closer.

"They completely cover the ceiling on the other side of this opening." He removed his hand from her mouth but slid it on around into her hair to keep her close as he explained.

"Sometimes they stay where they are, but I've had them fly. I don't know what determines their actions, whether it's noise or movement or what. But I do know we don't want to be standing in this opening when they come through."

Her hair lay soft on the back of his fingers while her breath scampered down his neck—just like he'd imagined all last night. And all this morning.

BATS IN FLIGHT? THE POSSIBILITY of a shot with bats in flight? Chance's breath playing softly around her ear and neck? Which experience was making her heart beat so erratically?

Until yesterday, it had been almost two years since she'd had anyone's breath around her ear, but this was no time to let a physical reaction get the best of her. Chance Brennan would never get the best of her again. She tucked her mouth in close to his ear, keeping her voice controlled. "I'll need some lighting to get it right. That'll be your job. I'll give you a lamp, and show you where to turn it on. When I give the signal, flip it to High. But I want to be inside that room."

"Hold on to my waistband." His voice froze at a flutter from the next room. They stood paralyzed, barely daring to breathe. When silence returned, he whispered again. "We'll move slowly through the door, down the right-hand wall. Be careful of your step. One stumble and they're on top of us." He hesitated. "Sorry. I'm being overly dramatic. Don't be afraid. If they come this way, drop to the floor and cover. Now get your camera and the lamp out. We'll leave the bags here."

Kyndal eased the zipper on her bag open and brought out the lamp. Wordlessly, she took Chance's hand and guided it to the switch, mimicking how to push the switch to the on position. She pulled the camera gingerly from the bag, looped the strap over her neck and shoulder. Her hand groped around Chance's waist until she was satisfied with the hold, then she gave his arm a quick squeeze to indicate she was ready.

They moved soundlessly through the opening.

The fecal smell, which had been a faint, musty scent in the previous room, now assaulted her nasal passages with a putrid blend of ammonia and sulfur that set off her gag reflex. She swallowed repeatedly, trying not to think about the toxic spores attaching themselves to her esophagus and the gooey guano clinging to her boots.

Chance snaked along the wall a few yards, turned to face her and pulled her lightly against him to anchor her position.

Her heart nearly galloped away when she hit the button to turn on the camera. The familiar high-pitched frequency signaling the battery charging was a sound she'd always taken for granted and barely noticed. Under these circumstances, it sounded like a warning siren.

Chance's hand rubbed her arm in a silent communication that everything was all right.

The battery charged and the red light glowed its go-ahead. The light was tiny, but in this utter darkness became enough for her to glance back at Chance with his look of intense concentration.

She smiled. He winked in return.

She took a deep breath and brought the camera up in front of her, simultaneously giving him a nod.

The lamp's soft light became a glaring sun, and for a moment she was blinded by it.

As her eyes adjusted, she had to fight the rising panic in her chest. The ceiling of this room was a black, lumpy sea—a solid mass of small mammals folded in upon themselves, dangling by their claws.

Kyndal snapped quickly, getting in four shots before there was any movement.

What caused the stir, she couldn't be sure—the camera shutter, the light or merely their presence?—but hundreds of sets of wings started to unfold and then the room swirled in a torrent of ebony movement. It was like being within two feet of a tornado. The wind from the flapping beat against her face making her gasp as she held the button for shot after shot.

Most of the bats stayed within the confines of the flock, but a few renegades dove toward her and Chance. She stifled a scream as something fluttered against her hair.

An arm like a metal bar circled her waist and pulled her against a body indistinguishable from the limestone wall except it was warm and inviting—and most definitely male. Somehow Chance managed to hold the light with his right hand as his left clutched her tightly. His chin closed down on the top of her head, covering her, protecting her from the onslaught. "Hold on, babe. They'll be gone in a couple of seconds."

As if obeying his command, the mass shot out of the opening, and the rush of beating wings faded to unnatural silence.

Kyndal fought to calm her breathing, which came in sputtering gasps, sobs without any accompanying tears.

Chance's hold on her didn't loosen, but his jaw slid down across her temple until his mouth hovered above her ear. "Shh. It's okay. They're gone. Shhhh." He took deep breaths, his strong arm pulling her in and then relaxing, setting a pace. When her breathing matched his, he finally eased his grip.

"I don't want to scare you." His chuckle made her swing around to face him. "They don't stay gone very long. In fact, they're probably on their way back now."

They ran from the room, scooping up backpacks as they passed. With the lamp still shining in one hand, Chance slung his pack over his shoulder and grabbed her. He pulled her out a different opening than the one they entered from and then ducked through another before switching off the lamp.

The sound of beating wings could be heard in the distance, coming closer with every breath. The sound grew to a roar then *whoosh!* It was gone. All was quiet again.

She could hear Chance unzipping his pack and fumbling around. In a moment, the soft light of his lantern showed her the small cavern they'd taken refuge in.

As if somebody had pulled a plug, the strength drained from her body. She sank to the floor and lay back, resting the camera on her stomach.

Chance squatted beside her, shining the light onto her face. "You okay?"

"Yeah. Just feeling the passing effects of the adrenaline rush." She pushed the lantern away. "Now get that thing out of my eyes."

"Reeeow!" Chance did a good imitation of a mad cat.

She hissed in return, and they laughed together as she sat up. "Let's see what we've got here." She turned the camera back on, and they scanned through the images of the bat cavern.

Several were of exceptional quality. One of a bat coming right at her.

"That's probably the little bastard that got in your hair."

"Eewww!" The thought sent a shiver down her spine. Then she remembered the feel of Chance's body against her, his arm pulling her close. "Thanks for shielding me and—and for steadying me."

"I'm glad to be a part of it. These are good, Kyn. Really good." The admiration in his voice made her face warm. "So when did you decide to drop pre-law and major in photography?"

She flipped the front of the camera toward her and blew on the lens, using more force than necessary to get rid of a couple of dust specks. The question was innocent enough, but it raised her ire just the same. If he'd been with her the way he'd promised, he would know why she changed majors.

She wiped the lens with the hem of her shirt, studiously avoiding eye contact.

But he hadn't been there. He couldn't know her disappointment when the financial aid counselor showed her how little the scholarship would actually cover considering the number of years of schooling law would take. He couldn't know her frustration when her lifelong dream lay shattered by a dollar sign.

He'd been at Harvard, not concerned in the least about finances…or her.

Living his damn easy life.

Her hands trembled as she replaced the lens cap and eased the camera into the security of the backpack. Sometimes those emotions rolled themselves into a fresh ball of anger that bounced around inside her head. Right then, it pounded against her heart, nauseating her with its rhythm.

Lashing out at Chance now would only make him mad enough to call off this venture. Retribution would come with the lost shots of the cave and the lost job.

She covered her mouth, pretending to yawn, opening wide enough to release the tension from her jaw but not quite wide enough to release her anger. "I took a photography class as an elective during my first semester, and I enjoyed it. Got hooked, you know?" She took her time zipping the backpack closed.

"At first, the attraction had to do with being able to arrange things perfectly and capture that perfection forever. With more classes, it became a fascination with the perfection of nature. A leaf hanging in midair by an invisible thread of a spider's web. A cave with walls of crystal or a swirl of bats. It's just the kind of match for me that law school never would've been."

She let the subject drop there. Her passion for photography was difficult to explain, especially to people who'd known her when she was younger and determined to be an attorney. Most people's occupations caused their anxiety; photography eased hers. "I'm lucky to have found an occupation that doesn't just earn me money. It fulfills me." She breathed easier, amazed at how much her thoughts had cleared.

Time to get her thoughts back on track. She'd let her past with Chance obscure her passion for this mission. That he left her nine years ago had no bearing on what was going on today. He was someone she'd had a relationship with over a third of her life ago and who now owned the cave. He was the means to an end. That was all.

The past twenty-four hours had been trying. She needed some time to relax and get her head clear before updating her portfolio. "C'mon. Let's get to that vug. I need to get home."

She was surprised to see relief shadow his face before he answered, "Yeah. This way." He was as anxious to get this over with as she was.

He led the way through several more caverns. One they had to squeeze through sideways. Another required more crawling. It wasn't the way she'd come the day before, but he seemed to know where he was going. She drew a deeper breath when she saw the limestone column formation in the middle of the room. Taking the lantern, she shone it toward the crevice. Crystals winked on the other side, giving the cavern thousands of tiny, watchful eyes. She and Chance stood silently, watching back.

He moved toward the sight, lured by the same force she'd experienced the day before. He jumped, caught the rim and pulled himself up, biceps bulging under the exertion, muscles in his back rippling under the stretched cotton. It took some manipulation to wedge those broad shoulders and the arm with the lantern through the narrow gap.

"Damn! This is more amazing than I imagined." He flashed the lantern around the room, and his voice held the same wonder she'd felt with that first glimpse. "I can't believe I've never noticed this."

Fragments of light escaped between Chance and the wall surrounding him, haloing his body with a silver lining. Kyndal fought the part of her that wanted to do some noticing of its own. With him hanging there in front of her, oblivious to her ogling, it was difficult not to notice the way he filled out those jeans, especially as he bent at the waist, his legs taut, gripping the wall. His slim waist tapered up into a broad back. And it took no great stretch of the imagination to picture the muscled thighs and calves hidden beneath the denim.

Her face warmed when she felt her body's reaction. She fumbled aimlessly with her backpack as he jumped down.

"Incredible!"

Wonder and excitement glowed in his eyes as he moved toward her, and for a brief moment Kyndal was transported back to the day they first made love, realization gripping her heart. She wanted to touch him the way she had then. A lover's touch. One last time.

The stubble along his jaw deepened in the hazy light. She drew the back of her fingers through it a couple of times, enjoying the way the scratchy texture left a tingle on her skin.

Their gazes locked and she answered the question in his eyes. "You had some dust in your whiskers."

She read the almost imperceptible movement in his body. The slight bend of his torso toward her in invitation. He was going to try to kiss her, but she couldn't let that happen.

She'd loved him, and he'd left her. She wouldn't travel that road again.

Snatching up her pack, she moved out of harm's way.

CHANCE KICKED HIMSELF for making the move. She'd wanted him for a split second. He'd seen that look enough times to have it firmly engraved in his memory. The way she'd touched his face…

He'd have to be more careful.

Heeding the warning, he picked up his pack and went to stand beside her under the opening.

"I don't think I can go through headfirst." Her voice was all business again as she studied the crevice. "There's nothing to grab on to on the other side."

He'd noticed that also and nodded in agreement.

"So, if you'll give me a foot-up—" she interlaced her fingers in demonstration "—I'll get a leg through and let myself down feetfirst. Pitch me the lantern and the packs, then I can grab your hands and help you maneuver through."

He leaned down as she placed her foot into the stirrup of his interlaced fingers. Her hands braced against his shoulders as he tried not to think about how the position brought her breasts into perfect alignment with his face, his mouth within reach of the peaks protruding through the material of her shirts.

"Ready?"

Her hand trembled slightly, and his mouth, which had been almost watering three seconds ago, went suddenly dry. "I'm ready," he answered, then added, "You be careful."

"One, two, three." She pushed down on his shoulders as he straightened.

The nymph weighed almost nothing—far less than the barbells he worked out with at the gym.

She shimmied through the crevice like a kid on a climber.

He eased the lantern through first, then their packs.

"Ooooo." Kyndal's voice took on a childlike quality as it floated through the gap. He could hear her moving around the small cavern. "The floor is weird-feeling—kind of spongy."

Spongy? That didn't sound right. He jumped and grabbed the rim. This was a limestone cave. The floors should be dirt and rock. Not spongy.

His memory raced to what he'd read about vugs. Bubbles left over after volcanic activity. Bubbles. Shells. Over thousands of years, what if the limestone and dirt underneath washed away? How thick would the bubble be? What if there was nothing left to support the shell? He scrambled to maneuver his head and shoulders through the opening.

The lantern and backpacks sat in the middle of the small oval cavern. Kyndal tiptoed along the far wall, running her hand along the snowballed contours.

Instinct told him the floor might not hold his weight, but she was so small…

"Kyndal, come back to this side." He fought to control the panic in his voice. "Come back over here, babe." Knees braced against the outer wall, he stretched his arms toward her.

She shot him a quizzical look over her shoulder.

An ominous cracking sound ricocheted off the walls.

Kyndal spun around to face him. She took a couple of steps in his direction, then froze. "Chance, something's happening." Terror vibrated her voice.

"Kynd—"

Another crack brought a scream that ended all too abruptly.

Panic exploded like a bomb in Chance's chest. He propelled himself through the opening and plunged headlong into darkness.

CHAPTER SEVEN

THE SILENCE WAS DEAFENING, compounding the sound of blood rushing through Chance's ears.

As if diving from a high dive platform, he'd somehow coaxed his body into a partial flip, allowing him to land on his back and side rather than his head. His left hip and torso took the brunt of the fall. He gasped to get the air back into his lungs.

Wiggling fingers and toes told him he wasn't paralyzed. The searing pain that cut through his chest when he pushed up on an elbow was possibly a broken rib but most likely a bad bruise. He'd live.

Fear gripped him when he realized he hadn't heard anything from Kyndal. "Kyn?" The darkness swallowed his word, making it almost inaudible even to him. He breathed deeply, holding his side, and forced his voice. "Kyndal!"

A low moan came from somewhere to his left. He eased up onto his feet. As he raised his arm to wipe his face, the hands on his watch seemed to float in midair. They put off a ghostly glow, but it gave him something to focus on as he stepped gingerly in the direction of her sound, keeping his arms out to feel his way. "Kyndal? Where are you? Talk to me, baby, so I can find you."

"Uuungh."

He turned his ear toward the sound and redirected his steps. "That's it. Lead me with your voice."

"Chance? Ooowww."

His heartbeat went wild. He didn't know whether to be thrilled that she'd spoken or terrified because she was in pain. "Keep making noise, Kyn. C'mon, babe."

"Chance!" Kyndal's voice grew to a cry of alarm. "I hit my head. Everything's so black, I'm afraid I'm blind!"

"No, you're not." Spurred by her fear, he groped his way toward the voice through the enveloping blackness. "It's just the dark, Kyndal. We'll find a way to get some light. Just let me find you first."

Her soft sobbing pulled him to the right this time. The thick darkness was nearly tangible, like a living creature. It wrapped around him and squeezed, made his breathing come fast, licked at the sweat on the back of his neck. He needed to touch Kyndal. If he could touch her, things would be okay. "Are you wearing a watch?"

"Ye—yeah." The word broke on a snubbed breath. She wasn't too far away. A few more feet.

"Look at your watch. Are the hands glowing? Can you see the hands?"

"No!" A panicked shriek this time. "Oh, my God, Chance! I can't—I can't see them! Ohhh."

Something soft against his foot. He dropped to one knee and felt. A backpack. *Please let it be mine.* "Kyn, listen to me. Shhh. Don't panic." He could hear her panting—maybe going into shock. He located a zipper and jerked it open. "I've found one of the bags, and I've got it open. If it's mine, there'll be a light in just a second."

He took a blind inventory of the contents. Two bottles of water. One crushed and leaking. A small first aid kit.

He plunged through the contents to the very bottom and grabbed the emergency flashlight his mom had put in his stocking last Christmas. A novelty item—a flashlight with no batteries, modeled after ones used in World War II. He'd thought it pretty useless at the time but had put it in the "cave bag." Now, as he squeezed the hand pump on the bottom and watched the tiny bulb begin to glow, he thought it was the most wonderful item ever invented.

The beam broke through the inky blackness and landed on Kyndal about ten feet away, huddled into a tiny ball, knees pulled to her chest. Her head jerked up at the sound of his movement toward her. She squinted and then her eyes grew wide as she jumped up to meet him, flinging her arms around his neck. "Oh, Chance," she sobbed, "I'm not blind. I was so scared."

He pulled her against him, lifting her completely off the floor and buried his face in her hair. "Shhh. It's okay. You're okay." He gritted his teeth against the pain in his side, but he couldn't bring himself to let her go. He held her, breathing deeply, stroking her hair. His stomach did a somersault when his hand came away wet.

Gently, he set her on her feet. "Kyn, I think you're bleeding."

She winced and eased herself down into a sitting position. "Yeah. My ankle's hurt. I landed on one foot, I think, then fell backward and hit my head." She sat down, removed her hiking boot and sock, and pulled up her pants leg. He stooped to examine it, noticing the shattered lantern behind her. Her ankle had already begun to bruise and was puffy.

"Could be broken. Might be a sprain. But I need to check your head first."

Her hand groped the back of her head. When she pulled it away, it was covered in blood.

Chance steeled himself for her reaction, but she surprised him by taking a deep breath and biting her bottom lip.

"Let me have a look." He kept his voice low and even. If she could keep from panicking, so could he.

He knelt behind her, pumping the flashlight up to its maximum. His fingertips and thumb began a gentle probe. "Tell me where it hurts."

"Up and to the left."

He moved his fingers as she directed and soon found a lump just behind her left ear. Roughly the diameter of a golf ball, from what he could judge. His fingers parted her hair. A nasty gash ran along the top of the swollen area, not too long, but still oozing blood.

He pulled his T-shirt over his head and wadded it into a ball, which he pushed gently against the wound. "Hold that firmly right there." He took her hand and guided it to the makeshift compress.

"It's chilly in here," she protested. "You need your shirt."

The adrenaline flooding his body had him drenched in sweat. The cool felt great for the moment, but it wouldn't take long to get chilled. "I've got a flannel in my bag. It's in a side compartment that shouldn't be wet." He took the flashlight and went back over to his bag.

THE IMAGE OF CHANCE WITHOUT a shirt was better than any painkiller Kyndal could have taken. Her throbbing ankle and head were momentarily forgotten as she took advantage of the blackness, covertly studying his sculpted abs and pecs, gleaming with sweat in the dim yellow glow. Shadows played along the ridges and the hollows, defining every muscle, highlighting each ripple. Mmm. Hunk calendar material. Instinctively, she reached for her camera.

Chance shrugged into the extra shirt from his pack, and the pain in her ankle and head returned full force along with a sickening lurch in the pit of her stomach. "Chance, have you seen my pack?"

She heard the pump of the flashlight and watched the

light grow stronger. She held her breath as he flashed the beam around and brought it to rest on a black lump resting against a gray wall. Her pack! She dropped the wad of T-shirt and scrambled to her feet, only to sink back down to the floor when pain stabbed through her ankle.

"Stay there."

Her teeth gritted at the command in his voice, an unfamiliar sound that would never have come from the Chance she used to know.

He knelt and set the bag in front of her. "Want me to open it?" No gruffness this time. His voice was soft and gentle and full of sympathy. He didn't know about her dire financial straits, but he seemed to understand what the loss of this camera would mean. She shook her head.

Her breath came in spurts as she started unzipping the middle compartment. Her hands trembled, giving the stubborn zipper a mind of its own. Chance's hand covered hers, calming the tremor, bringing the zipper under control until it parted completely.

He focused the beam into the bag. The two tripod lamps lay on top, legs slightly bent, but not irreparable. She laid them aside. Both of the expensive bulbs were shattered.

Turning the pack and giving it a little shake, she prayed only the glass from the bulbs would fall out. Her breathing stopped as she pulled the camera out and examined it. Everything looked intact. The lens wasn't broken.

She flipped the switch. Her heart sang to the strains of the charging battery. When the indicator light showed "ready," she pressed the button. A flash and then an image of gray walls appeared on the screen. Not a prizewinner, but a beautiful sight to her eyes.

Chance's breath exploded in relief, and she gave a giddy laugh. It wasn't until he brushed a tear from her cheek that she realized she was crying. "So now we can worry about the really important stuff like where we are. And how do we get out of here?"

Chance pumped the flashlight as bright as it would go and traced the hole in the ceiling. Jagged, brittle edges surrounded a gaping hole ten, maybe twelve feet above their heads. Climbing out didn't look promising.

"What happened exactly?" She snapped several shots of the hole. The crystal dome winked mocking eyes at them.

"The outer shell of the vug gave away. There was nothing underneath. Maybe never was."

She recognized the tension in his voice, and her stomach tightened. It was one thing to get herself into this predicament—something else to drag someone with her into this hellhole. "People warned me not to do this, said it was dangerous. Oh, Chance, I'm so sorry." She swiped her hand through her hair. The knot behind her ear throbbed, but the bleeding had stopped.

His arm came around her shoulder with a comforting squeeze. "Not your fault. I should've thought faster and stayed behind. I could've gone for help. It was just… when I…when I heard you scream…I…" His deep voice cracked, and he finished his statement by kissing her on top of her head.

The emotion in his voice, the touch, the kiss. It was too familiar and too much. A lump in her throat grew as large as the one on her head.

They had to get out of there.

CHAPTER EIGHT

"I'VE SEEN MOVIES WHERE people tied their clothes together and used them as ropes."

She couldn't be serious. "If I get you to take your clothes off, I'm sure as hell not gonna worry about making a rope, or even try too hard to get out of here." Chance laughed, meaning it as a joke—sort of.

"Maybe if I stood on your shoulders…" Kyndal's voice broke in panic.

Chance studied the distance from where he stood to the opening in the ceiling. "We still wouldn't reach it. Besides, it's too dangerous with that ankle of yours."

"Did you know the cave had a section deeper underground? Have you ever explored it?"

He shook his head to both questions.

"So what do we do?" A tremor rattled her question.

"We wait. The best thing to do is stay put. Let's hope Sheriff Blaine takes the day off, and the teenagers like to party on Sunday."

"That could be hours from now. Late tonight."

"People know we're here. Jaci and Bart…and you're dating someone, right? Surely, he'll get worried when you don't come home."

"We're not living together. And he's working a lot of nights, so I'm not sure when he'll call." Kyndal took a deep breath, closing her eyes for a long moment. Even when she opened them again, an impenetrable veil behind them stayed down. A defiant tilt of her chin let him know her love life wasn't up for discussion. "What about you? Did you tell anyone?"

Chance rubbed his hand down his face in frustration. "The office is closed until Wednesday. Mom and Dad have already left for New Orleans, and our secretary's father is having surgery tomorrow." Another flicker of hope came to him. "Don't you and Jaci talk all the time?"

Kyndal's sigh extinguished the flicker. "Usually just once a week, unless something important comes up."

She didn't say being with Chance Brennan wasn't important enough, but the implication stung just the same.

"Your mom?"

She shook her head. "On one of her trips. I don't know where she is."

Chance well remembered Mrs. Rawlings's unannounced little trips. Kyndal would come home to find a note, and her mom would be gone. Damn woman missed her daughter's high school graduation—valedictory address and all. His own mom, bless her heart, took Kyn shopping and paid for her dress for their senior prom.

"So…we're stuck. Until somebody figures out we're missing. Or the teenagers decide to party…" Kyndal's words trailed off to a breathless whisper.

Chance's mind raced. Was it possible they'd actually have to stay there overnight? Or longer? Without supplies? Water. They'd need water.

He found the bottles he'd stuck in his pack. One was crushed and had lost most of its contents into the pack. He pulled it out and laid it on its side to preserve what was left. The other was still intact.

He removed the small first aid kit, replacing it with his soiled T-shirt to soak up the precious liquid. He could use that to cleanse Kyndal's head and put some of the medicated ointment on it. The ibuprofen would ease her pain for a little while. No food, though. "Do you have anything to eat with you?" She didn't have enough meat on her bones to last too many days without food.

"A couple of granola bars."

"And I have a bottle of water. We won't starve, but we'll have to conserve."

"You don't really think we'll have to stay in here that long. Do you?"

She groped for reassurance, and he wanted desperately to give her what she was looking for. His gut told him they needed to play it smart, and play it right. He forced some levity into his voice. "I think we're gonna be fine. We just need to keep our heads. We can't panic. I've read a lot about caves, so I'm not completely in the dark about this."

Her response was a sarcastic snort.

"Okay, so I'm in the dark, but not completely." He sat down and patted the area bedside him. The way she hobbled over and plopped down so quickly alerted him she needed medical attention. "Let me see that ankle."

Kyndal pulled up her pants leg again, exposing an ugly purple-and-black area where an ankle should have been. He couldn't tell where her calf ended and her ankle began. It appeared to be broken—and painful from the way she chewed her bottom lip. Although he tried to be gentle, she flinched at his touch.

The foot needed stabilizing. His first aid kit lacked any adhesive tape, and the tiny gauze bandage wouldn't go very far. "Do you have any first aid supplies in your bag?"

She shook her head. "I've got some masking tape."

"That'll work. I can wrap the ankle. But it would be better if we had a splint of some kind." He scanned their surroundings with the light, looking for anything useful.

Just a mass of smooth limestone and dirt as far as the meager light reached.

The beam fell on Kyndal's lamps. "How much do those lamps cost?" He flashed the light over the bent frames, evaluating their usefulness.

"A couple hundred apiece. But they're not mine. They belong to— Chance, you can't—"

Before she could protest again, he'd grabbed one of them and snapped off a leg.

Kyndal gasped as if she'd been slapped.

"I'll buy a new one." He grunted and broke off another one.

A quick shuffle through the photography paraphernalia in Kyndal's bag produced a sizable roll of masking tape. A strategically placed rock kept the flashlight aimed at her foot as they worked, but he had to keep pumping it up.

A penknife allowed him to rip her jeans leg to the knee, then he stripped her hiking boot of its shoelace and spread the tongue area as a cradle for her foot. The padded top was a good support around her ankle. He slipped the sock over her toes and up to the arch to keep her foot warm. Following his directions, she held the two broken lamp legs on either side of her leg as he secured them with the shoelaces and rolled the tape around until he'd fashioned a makeshift splint.

"With no ice to keep it from swelling, we'll likely have to remove the tape eventually. I don't want to cut off the circulation." He pumped the flashlight and spotlighted the area, eyeing their handiwork critically. It would have to do. "Does it hurt much?"

She shook her head. "Not too bad." When the light reached her face, her eyes said she was lying.

"I've got ibuprofen." He indicated the first aid kit.

"I'm okay. I'll save that for if and when I really need it."

"We need to keep it elevated as much as we can." For lack of anything better, he located a boulder of manageable size and eased it under her foot. She winced and his stomach rolled. Knowing she was hurting was almost more than he could take.

"Thanks." Her face was in shadow and he couldn't see her expression, but her voice was soft with gratitude.

"It's not great, but maybe it will help." He sat down beside her and pumped the flashlight up again to its max. She shivered against him. "Are you cold?"

"A little."

"It stays fifty-three degrees in here year-round, so we won't freeze." But they wouldn't be comfortable, either. Unless he could convince her that sharing body heat in a time of crisis was necessary.

He put his arm around her and pulled her close. She didn't protest but instead leaned into him, and he heard her quick intake of breath. "Take some of the ibuprofen, Kyn. There's no use sitting here in pain."

She turned her face toward him when she spoke. "I'm okay. Really."

Her mouth was, what? Two inches from his? All he had to do was angle his head downward a little more and he would kiss her lips.

His eyes moved upward from her mouth and their gazes locked, brought together by this trauma, held by memory. He touched his forehead softly to hers. And then, as if it were the most natural thing in the world, their noses met, and then their lips. It wasn't a kiss of passion as much as one of compassion and support. A soft coming together, a symbol of the need for them to press through this together. Her lips trembled under his, shaking him to the core.

They sighed in unison when their mouths parted. "We're gonna be okay," he whispered.

She nodded, then wiped away a tear.

Damn it. Now he'd made her cry.

KYNDAL RAISED HER EYES to the hole in the roof in an attempt to stop the tears. Crying wouldn't help this situation at all. It wouldn't ease the searing pain in her foot or the throbbing in her head. Wouldn't erase the bittersweetness of Chance's lips on hers or stop her desire to press him closer.

She held the tears in check by logic and an upraised chin.

Chance stood abruptly. The sudden movement changed the mood and shocked her system back into panic mode. His attention was on the flashlight as he examined it closely. He moved something on the side and the beam held steady. "Ha! I knew there had to be a way to make the light last longer so I won't have to pump it constantly." His voice held a note of triumph. "Kyn, if it's okay with you, I'm going to explore a little."

"No! Please don't leave." Her breaths were coming fast, but it didn't feel as if any air was getting into her lungs. "I—I'm scared…don't want to—to be alone."

Chance laid the flashlight in her lap as he knelt down and took her face in his hands. "You'll be okay. I won't be gone long, I promise, but I'd hate to think I sat here doing nothing when there might be a way out."

His words—his touch—calmed her and brought her breathing to almost normal. She nodded, but fought down another surge of panic when he stood and picked up the flashlight. He would need the light, of course, and the thought of being left in the hellish darkness gave her an idea.

Her foot weighed as much as the rock it sat on, but with some effort, she raised it and pulled her backpack from the pile. "I'll get the flash from my camera. It's got a good battery that'll last a long time. If I need to see, I'll just set off a flash."

Her fingers worked nimbly in the shadows as she disengaged the flash from the rest of the camera. The battery hummed its high-pitched frequency, and the indicator light winked at her. She held it up and let it flash, catching Chance's face in a look that softened from surprise to admiration.

"Be back soon, I promise."

As he moved off into the darkness, his last words echoed around her.

He will. He'll be back soon.

She'd thought those exact words nine years ago, and they hadn't been true then.

The pale beam of light grew smaller with the distance, and the smaller it grew, the more quickly she breathed. When he got completely out of sight, the blackness crushed in on her, leaving her gasping for air. What if something happened to him? What if a boulder fell—or what if he got lost and didn't come back? Ever?

She opened her mouth to call to him but forced herself to take a deep breath instead. He would come back. He *would* come back…this time.

CHAPTER NINE

SMALL CAVERNS. LARGE CAVERNS. Caverns of every size and shape. The lower level of the cave was as intricate as the one above. It was risky to go farther without something to point the way back, and Chance's pockets were empty.

He did an about-face and retraced his steps, following the coins he'd placed as markers but not picking them up. They would stay as indicators of the area he'd already explored. In a little while, he'd come back and go deeper, but right now he needed to get back to Kyndal. Even more, he *wanted* to get back to Kyndal.

Like a lab rat sniffing for cheese in a maze, he swept the ground with the light, watching for the glint of metal. Shiny pennies had never been so valuable.

The trail ended, and he squeezed through the narrow opening into the large cavern where they had landed.

The flashlight beam found where the packs had been, but they were gone...along with Kyndal.

Had someone come? His heart beat furiously as he scanned the jagged hole above his head. He held his breath, listening for sounds from above—sounds of rescue. It was crazy. He hadn't been gone long. Surely he would have heard shouts.

His heartbeat surged into a panicked rhythm. Where was she? "Kyndal!" he shouted.

"I'm over here."

He moved toward the sound, straining to see past the confines of the narrow light.

He found her, yards away from where he'd left her, leaning against a boulder, taking shots of…a wall?

"Spiders." She kept her voice low as if she were afraid of giving her location away to the enemy and pointed. "There."

Chance peered in the direction she indicated, swirling the light around the base of the wall until it fell on a place where the texture seemed to change, even from a distance. The reason for the difference caused his throat to constrict.

The wall was no longer an inanimate object. It had come to life, covered by a multitude of white, scurrying bodies.

Chance stepped back enough to have a head start should they decide to give up their exploration of their home for the promise of fresh meat. He slid the light up the wall and drew a sharp breath. The limestone edifice was a solid mass of intricate webbing, teeming with shimmering, eight-legged bodies.

For reasons he couldn't quite fathom, the one wall seemed to be the habitat of choice. None of the other areas had any sign of spiders or webs. A water source perhaps? Deep within the rock? The idea made his throat go dry. He and Kyndal would have to be careful with their water. Doing battle with this number of enemies would be an exercise in futility.

"Aren't they beautiful?" she whispered.

"Ghastly. Creepy. Hideous." He shuddered. "Only a tree hugger could see beauty."

"Only someone with his head up his ass couldn't." She continued taking her shots.

"And yet I still manage to keep my nose clean."

"What's that supposed to mean?" She leaned against the boulder and turned toward him.

"I searched you on Google you last night—interesting article, by the way. All about a scandalous end to your beloved website."

"I haven't read it so I'll take your word. Oh, wait…I probably shouldn't make that mistake again." She snatched up her bag and stuffed the camera back into its chamber, keeping the flash out.

"I never lied to you, Kyndal." The tops of his ears started to burn.

"Obviously, saying you'll never leave means something different in Brennan-speak."

"Damn it, Kyndal. You haven't been entirely truthful, either." He caught her arm as she pushed past him, but she jerked it out of his grip and hobbled toward the far end of the cavern, which they hadn't explored yet.

He moved faster, checking the area for additional spider colonies or any other movement. "Why didn't you tell me you were out of work?"

When Kyndal plopped down against the wall, her face contorted in pain. "Why should I? I'm not out of work. I'm just out of the kind of work that supplies luxuries—you know, the stuff you've had all your life."

The gloves came off at that remark. "The people who lost their jobs because of your damn website needed to eat, too—or didn't that occur to you? Maybe you're just reaping what you sowed."

"If that's true, your storehouse would be full of bullshit."

They glared at each other for a long, angry moment, the past hanging between them like a piñata waiting to be broken.

Chance drew a long breath, his own words eating at him as much as her retort. "I'm sorry. I really don't think you deserve what's happened. But bad choices follow us—"

She held up her hand to stop him. "I'll live with my

choices and you live with yours." She waved at the openings. "Now go find us a way out of here. There has to be one."

Light played off the wall he had yet to explore. Three openings offered hope of a way out—or at least a smaller cavern where they might be warmer.

"Someplace free of spiders," he grumbled. "They won't listen to reason, either."

KYNDAL LET OUT HER BREATH as Chance disappeared into the wall.

What was it about that man that made her lose control and go off the deep end? One part of her wanted to get as far away from him as possible while another part relished the feel of him against her.

Talk about bad choices. Coming to this cave with him was one of the worst she'd ever made—and not just because of the accident.

Maybe the bump on her head had given her a concussion that had scrambled her thoughts. Or maybe, she'd never gotten over Chance Brennan in the first place. Whatever the reason, she had to get her emotions under control and keep steering the conversations toward the present and not the past.

The teenagers probably wouldn't be partying until dark—around six o'clock. Her last glimpse at Chance's watch was maybe half an hour ago. About one-thirty then. So how to keep the conversation light for another four hours? Games? Chance had always been pretty competitive. I Spy was out. Twenty Questions? Too risky, as was Truth or Dare. Rock, Paper, Scissors had possibilities, but her skin crawled at the thought of four hours of it.

Man, a beer would taste so good right now.

A song popped in her head. She hummed a few bars,

and then started to sing softly. "Ninety-nine bottles of beer on the wall, ninety-nine bottle of beer. Take one down and pass it around..." She made it down to seventy-one before she heard shuffling noises to her left. With any luck, it would be Chance and not a backup horde of spider recruits coming her way.

But luck hadn't exactly fared well for her lately.

The pinpoint of light expanded as Chance scrambled through the far opening, and her heart pounded with relief at the sight of him. But only because he might've found a way out.

He motioned with the light toward the gap he'd come through and started gathering their packs. "There's a small cavity not too far away that I think will be warmer. Let's move in there."

She trembled at the thought of moving farther into the depths, away from the crystal opening with its connection to the upper level. "But if somebody comes, will we hear them that far away?"

"I'll come out every half hour or so. I'd feel safer if we were farther from the spiders." He held his hand out.

She took it and immediately regretted the action. His thumb brushed lightly across her knuckles as his gaze found hers. Thoughts of touching him had her primed, so the actual occurrence ran a surge through her. She felt her breath catch in her throat. The electric current followed his hand to her hip where he held her while she balanced shakily on her good foot.

She gave a nervous laugh, much too aware of him. In the stillness, she heard him swallow.

The slight tug pulled her off balance, and she came up hard against him. His free hand caught her around the waist, holding her close, his eyes searching hers, trying to see beyond the shadows. "I can't deny you still have an effect on me, Kyn. Even after all this time."

"I know. I feel it, too."

"Is it wrong? Wrong for me to want you?"

She heard the backpacks and flashlight fall from his grip an instant before his fingers traced a path from her chin to her cheek and into her hair. The light faded away as she closed her eyes. *Wanting wasn't wrong.* Wanting was a feeling, and feelings couldn't be right or wrong.

She shook her head in response to his question, melting into the familiarity of his embrace. His breath hovered just above her mouth, and she rose on tiptoe to capture it, not caring how many others there had been because at that moment, there were only the two of them.

She slid one arm around his waist, the other across his shoulder. Her fingertips played across the back of his neck before gliding into the damp fringe just above it. His back muscles shuddered then relaxed under her palm as she pressed her mouth more firmly against his and parted her lips in invitation.

The darkness wrapped around them, pushing them closer.

The kiss outlasted the first few moments of fevered intensity and settled into a rhythm of languorous sensuality.

It ended as softly as it began.

Their clutch loosened, and Kyndal lowered her weight back onto her good foot, still supported by Chance's arms.

She could feel his eyes on her even in the dark, knew instinctively he was about to kiss her again. If she didn't stop it she'd be laying herself wide-open. And, despite what she'd thought a moment ago, that would be wrong. "I can't…" *Trust you with my heart again. You left me,* she wanted to say, but this wasn't the time for an argument. "I can't do this." She pushed at his chest, heard his sigh as his hands dropped from her. A searing pain shot through her foot as she placed her toe down to balance.

"You and this guy..." The huskiness in his voice was magnified in the surrounding blackness. "What's his name?"

"Rick Warren."

"You and Rick Warren have a good thing going and you don't want to screw it up. I understand."

"No, you don't." She didn't want to pick a fight, but she wouldn't let him believe a lie. In the dark, it was easier to say things the light might not allow. "It has nothing to do with Rick. We haven't even been on a date yet. He just asked me out yesterday."

"But Jaci..."

"Was just being Jaci."

His fingers touched her arm again, worked their way down to grasp her hand as he stepped against her. "So what's stopping you? Why can't you do this?"

She shook her hand loose. "We've moved on. No use going back."

There was a long pause and then his voice cut through the darkness. "Enough said."

The finality in his words lingered, holding her motionless, and she sensed a sudden loss, as if he had vanished from her life again. When she heard the pump of the flashlight, she realized he had only bent down to retrieve their bags.

They avoided eye contact as he took her arm and helped her to the opening.

"It's sort of a tight squeeze, but it's not far. We'll have to crawl." He shone the light into the tunnel, angling it toward what looked like an indentation in the right-hand side. "That's where we're going. Think you're up to it?"

Kyndal nodded and dropped to all fours. Her knees were

already tender, but crawling was a lot easier than hobbling, and she needed some distance from him, even for only a couple of minutes.

She moved slowly, lifting her knees clear of the ground rather than scraping them on the stone beneath. Chance stayed well behind, keeping her path illuminated.

The tunnel continued to a point where it faded into nothingness. Another larger cavern? Did this cave never end?

She followed the angle of the light to the indentation, a quasi-rectangular hole that required her to turn on her side to scoot through. Inside, the small niche appeared to have been formed by a giant ice cream scoop.

Chance followed her in, filling up a large part of the small space while the fresh memory of the kiss they shared lingered in the air, taking up the rest.

Kyndal gave a mental groan at the forced intimacy and sent up a prayer that someone would find them soon.

CHAPTER TEN

"THE KIDS' CANS WERE EMPTY, but who in their right mind has a family portrait taken with everybody holding up cans of Skoal?" Kyndal threw up her hands in mock wonder.

Chance laughed, not only at the story, but at Kyndal's animated way of telling it. She'd finally dropped her cool facade and relaxed into the Kyndal he remembered—the one who did everything with zeal.

What he hadn't been able to reconcile in his mind was that, since college, the brilliant girl he'd known had already been involved in a scandal and was eeking out a living by taking family portraits at a Walmart wannabe. That bothered him more than a little.

"So, if you get this job, will you move back to Paducah?"

She smoothed a hand down her hair and leaned her head against the wall. "Yeah, or somewhere close."

Kyndal…back in Paducah…unattached. That thought was disconcerting, considering the attraction between them. Any contact would have to be limited. Affiliation with her scandal would be all he needed to blow his political ambitions to Never Never Land. Paducahans wouldn't take kindly to anyone who worked against the river industry.

Before he could delve too deeply into the matter, her stomach let out a roar that sounded as if an animal had them cornered.

"Sounds like somebody's hungry."

She pulled her pack into her lap. "You set up the house—" she nodded toward the T-shirt he'd taped across the doorway to hold in their body heat "—so I'll cook. How do you like your granola bar?"

"I prefer sunny-side up, but since all we have is this flashlight, however you fix it is fine." He moved to his knees and stretched his arms over his head, brushing his fingertips on the ceiling.

While Kyndal fished around in her pack, she motioned again to the T. "That was a good idea. It's actually pretty warm in here. Are you warm?"

He nodded.

She gave an impish grin. "Do you think it'll keep the spiders out?"

"Damn it! Would you quit mentioning the freaking spiders? They're not going to come this far."

She gave a playful laugh and held out one of the granola bars to him. He reached for it, then hesitated and waved it off. "I'm really not very hungry yet," he lied.

She saw through his charade and rolled her eyes. "This is no time to be gallant, Chance. With this ankle, you might have to carry me, so you need to keep up your strength. Here." She brandished it toward him again, but he didn't take it. She needed it more than he did, and if she got hungry enough, maybe he could talk her into eating it.

"If you're not going to eat, neither am I." Her lips pressed together in a firm line.

Damn her stubborn streak. He took the package from her with a disgruntled huff but held off tearing into it until she had hers open and had poured a few pieces into her hand.

His bar, too, had been crushed and was more of a granola pack. Luckily, the wrappers had held up even if the contents were battered. “I’m glad you brought these.” He tossed a few bits into his mouth. “I had a big bag of peanut M&M’s to share with you when we got back to the house. Too bad I didn’t put them in my pack.”

“Oooo, not sure I would’ve shared them, anyway.” She rolled her eyes dreamily. “Those are my favorite.”

“I know.” He smiled and gave her a playful wink.

She rolled her eyes again, this time in vexation. “You thought you could seduce me with chocolate?” She turned the bag up and released the last few morsels of oat-and-honey clusters into her mouth.

“Actually, I remembered how you always wanted candy…um, afterward.”

A flash of anger shot from her eyes. “Of all the nerve!” She wadded up the cellophane wrapper and launched it at his head. “You are the most single-minded, self-assured, hopeless egomaniac I’ve ever…ever been stuck in a cave with.” She shook her head. “You honestly thought I was going to sleep with you?”

“Not sure there was going to be much sleeping involved, but I thought we might have sex.”

“Augh!” She crossed her arm tightly across her chest, her back pressed against the wall.

“Oh, c’mon, Kyn. Don’t tell me it didn’t cross your mind. I felt that kiss out there.” He wiggled his finger between them. “We’ve got chemistry. We’ve always had chemistry.”

“Yeah, well, chemistry doesn’t heal broken hearts.” Heat emanated from her words as her voice became louder. “And you didn’t just break mine. You ripped it out of my chest and stomped on it.”

What had started as a little sparring was turning into a full-on argument, but that was okay. He was tired of tiptoeing around this issue—and damn tired of the guilt he'd carried for nine years.

"You don't think it hurt me?" he rebutted. "It did! But it was the only way, Kyndal. Between you and Dad, I was suffocating! He was pushing and you were pulling…no, you weren't just pulling, you were clinging…so…damn…tight. I felt like I couldn't breathe. I had to get away." He stopped, aware he'd said too much, but letting the truth out had released a ten-ton weight from his chest.

"I've always believed—or at least I've always told myself—you broke up with me because of your dad. I was always a nobody to him. Never good enough for his son." The clipped staccato of her words pushed him over the brink.

"Hell, *I* wasn't even good enough for his son." His angry words hit the close surrounding walls and bounced back at him. "My whole life, all his dreams were pinned on Hank, and that was okay. He pushed me, wanted me to excel, but the major attention went to Hank. And then after Hank died…" His throat constricted at the words. *Damn it...damn it...damn it! Not now.* He ran his hand down his face. He was exhausted from the stress of the day, nerves stretched to the breaking point. His emotions were too raw for this. But something snapped, and words poured out. "His drive for me doubled. No, it tripled…quadrupled. He and Mom fell apart. I became all he had."

He paused, but Kyndal didn't say anything. He fought to gain control of his words. He had to make her understand. "Dad didn't think you were a nobody, Kyn. You scared him because you were my…my everything.

"Losing you on top of losing Hank was unbearable for a while. But I threw myself into my studies. I took all the time and energy I would've spent on you and used it to keep my grades up. And it worked. I kept a high ranking all the way through, which kept Dad satisfied. Every time he talked to me, he'd tell me he was counting on me to come back and practice law with him…that Hank would've wanted me to be there. He reminded me of my ambition to become a judge…and how proud Hank would've been of me."

Emotions spent, Chance drew a long breath. Kyndal didn't say anything, and he wondered if she would ever speak to him again now she knew the truth.

"Thanks for being honest with me," she said at last, her voice tight with emotion. "I needed to know." He watched her throat convulse as she swallowed. "And, like I said before, we've moved on. There's no need to go back."

KYNDAL HELD THE T-SHIRT UP as Chance crawled through the opening for the fourteenth time since they'd set up camp in the niche. She didn't have to ask. She'd listened and had easily heard his long blows on the emergency whistle he kept in his pack.

There had been no answering shouts any of the previous thirteen times, and this one was no different.

It was almost ten o'clock. Rescue wasn't going to come tonight. She was almost glad her stomach was near empty because it drew into a hard knot that would've forced any contents upward.

Chance gave a resigned shrug. "Nobody out there. I don't think there's much chance of anybody showing up tonight." He rubbed his hands together, blowing on them. "Are you cold?"

"Not too."

The earlier argument, his confession, her realization his life hadn't been so easy… Those things had broken down some barrier between them and made the past few hours much more amiable. Kyndal had never had anybody around long enough to tell her what to do—listening to him gave her a new understanding of what life would be like with a father like Bill Brennan. No independence. Little privacy. Unbearable.

Chance picked up the deck of cards he'd produced from his backpack earlier along with a small wooden case of dominoes. The games had helped the hours pass.

"It's probably safe now to get into a serious game of Strip Poker."

She glared at him. "Don't start with me again. No Strip Poker. No Strip Crazy Eights. No Strip Hearts or Strip Spades."

His low chuckle mocked her outburst, which infuriated her even more. "You're cute when you're all huffy like that." He scooted up beside her. "All joking aside, if we took off our clothes and cuddled, we'd probably stay warm. Your jeans would have to stay on, but we could use our shirts as blankets, and my jeans could be a pillow. You need some kind of cushion under your head, and we need to leave the packs under your foot."

The thought of them even partially naked sent a heated flush through her body, but the idea of laying her head on the ground made her pause. The ibuprofen had helped the pain and the swelling of both her ankle and her head. Neither one throbbed much anymore, but both were sore.

"Or you could lay your head in my lap."

"No, thanks. Too hard and lumpy. And no nudity." She answered his smug grin with a sweet smile. "Here." She pulled one of the packs from beneath her leg. "You can use this so you won't think about putting your head in *my* lap."

She was still all too aware the chemistry he spoke of was indeed there. The hours of close proximity had her wound so tight she would explode on contact if his warm breath so much as flickered against her skin.

"We need to get some rest."

Hearing the weariness in his voice, she scooted down and lay back carefully, placing her arm behind her head.

Chance placed the flashlight between them. "Do you want this on or off?"

She didn't expect to sleep a wink, but maybe he could get some rest if the area was dark. "Off," she said.

He flipped the switch that plunged them into absolute darkness.

Kyndal swallowed the surge of panic that rose in her throat. It was so dark. So freaking dark. "Chance?"

"Yeah?" His breath touched her cheek, which told her he was lying on his side facing her.

"Would you think I was being too clingy if I asked you to hold my hand?"

She heard the scrape of the pack on the floor and felt his body slide even closer to her. She tensed. He raised her head gently, placing it in the nook of his shoulder. He rested the flashlight on her belly and covered it with her right hand. Drawing her close against him, he clasped her left hand, relaxing his arm across her middle.

The tension left her body. She felt safe in his comforting embrace.

KYNDAL'S ANSWERING MACHINE picked up for the third time in three hours. Jaci looked at her watch. Ten twenty-eight and still no Kyndal. "Should I be worried?"

"If I say no, will it make any difference?" Bart adjusted the pillows behind him and laid the book he'd been reading to the side.

"But she's still not home." She placed her cell phone into the cradle to charge. "And she needs to get a job that will let her afford a cell phone."

"You're not her mother, Eight Ball."

His use of her old nickname lightened the mood, making her smile as she turned back to him. "Somebody's gotta be." She threw the covers back and climbed on top, straddling her husband. "You think she's spending the night with him, don't you?"

Bart nodded. "Yep."

"That's not good."

His lips twitched, and he wiggled his eyebrows suggestively. "Oh, I dunno about that. Things used to be pretty hot between them."

"You know what I mean." The past two days had been so frustrating, worrying about her best friend, which was nothing new. She pushed her bottom lip out in a pout. "Kyn's finally put him behind her, and she and Rick finally have a date. Sleeping with Chance will mess everything up." She locked her arms across her chest with a huff.

Bart pried her arms loose and interlocked his fingers with hers. "What happened to that everything-happens-for-a-reason philosophy you always pull on me?"

"I just can't stand the thought of him hurting her again."

"And you think that will happen if they do the nasty?" he growled, and proceeded to nibble on her knuckles.

The sensuous sound and actions made her lose her concentration for a moment. She poked his chest, causing him to groan in mock pain. "It won't be *the nasty* for Kyndal. This is Chance, remember? For her it'll be making love. You yourself told me he had political aspirations. They're on opposite sides of the political fence."

"True, *but*—and I say this with all the love and burning desire I feel for you—you need to back off and let Kyndal make her own decisions and quit feeling responsible for her. She's a grown woman. She'll figure it all out, and she'll call you when she's ready to talk."

He tossed her off of him onto her back and stifled her

response with a kiss. As soon as his lips left hers, he continued. "And, while we're on the subject, I know you care about Julia, but you need to take care of the business, and let Stuart take care of his wife."

She shuddered. "Stuart makes me uncomfortable."

"All the more reason you need to stay out of their private affairs." Bart kissed her and brushed the hair back from her face, the earnest look in his eyes melting her heart. "You try to mother everybody. Maybe it's time we tried again."

A lingering pain stabbed at her heart, the miscarriage five months ago still too fresh. "I'm not ready yet..." Her throat convulsed. "I may not ever be ready."

She saw the disappointment in his eyes, but he covered it almost as quickly as it appeared. "Why, babe? Talk to me."

It wasn't just the pain of the loss that had been troubling her lately. "I'm afraid."

Bart's slightly crooked mouth tightened in concern, and blurred in her vision. "Of what? You're okay, aren't you?"

The panic in his voice spurred her. "I'm fine *physically.*" He brushed a tear from the corner of her eye, making her voice catch. "But if everything really happens for a reason, maybe the miscarriage happened—" her control broke, and she began to sob "—because I'm not meant to be a mom."

Bart gathered her against his chest, letting her cry it out while he rubbed her back, waiting for the quiet after the storm. When her tears started to subside, he said gently, "If that's true, babe, then it won't happen, and if it happens, it was meant to be, right?"

"But what if it never happens, or what if I'm never ready? I know how much you want kids."

"I want *you,* Jaci." He kissed her forehead...her eyes... the tip of her nose. "I'll take whatever life gives me as long as I have you." He kissed her mouth softly.

She closed her eyes and allowed herself to get lost in the feel of his lips. God, she loved this man. If only Kyndal, and Julia, and every other woman on earth could find this kind of love.

"You're okay if it doesn't happen?" she whispered because his kisses were making her breathless.

"As long as we can keep practicing."

"I never want to stop practicing," she admitted, feeling his muscles quiver in response to her gentle scratching. "In fact, I think I'm ready for a session right now."

CHAPTER ELEVEN

CHANCE WAS SO ANGRY and frustrated he could spit—that is, if he could work up enough moisture in his mouth to form any spit. Even at the rate they'd agreed on—one swallow every two hours—the second water bottle was almost empty.

He kicked the wall instead, but it didn't make him feel any better and only hurt his toe. He'd promised Kyndal he'd find a way out or find some water today and now the day was almost over. Failure—both counts.

The muscles in his legs and back cramped as though he'd covered miles, squeezing through gaps, crawling through holes, climbing over boulders. Nothing. No hint of moisture. No sign of light. No flicker of hope to ease the panic pounding in his temples.

Each time he went back to check on Kyndal, she looked so hopeful. And each time, he faced the disappointment in her eyes. No tears. Probably too dehydrated to make any. She smiled and said it was okay.

But it wasn't okay, damn it. Damn it to hell, it was *not* okay! Fifteen hours of exploration should've brought him something other than sore muscles and an aching toe. He should be able to fix this. His dad would say he shouldn't have let this happen. What kind of man was he that he couldn't get them out of this? Guilt slammed a one-two punch into his empty gut.

He kicked the wall again with his other foot.

Almost eight o'clock. Water time. The last one. He'd lie and tell Kyn he'd already taken his turn. That would leave one more, and he'd make her go first next time.

He followed arrows he had scratched in the dirt back to his coins. From there he knew the path by heart, he'd followed it so many times today.

In the big room—Kyndal's name for the cavern they'd fallen into—he stopped under the hole in the ceiling and let go a few blasts on the whistle. He listened after each one, hoping someone would hear and call out. There was no answer.

He trudged past the spiderweb, admitting defeat. Tomorrow he would explore the area on the other side of the big room.

There had to be a way out, and if it was there, he would find it.

He took a deep breath and settled his face into what he hoped was a look of confidence before crawling once more through the T-shirt covered hole. "Honey, I'm home."

The air in their niche was several degrees warmer than outside—or maybe being near Kyndal warmed him up.

"And I'm glad, but don't expect me to be cooking your dinner. You promised we'd go out tonight." Her voice sounded scratchy, but she smiled. The light illuminated her dirt-smudged face and the dark circles under her eyes, but she was still beautiful. Maybe her attitude added to the allure. All day, she'd been excited and hopeful every time he returned. Not once had she whined or cried or complained. She smiled and joked like now, no doubt trying to make him forget she was in pain.

Nothing could make him forget what a miserable failure he'd been today.

"You're not going out again, are you?"

He shrugged. Now that he'd seen her, he wasn't nearly as tired. He might be able to manage one more excursion.

"Please don't go. I feel totally useless sitting here." She combed her fingers absently through her hair. "You're giving it all you've got, and I'm sitting here doing absolutely nothing."

"Quit berating yourself. If you could, you'd be out there with me in a heartbeat." He handed her the water bottle. "How's the ankle?"

She eased a pill from her jeans' pocket and popped it into her mouth, taking a small sip to wash it down. "It hardly hurts at all unless I put direct pressure on it." She held the bottle out to him.

"No, thanks. I've already had mine."

"You're lying." Her eyes narrowed to slits, and the bottle didn't move. "You haven't been drinking your share. I've been watching."

"And you're lying about your ankle not hurting."

The corners of her mouth turned up. "Okay, we're even. Drink the water, and no more lying."

Why did the woman have to be so pigheaded? He took the bottle and swallowed the last bit of water then threw the bottle against the wall. It bounced back at them defiantly. He caught it the instant before it hit her injured foot. Her face was already squinched in anticipation.

"Doesn't hurt much, huh?"

She shrugged. "Not like it did yesterday. Honest. I think it's kind of numb."

He'd had football injuries like that. After the initial excruciating pain, things settled into a rhythmic throb, which led to a dull ache and eventually numbness. He pumped the flashlight and focused the beam on her foot. "The masking tape's holding up well considering all the dust." Though it had started to loosen in some areas and fray in others. "If it'll last a few more hours, I'm sure we'll be out of here."

"I couldn't stand sitting here in the dark any longer." She rubbed her hands up and down her arms. "I got so desperate, I crawled out and took some more shots of the spiders."

"You what?" He never dreamed she'd take such a chance. "We don't know if they're poisonous, and we sure as hell don't want to find out the hard way. I told you to stay out of there."

"I didn't get close to them. I used my longest lens. But if you go out again, I'm going to go, too—even if I have to hop alongside you."

The image eased his irritation and made him chuckle. "Well, I don't want you to do that, and I *am* pretty tired." The muscles in his calves started to cramp. He took off his boots and stretched his legs by holding his toes and pulling back. The muscles loosened and relaxed. "Do you want to play cards?"

"No."

"Dominoes?"

"No." She sighed. "I just want to talk."

The way she spoke so solemnly jarred him. "Okay, we'll talk." He watched her take a deep breath. What did she want to say that was so difficult?

"You were right about what you said yesterday." She paused. "I was far beyond clingy. Insisting we have every class together our senior year. Planning every class at Harvard together. Wanting you with me to the point you never had time with your friends. I held you way too tight, and I'm sorry."

She *had* understood what he said yesterday. He was glad they'd cleared the air. Now maybe they could remain on friendly terms. "It's okay." He shrugged, and his shoulders ached at the slight move. "We were young, and it was first love, which comes with a huge learning curve."

"What really bothers me, though, is how much I thought I loved you, yet how self-absorbed I was. I was so wrapped up in my cocoon of self-pity, I never thought about the pressure you were under or how much you were hurting. Basically, I guess your dad was right. I wasn't good for you."

The conversation had taken a serious turn that Chance wasn't up for. The mention of his dad reminded him of his failure today and how much work was piling up at the office. He rubbed his shoulders, trying to ease the tension. "Young love's tough. My biggest regret is breaking up with you with no warning. It had to have been a shock."

"Yeah, but if I'd been warned, I would have talked you out of it." Her laugh held a bitterness that made him cringe. "It was the only way for you to break free of my hold."

They were silent for a while, and then she cocked her head. "Do you regret that we had sex so young?"

"Not at all." He shook his head and felt the movement deep in his shoulders.

"Neither do I."

He smiled and gave her a wink. She winked back.

"Do you think about him a lot?"

Chance closed his eyes, running back through the conversation to locate the *him*. "My dad?"

"Hank," she whispered.

Phantom pain shot through his heart, imagined, but somehow real. "Yeah." His breath caught. "Every day."

WHEN CHANCE'S VOICE BROKE, Kyndal felt it in her throat. All day long, she'd been softening toward him...playing yesterday's confession over and over in her mind as she sat motionless in the dark. He *had* loved her, truly and deeply.

"You were my everything," he'd said.

Like water had eroded the walls of the cave thousands of years ago, those words started eroding the protective covering around her heart. She felt it open toward this man she'd worked for nine years to keep out, felt it reaching out to him in sympathy.

His body was a study in anguish: furrowed brow, tightened jaw, hunched shoulders, fisted hands. God, he'd worked so hard today. He needed to relax.

And she needed a reason to touch him.

Kneeling, she eased around behind him, careful not to jostle her ankle too much, and began massaging his shoulders. "I think Hank is very proud of the man his little brother has become."

The flashlight rested on the ground, throwing its light away from them. And yet, she could feel his unfathomable sorrow as the silhouette of his shoulders moved slowly up and down. "I hope so."

She kneaded harder, trying to let her fingers absorb the tightness she heard in his voice, but the shirt made it difficult to reach the knotted muscles.

"Take off..." She cleared the lump from her throat. "Take off your shirt. The flannel won't move around."

Until the material slid from his shoulders and her fingers rested on bare skin, she didn't realize how dangerous the ground she treaded on was.

Her thoughts today hadn't stalled on his confession; they'd been inspired by it. Under the cover of this intense darkness, she'd allowed herself a freedom she hadn't experienced in nine years—hours of remembering their good times together. Until today, she'd only permitted herself to think about the bad times, keeping the ego pain fresh and the heart pain at bay.

Today, she'd remembered the sweetness of that first

time together, and their excitement and amazement as each encounter brought new discoveries. She remembered how they'd been open to new things and honest with each other about everything.

Never far from her thoughts were the present fears she kept submerged. Their food was gone. Water was gone. Time was running out. She wouldn't let herself think about dying, but even rescue meant saying goodbye to Chance again…this time with the painful insight of a newly discovered truth—he'd loved her as much as she'd loved him. But he'd left her just the same. Because she'd been too clingy? She was guilty of that, and he'd rationalized himself into believing it was the reason.

But she'd been his *everything*...and even that wasn't enough to make him want to stay with her.

She'd pieced together the others things he said—the cracks about her politics and her job…and her lack of a job.

Being everything to him wasn't enough to hold him because she wasn't good enough. Never had been…never would be until she became that somebody she'd always dreamed of being.

The truth hurt, but she could accept it because now she understood.

She splayed her fingers and pressed her thumbs firmly along his spine at each vertebra. He grunted hard with each compression and sometimes added a pleasure-filled moan.

The sounds weren't lost on Kyndal. They were the same sounds he made when they used to make love. Each grunt and groan stirred her more until she was holding her breath in between and releasing it to his rhythm.

They'd be rescued, and they'd say goodbye again, and he'd go back to his law practice with his dad, and she'd go back to her photography.

She wanted him to leave this place with a new opinion of her. One that would erase any previous memory of her clinginess.

Maybe that's why they were stuck in this cave—karma's way of letting them walk away in peace.

She took a long breath and smoothed her palms up his back, across his shoulders, along his neck. Then her fingers spread, and she slid them from the nape into his hair.

He groaned as her lips made contact with the back of his neck.

CHAPTER TWELVE

CHANCE NOTICED THE SUBTLE difference in Kyndal's touch as her hands moved up his spine, but he expected it to be followed by another sweet assault of thumbs plunging into his shoulder muscles. He hadn't prepared himself for the softness of her lips.

His groan escaped—a sound of unbridled passion edged with confusion. What was she up to? They'd *"moved on. No use going back."* Her words. And now this?

God, she was making him crazy.

He'd pushed himself all day in an attempt to keep his distance, respecting the line they'd drawn. Then the line vanished. Her lips were against his neck. Her warm breath scampered down his bare back. It might as well have been a freakin' bellows, the way it set him on fire.

He had to stop her, had to get her off him. He grabbed her wrists tightly with each of his hands. "Don't, Kyndal. I'm not in the mood to be toyed with." He flung her hands away and reached for his shirt, but she moved faster, snatching it up and tossing it against the wall.

He stretched to the side and dragged the shirt back to him, letting out an exasperated sigh. "I'm not playing, Kyn."

"Neither am I." The quiet way she spoke the words pulled him around to face her.

She held the flashlight—it took both of her hands to pump it up. Starting with his face, she ran the beam slowly, seductively down his body. "We're not kids anymore, Chance. We've changed. I want to make love. As a man and a woman."

Her words echoed back to him and filled his brain. Did she realize what she was saying? He lowered his eyes, watching as the light made its way down one of his legs and up the other, wishing her hands were skimming over him rather than the damn light. God, he wanted her.

But if he made love to her—and that's what it would be rather than casual sex—what then? He didn't have time for a relationship. He had too many demands now. Workaholics didn't make good bedfellows. His dad taught him that.

But the real reason niggled at him—his ambitious plans wouldn't allow a relationship with this particular woman. Any breath of scandal would be a problem, but a scandal that involved taking jobs from the river industry would be a death knell.

Shame and embarrassment at his condescending attitude heated his face, and he shook his head. "Nothing's changed since yesterday, Kyn. We've moved on."

"Exactly," she agreed. "That's what makes it okay. Don't you see? There's nothing between us now." She crawled closer, laying the flashlight to the side and sitting down in front of him. Her knee brushed his shin as she curled her good leg under her. "All the old ties are gone. All that's left is the chemistry."

The touch, the nearness of her, intensified the conflict in his mind. "It's a mistake, Kyndal. That chemistry's liable to stir up emotion. We'll regret it."

She flinched and swallowed. "On the contrary, Counselor, I'll regret it if I let this opportunity pass me by." She held his eyes with a steady gaze and eased up onto her knees until her mouth was even with his. "I'm not asking for a relationship, Chance. No phone calls, no demands…

absolutely no clinging after we get out. I just want your body."

Just bodies…nothing but chemistry

Her arms circled his neck, and she leaned into him and pressed her mouth to his. When her tongue brushed his lips, the heat rushed through him, burning away any trace of resistance. His hands plunged into her hair, and he pulled her to him, sucking her sweet softness into his mouth.

Despite their intended message, her words flung him back ten years to a time when Kyndal was his ambition… his life. She was the sun and the moon, the universe of his existence. He had to have her. Now. He'd laid first claim to her long ago. Tomorrow—if there was one—she would go back to her photographs and he would go back to his practice. They would go their separate ways to their separate lives tomorrow.

But tonight, she was his.

"NO PHONE CALLS…*no demands...absolutely no clinging after we get out. I just want your body."* The words tightened Kyndal's empty stomach, but they obviously had the desired effect on Chance. Absolving him from any responsibility in the act was all he needed in the way of permission it seemed.

He'd tried to talk her out of it, but she was the one who had insisted…seduced…so she was going into this with her eyes open—or rather closed since Chance had her locked in a deeply erotic kiss.

The boundary to the emotional danger zone grew fuzzier by the minute. In a fleeting moment of clarity, she realized he'd snuggled her onto his lap. She lost sight of the boundary again when his hands tangled in her hair. Just when she thought she would suffocate from the passion in his kiss, he moved to her neck and took her breath completely.

His warning words flashed back through her mind. *"That chemistry's liable to stir up emotions."* He was right. She was hungry with emotion. Maybe she should stop this.

But she didn't want to stop. This was her Chance. The irony of the words spurred her into action. Grabbing the bottom of her thermal top, she jerked it over her head. Chance had her T-shirt pushed up and her bra unsnapped by the time the top layer slid off. The others came off quickly with his help.

When the tip of his tongue made contact with her breast, the powerful current tore through her, causing her to cry out. He responded with sweet attentions to the other. Her hands raked through his hair, pressing his mouth closer.

His hard ridge bulged in the confines of his jeans, and she moved against it. But when she started to loosen the button at his waistband, he guided her hands away. Not to be deterred, she went to work frantically on her own jeans then, but he closed his hands around hers and stopped her again.

What was he doing? Frustration catapulted her into a sitting position, her eyes only inches from his. She used the most threatening tone she could conjure up through her erratic breathing. "If you stop now, Brennan, you're a dead man."

His eyes narrowed, but she caught the slight twitch of his mouth at one end. "I'm not stopping. Just slowing down. It's been too long to rush through this."

His words warmed her, yet also chilled her. They *had* waited a long time for this…this one, last time.

Her brain advised her to slow down and make it last, but her body resisted the delay. She pressed herself to him, absorbing his heat, catching his fire, shaking her head in protest. He nodded in response and languidly lowered his mouth to hers.

This kiss was deeper than the first. He seemed not to notice her pitiful whimpers as his tongue swept her mouth again and again.

His chest had grown more powerful through the years, bulging with delicious pectorals that added both depth and width—a suit of armor protecting his heart. She understood then that she couldn't get through even if she wanted to—which she didn't. This would be sex and only sex. She'd promised. She relaxed, and he seemed to sense the surrender. Only then did he release her mouth.

"That's better." His breath was warm against her ear as he rocked her slowly, holding her like a treasure.

She nuzzled her lips against his neck. Chance wasn't a get-set-and-go kid anymore, but a man who had obviously learned a lot over the years. Unbidden and alarming jealousy ripped through her at the thought. Jealousy of every woman he'd ever touched. She gritted her teeth, panting her way through the renegade thought and back to logic.

Might as well enjoy what they taught him. It's only for this one last time.

His knuckles brushed the side of her face, bringing her breathing down to a soft purr. "You're beautiful, Kyn. I thought you were hot at eighteen, but now..." The way he stroked the valley between her breasts with the back of his fingers completed his unspoken thought. She fought to remain still, letting his touch move through her. But when his fingers dipped below the waistband of her jeans, she writhed in agony. "Chance—"

His mouth closed down on hers, his tongue countering her exclamation as his fingers undid her jeans and dipped farther. She wriggled in an attempt to move his hand deeper than the just-below-the-navel position it held.

"Uh-uh-uh." He pulled his hand out. "Slow down, babe."

She closed her eyes and sucked in a ragged breath as he brushed his fingers through her hair.

"We don't have anywhere to go. We can make this last all night if we want."

His soothing strokes brought her out of her frenzy and calmed her to the point that she could focus on what he said. "Mmm. You can go all night?"

He gave a sensuous chuckle that tingled the base of her spine. "One of the more useful things I learned at Hahvahd."

She smiled at his gentle tease and traced her finger down the curve of his face. "Touché."

"Touché, indeed." He turned his face and kissed her finger. "I intend to touché you. All over. Now, stand up." She couldn't stand completely upright, but he helped her, positioning himself on his knees in front of her. "Put your hands on my shoulders and balance on your good leg."

He slipped her jeans and thong down over her hips, planting kisses on each new patch of exposed skin. She shivered at the thrilling contradiction: her cool skin, his hot mouth.

When the jeans dropped around her ankles, he sat back on his heels, allowing his gaze to roam over her unabashedly. Like a champion claiming the winner's cup, he planted a kiss on her navel.

Where his mouth grazed, a coil of heat centered and moved outward. "Oh, yeah," she moaned, encouraging him to go lower. Instead, he went to work unlacing the hiking boot on her good foot.

"Bend over my shoulder," he instructed.

The position was a new one to her, but if it meant relief from this torture, she was more than willing to experiment. She couldn't contain the squeal when his weight shifted back, leveraging her off the floor enough for him to remove her jeans, being extra careful with her ankle.

He tilted forward until her bare foot rested on the smooth, cold surface of the limestone floor. A warm flush moved through her as she wiggled her toes, remembering the first time they'd done this and the same exhilaration of total abandon. But her left foot still bore the encumbering weight of the hiking boot. "What about the other one? I want to be naked."

Chance shook his head, smoothing his palms up her calves and around her thighs. "No way I'm going to take that one off. We might not have enough tape to get it back on properly."

She wrinkled her nose at the clunky mass. "That doesn't make me feel very sexy."

"No?" His eyebrows shrugged playfully. "Just spread your legs a little."

She obeyed. And when his tongue started a slow ascent on the inside of her thigh, she ceased to care how she looked.

She relinquished her body completely to his exploration. And explore he did.

His hands, his fingers, his lips, his teeth, his tongue, his breath...all became instruments of sublimely erotic torment that manipulated every erogenous zone she'd ever known.

And then he introduced her to a few more.

The black stubble around his mouth and chin blended with the shadows of the cave to heighten her sensation. She was being devoured by a ravenous sexual beast in a labyrinth of stone. But she needed no fantasy when reality was this perfect. Chance and Kyndal. The way they used to be, only better.

One last time.

The heady experience made her dizzy from too many quick breaths. "Chance…I'm…ah…ah, going to fall." She ground the words out between gasps.

He swept her up and laid her on top of their discarded shirts.

"Take off your jeans." Emotion blocked her voice to only a whisper as she held her arms out to him. "My turn now."

"TAKE IT EASY ON ME," he said, but the desire in her eyes told him his warning had fallen on deaf ears.

The simple act of pulling off his jeans and stretching out beside her took on a surreal quality as he gathered her to him, feeling her heat—reminding himself that the woman in his arms was Kyndal Rawlings. After all those years, here she was in the flesh.

The hands stroking him were Kyndal's.

The tongue flicking along the inside of his rib cage, moving down his stomach, causing him to lose his breath was Kyndal's. Her hot mouth was a brazier branding him, searing her name on his heart. It would take no effort to let go and allow her flames to consume him.

No, not yet. He couldn't promise her the things she probably wanted, but he'd promised her all night. He grasped her head and pulled her mouth up to his.

Kyndal responded to and reciprocated his every touch with an intensity he'd never experienced before, yet still his heart hung heavy in his chest.

His tongue, his lips, his fingers—he used them all to bring her to climax after climax, until her body was a writhing mass of unbridled ecstasy. And time after time, she took him to the brink with her mouth and hands, and the gnawing need to be inside her struggled with his rational side. They didn't have a condom.

He held back, not wanting this to end. But when he deepened his kiss, Kyndal's sensuous moan nearly drove him over the edge. Her hand clutched him, drew him close enough to enter. One thrust and he'd be in and there would be no turning back.

He tore his mouth from hers and shook his head. "No, baby. We don't have protection."

The beam from the flashlight had dimmed to a flicker. Her hard breathing came warm and moist against his chest. "I'm not worried if you're not. I'm on the Pill."

He swore inwardly at the revelation. She was a woman prepared for opportunities that might arise. Of course she would be on the Pill. The words pierced his heart even as they stirred his passion. No condom. Nothing between them. Just the two of them making love the way he'd fantasized for so long.

One last time.

He grabbed the flashlight and pumped it to full beam.

"What are you doing?" Her words came out in a breathless rush as her teeth grazed his neck.

"I want—" he ran his hand down the back of her thigh, lifting her leg and positioning it atop his "—to see your eyes—" he slid slowly into her, relishing her tightness and the excitement of her gasps "—when we come together."

He held her gaze, letting her body language tell him when to speed up and when to slow down. Their breathing synchronized. She clawed at his arms and back with mewling sounds. He quickened his thrusts.

She met each one, driving down onto him until her moves became wild and frenzied, making him rigid almost to the point of pain. He couldn't hold back much longer.

Her eyes opened wide. "Oh, Chance! I'm going to—" He felt her body curving into him as her back arched.

Now! Make her yours. One last time.

Her muscles contracted around him, and, with a final plunge, he released nine years of pent-up passion…along with the silent, secret contents of his heart.

Their names echoed through the chamber as wave after wave shook them until they collapsed in a sweaty heap, exhausted and speechless.

She gave him a dreamy smile, and he kissed away a tear leaving its track along her flushed cheek. "Don't cry, Kyn. It's okay. We needed this."

"I know," she whispered. "It's just the irony…that the first place we made love is also the last place we'll make love. We talked about things coming full circle and…and they have."

The truth brought an ache to his chest. The whole situation was ironic—a twist thrown into the natural order of things. The woman he worked so hard to get out of his life was back in his arms. She felt so right despite being so wrong.

And the closure she'd promised didn't feel like closure at all.

His heart felt as if it had been laid wide-open.

CHAPTER THIRTEEN

THE PHONE RANG, AND JACI reached for it, abandoning her search for the perfect shade of puce from among the endless set of color swatches. "Decor and More."

"Hi, Jaci. It's Erlene Moore."

"Hey, Erlene. It's good to hear from you." Flashes of the precious nursery Julia had designed for the Moores filled Jaci's memory. Surely, the woman wasn't calling to complain about anything. "How's that baby boy?"

"He's getting to be a big boy now, which is why I called." There was a short pause. "I'm pregnant again."

"Wow, it's been longer than I realized. Congratulations."

"Thanks. This one's a girl, so we want to have the nursery redone, and we also want Cody to have a room of his own."

Handling the child's room would be no problem, but nurseries were Julia's forté. "Are you in a hurry for this? Julia's away for a few weeks."

"I'm seven months already."

Exactly the same as I would have been... The acknowledgment brought a pang of something that felt as if regret and guilt and fear made a fist and punched her in the stomach.

Erlene's tone became apologetic. "I shouldn't have waited so long to call, but Cody and my job take up so much time. Then finding out I was pregnant again was like being caught up in a whirlwind, and before I knew it, there were only two months to go and nothing's been done." Her voice raised an octave. "No, no, Cody. Give Mommy her keys." Erlene paused, then continued in her normal tone. "I looked for my keys for three days last week before I found them inside an unzipped teddy bear."

Jaci pushed through the discomfort as she flipped the pages of her appointment book. There was no use dwelling on what had happened, and the thought of designing a nursery by herself had a certain appeal. She might never get to design one for herself, but doing someone else's might give her vicarious satisfaction. She found an opening for the following week. "I'm open a week from today at two-thirty."

"Cody goes down for… Not right now, Cody. Mommy will be off the phone in just a minute. Yeah, I'm off on Tuesdays, and Cody takes a nap at two, so he should be asleep. That would be good."

"Would you like me to come to your house?"

The response was an emphatic "No."

"No?"

"No, Cody. Leave the lamp cord alone. We mustn't pull on cords. That would be great, Jaci. And I'm desperate for suggestions on more ways to baby-proof things."

"I'm sure if you search Google—"

"I've got to go, Jaci. See you next Tuesday. Cody, come back with that." The last sounded as if Erlene had broken into a jog.

Jaci moved the color swatches off her lap, and typed "baby-proofing the house" into a search engine.

"Oh, dear Lord!" She gasped as her eyes fell on the results—all 881,000 of them—and the sense of ineptitude she'd repressed for the two days since she and Bart had talked came out again swinging.

"Who in their right mind ever convinces themselves they can do this?"

The blow came hard and fast, an uppercut to her heart.

Certainly not me.

KYNDAL LISTENED TO CHANCE'S deep breathing, taking comfort in the sound. There hadn't been many times they'd actually awakened with each other after making love. Occasionally, he'd managed to convince his parents he was at a friend's house when he'd really spent the night with her. With her mom gone so much, getting time alone wasn't a problem. But spending an entire night together had been nearly impossible.

After Hank's death, Chance's parents kept him on a short leash. No other seniors had a midnight curfew, but Chance did. And, on the rare occasions when her mom was home, they had to make use of the car's backseat or secluded beaches on Kentucky Lake.

Waking up naked next to him now would've been a dream fulfilled, but the coolness of the cave had forced them to put their clothes back on.

She tried to ignore the thirst and the excruciating pain in her head that kept her awake most of the night, the gnawing emptiness in her stomach…and the hollowness in her heart when she thought about leaving this place and going back to a life without Chance.

Nothing's changed. Don't even try to convince yourself this will last.

The truth, as taught by her mother, was that men came and went, moved in, moved out, but none ever stuck around for more than a couple of years. It was okay to love them, but the unwritten law said never to need them or depend on them.

Her mother had tried to warn her when she first started

going out with Chance. "Don't get wrapped up in that boy, baby," Mom would say. "He lives in a different world than we do, and bad things happen when worlds collide."

Then she would take off on one of her road trips, and to combat the loneliness, Kyndal would wrap herself even tighter around him, hoping desperately to prove her mother wrong.

Clinging.

She edged farther away, mentally and physically distancing herself from the man who lay beside her.

Chance stirred, reached out to her and scooted closer. "You awake?"

"Yeah."

"How come? Your ankle hurting?"

She felt him push up on his elbow, his hand resting warm on her stomach. "A little. Not too bad."

His hand slid under her shirt and stroked her bare skin. "I'm rested, and I think I promised you an all-nighter." His breathing was soft on her face just before his lips closed down on hers.

Much as her body tried to convince her otherwise, her mind screamed that no good could come from making love to him again. It would be like jumping into an emotional abyss.

Logic backed her away from the edge. "I have a headache."

He groaned then gave a low chuckle in her ear. "It's the old I've-got-a-headache, is it?"

She nudged him with her elbow, eliciting another groan. "I really do have a headache. In fact, I'm sort of hurting all over."

Chance sat up quickly. She heard the pump of the flashlight, and then the light blinded her. He pressed his thumb along the bottom ridge of her eye socket, and, when the light shifted, she read fear in his expression.

"What? What's wrong?"

He swore under his breath. "You're dehydrating, Kyn."

"How do you know?"

"I had a malpractice suit against a nursing home where a patient died of dehydration. I had to learn all about it." He located his socks and boots with a sweep of the light and rushed to put them on.

She tried to keep her tone light. "I'm not that old."

"Symptoms are the same. Headache usually followed by muscle cramps. I've got to find you some water."

Another day, or even another hour, alone with her thoughts would cause her to pull her hair out one at a time. "I'm going with you." She jerked her abandoned sock free from a boot and donned it quickly.

"Kyn, I can search faster without you." He brushed his knuckles down her cheek gently, but his firm tone said she would be a hindrance.

"I know I'm a pain in the ass, but I can't sit alone in this crypt for one more nanosecond." Through the shadows, she watched his mouth tighten, but she pressed on. "We'll move to the next cavern. I'll stay there, and you can explore that area. Then we'll go on to the next, and the next if we have to. Leave me when you have to, but not here." His eyes drew in with concern. She could tell he still wasn't convinced. "If you found water somewhere far, you'd have to come back here to bring it to me. This way, I'll be closer. I won't be any trouble, I promise. I'll busy myself taking some more shots."

He rubbed his hand roughly through his hair and down his thickly stubbled jaw. Finally, he threw up his hands in surrender. "Okay. Let's take our stuff with us. If we find the way out, we won't have to come back for it."

She smoothed out one of the discarded granola bar wrappers. "If anybody comes looking for us from this direction," she tore the wrapper into several thin strips, "we'll leave these to mark our way."

Chance left her briefly to drop a marker in the spider room by the opening they'd chosen to follow. He was only gone for a couple of minutes, but they seemed interminable. She didn't realize she'd held her breath the whole time until she let it out when she glimpsed the tiny beam headed back her way.

The tunnel wasn't large enough for them to move abreast. Chance crawled in front, his body blocking most of the light.

Kyndal concentrated on his grunts and his breathing. They tethered her to reality in this surreal landscape, kept her from crying as her movements jarred pain loose from every sinew.

Is this the way a baby feels moving through the birth canal? She found comfort in that thought. They were moving through a birth canal and would emerge back into the world at the other end. Tunnels always had light at the end of them, didn't they?

This one didn't. When they finally broke into an open space, Chance scrambled to his feet and helped her to hers.

She clung to him, fatigued and unable to hold her balance as blackness whirled around her. A wave of nausea swept through her, and she convulsed in a dry heave.

"Oh, baby, don't. Please don't."

The desperation in his voice rallied her strength. She contained the lurches to her stomach and swallowed until the spasms passed. "I'm okay now." She leaned her head against his chest. "I just got up too fast. I'm really tired."

"Rest a minute." Chance supported her with one arm as he flashed the beam around the cavern. Although not as large as the one they'd fallen into, this one had more stalagmites and stalactites than they had seen anywhere else in the cave. Like teeth lining a giant mouth.

The odd, bumpy growths were evidence of some type of water activity years ago, which Kyndal found reassuring. The openings littering the wall gave her comfort, each one promising a way out. She took a relaxed breath and pushed off from Chance, planting the toe of her injured foot firmly, showing him she'd regained her balance.

"I'm going to get some shots in here while you explore those doorways." She hopped over to the nearest knee-high "molar" and settled beside it, busying herself by assembling her camera.

"You're sure you're okay?" Chance's voice was once again smooth and composed.

She nodded.

"I won't be far."

Time passed quickly as she lost herself in shot after shot. The limestone growth served as a firm support, steadying her and acting as a prosthetic leg under her knee. The pain in her head and back eased. Perhaps standing up helped the blood flow. But she tired quickly and had to sit much of the time. Sometimes she became aware of Chance's shuffle in the background, and sometimes she became aware of the silence.

Darkness made for a strange working environment. She often gave in to it and shot intuitively with her eyes closed. The abstract angles and shadow play gave a dimension of hollowness and emptiness she'd never considered capturing before. It spoke volumes—like the white space of a poem. The results pleased her.

With her eyes closed, she didn't see the beam of light or hear Chance approach. Luckily the camera strap was around her neck when his hand touched her shoulder and she jerked around. He caught her hand as she steadied herself. His quick intake of breath focused her attention on the beam of light shining on her hand.

When he'd grasped it, a ridge of skin had been forced up on the top, starting below her middle finger and reaching to her wrist. It stayed put, hadn't smoothed back down like it should, looking like a worm had made its habitat under her skin.

"Another sign of dehydration." Chance's voice trembled, and he cleared his throat. "The skin loses its elasticity. I think we need to go back to the first room."

"The room with the spiders? There's no water there." She shook her head, which shot a dizzying pain through her skull. She ran an arm around his waist for support.

"The spiders chose that wall for a reason."

His voice was as hard as the arm clamped around her, and his intention finally cut through the fog in her brain. "Oh, God, no. Chance, you can't! There are too many of them." She took his face in her hands, forced him to look down at her. "If they're poisonous, you could die."

"And you could die if I don't find water."

And so it was out. The dreaded d-word. They'd both studiously avoided it until this second, but now it was out drawing a collective shudder through them both.

He gripped her tighter. "I'm not going to let that happen."

How could she convince him she wasn't near death, make him forget his plan of attacking the spider wall? He wouldn't believe her words. She had to show him. Impulsively, she pulled his mouth to hers, willing him to find a promise of hope. It took a few seconds, but she finally felt him start to respond with a hunger of his own. She kissed him deeper.

I love you. The words flooded her brain and dropped

onto her tongue where she bit them back. Saying that now would sound like a final confession, make him believe she'd lost hope, make him do something stupid—like fight ten thousand spiders for her.

She summoned the will to push every thought from her mind except survival and found it in his embrace. "No going back, Counselor. Remember?" She spoke the words precisely. "We've moved on."

Now, if she could just convince her heart to follow that advice.

CHANCE SNIFFED THE AIR. Two of the last three tunnels had a slight upward slope, but this one had a different scent than the others. Cleaner. Fresher. The aroma wasn't strong, but it reminded him of a spring rain.

That fragrance could only come from water—or his imagination playing tricks on him.

He loathed the idea of moving Kyndal again. They'd been at this for so long now, he'd lost track of time. His watch read two thirty-eight, but he didn't know if that was Tuesday afternoon, Wednesday morning, Wednesday afternoon. He'd lost track.

He hadn't meant to fall asleep after the last long trek through what seemed like miles of passages, but Kyndal seemed so exhausted. He'd just wanted to hold her through her nap. Then he'd dozed off.

A dull pain had awakened him as it pierced his back and followed his ribs around to the front with almost rhythmic precision. Kidney most likely. Whatever, it was taking a toll on him. He didn't want to admit his body was giving out, but he wasn't able to cover great distances bearing so much of Kyndal's weight as she hopped beside him.

Every time he left her now, he came back to find her asleep. That scared the hell out of him. What if she didn't wake up next time? Her speech was becoming a bit incoherent. Even now, she was mumbling something about Hamlet and life being a waking shadow.

A surge of adrenaline sent energy into his lethargic limbs. He had to get her through that tunnel even if he dragged her.

"Kyn." He raised her chin gently and shined the light directly into her eyes, which were clouded with confusion. Her pupils were enormous. "That tunnel slopes upward. It may lead to the surface." Her mouth moved in inaudible speech. "We need to take it, baby, but it's too narrow for me to carry you. Can you crawl a little farther?" He was thankful the darkness hid his lie. It might be twice as long as the last one, and that one had been agonizing.

The cloud lifted from Kyndal's eyes and she seemed lucid again. She gave a nod.

"Hold on to my feet so your hands don't get so cut up. I'll move real slow, okay?"

She blinked.

With both packs on his back, seeing behind would be impossible. And the narrow tunnel would make turning around difficult. He needed to feel her to know she hadn't collapsed.

"Okay, Kyn?" He jiggled her face until he felt a perceptible nod.

"'Kay, Couns'lr."

Her words were soft and slurred, but, in them, he found strength. He positioned her and started the slow ascent.

His original plan was to speak encouragement through the entire length of the tunnel, but that proved too demanding. He needed every ounce of strength he had left. So they inched their way in silence, their progress measured by the increasing pain in his back and sides and chest.

He prayed she would be able to keep her hands on his legs. Twice she slipped, but managed to regain her hold.

He became oblivious to everything except the feel of her hands around his ankles and the pinpoint of light in front of him. They were all that mattered in this world.

The tunnel widened and sloped upward abruptly. He held the flashlight in his teeth so he could use both hands to scramble onto a smooth plateau. He reached back and hauled Kyndal up the last few feet. His heart sank as he panned the area with the light.

A dead end.

One opening that didn't look promising—just a wide fissure really.

No water.

He'd chosen the wrong way, and Kyndal would never make it back down the passage and up through another one. She was too weak.

He'd failed.

"I'm sorry, Dad." His mouth formed the words of its own accord.

A faint ringing started in his ears as darkness closed in around him. "Can't pass out. Don't pass out." He ground the words out through clenched teeth as he threw the beam around aimlessly.

Dampness. Moisture. Close. He could smell it. Taste it.

Willing his head to stop spinning, he focused on the opposite wall. There was something odd about it. He put down the flashlight and crawled the short distance over to it, touching it with his finger. Not hard limestone. Not rock. Soft. Applying pressure, his finger sank into it. He spread his fingers and grasped a handful. Dirt.

A cave-in.

He lay back and shut his eyes, letting the sickening realization wash through him. At one time, this probably had been a way out, but now it was blocked. By how much dirt? How far to the surface? He could try digging up through it, but if it was unstable that could bring the roof down.

"Chance."

He opened his eyes.

Kyndal had taken the flashlight. He could barely make out her legs protruding from the wide fissure.

CHAPTER FOURTEEN

KYNDAL STARED AT...THE SUN? No warmth. No light. Yet it was the sun.

Her brain struggled to make sense of what she saw. A picture of the sun. A painting.

Still on her back, she dug her elbows into the soft flooring and scooted farther into the hole, protecting her foot as much as possible. Soft flooring? Fur. She was lying on fur.

"What is it, Kyn?"

She didn't answer, didn't know how—just drew her legs up out of the way to give Chance room to crawl in behind her.

When he did, she heard his sharp intake of breath. "My God!" He took the flashlight from her and pumped it to the max, scanning the wall with the light.

Red. Red all around. And black, staring eyes. Heads and eyes painted on the walls. Figures. Drawings of figures. Graffiti? Had the teenagers been here?

"I think you've found an ancient room." Chance's voice was thick with heavy breathing.

The light fell on tied bundles scattered around the base of the wall. Chance grabbed one up. "Animal pelts." He broke the ragged gut cord and shook the bundle open. The brown fur was beautifully preserved—full and lush. "Coyote."

Kyndal concentrated on forming the words. "Then there's a way—"

"Shh!"

"—out from here," she finished.

"Shhh!" Chance covered her mouth with his hand. His eyes were wide, and he cocked his head, looking like a deranged bird listening for a worm. She wanted to giggle, but her body couldn't muster enough energy. Instead, her eyes lazily followed the light.

Suddenly, Chance lunged toward a black streak on the wall. A small indentation at the bottom of it held a clay bowl, brimming over with liquid.

"Water!" Chance ran his hand along the streak. He reached out to the bowl, then pulled his hand away, touching his fingers to his mouth. They trembled violently against his lips.

"Kyn, you need this water." His wild-eyed gaze locked on to her. "I don't think I can pick it up without spilling it, and you need every drop." He laid the flashlight down and cupped the sides of her face, forcing her to look at him. His hands, which had been so warm before, were cool against her skin. "I want you to lie on your belly and sip it down a little. Can you do that?"

She nodded though whether it was under his power or her own she wasn't sure.

He maneuvered her until she was stretched out on her stomach. The soft fur begged her to snuggle into it, but she ignored the seduction of its warmth, straining to push the ten-ton weight of her body onto her elbows. She gritted her teeth as her arms wobbled, dropping her onto her stomach again, driving the breath from her. The bowl seemed to whirl as her eyes lost their focus, and the world around her started to fade.

Someone called her name a couple of times, but the voice was far away, as though she was hearing it from underwater. She floated facedown…in a pool of something soft…water?…surrounded…engulfed…sinking down… down. She struggled to swim, trying to free her arms, which were pinned beneath her.

"Kyndal."

The voice grew to a shout.

"Kyndal!"

She was rolled over and jerked into a sitting position. An arm supported her back. Hot lips touched hers and then her mouth flooded with liquid. She swallowed. The lips left for a second; then they were back, filling her mouth again with coolness. She didn't swallow immediately, letting the moisture soothe the parched tissue inside her jaws and along the sides of her tongue instead, relishing the texture and clean, sweet taste.

The water felt exquisite, sliding down her dry throat, cold enough to make its presence known as it passed between her collarbones and into her chest.

The voice called her name over and over, commanding her to respond, reeling her in like a fish on a line.

It took a few moments for her heavy limbs to respond to the demands from her brain. Once they did, she fought her way to the surface and broke through with a gasp and a cough, forcing her eyes to open. Cloudy at first, they finally cleared, and she saw Chance's contorted face.

She'd seen that look one other time. The day Hank died.

"Hold me." Hardly more than a whisper, her voice waved the magic wand that relaxed his face. He clutched her tightly to him.

"Did you…get water?" she croaked. "Shouldn't've drunk it all."

His fingers moved softly through her hair. "I'll get some next time. It's a slow drip, so it'll take a while."

She let her gaze wander about the strange room while

the water found its way into her system. "What's this place?"

His chest heaved as he took several long, deep breaths. "I think it was for Native American ceremonies." He focused the flashlight beam on various drawings that obviously represented male and female characters coupling. "Probably performed fertility rites here."

The thought of other people who'd been here brought hope back into her heart. "They didn't get in the way we did. There's a way out from here."

"Was," Chance corrected. He drew another long breath and pointed to the crevice they entered through. "There's been a cave-in out there."

"Oh." She swallowed her disappointment, noticing how dry her throat was already. She couldn't give in to despair now. The chance to stay alive more than ever lay in keeping their wits about them. "Nice place…to wait…for rescue. Warm. Cozy. Running water." She leaned back to give him a smile of reassurance.

He didn't say anything, but the grim set of Chance's mouth spoke volumes.

"IF ANYTHING'S HAPPENED to her, I'll never forgive myself." Jaci turned away from the sight of Emily and Bill Brennan's grief-filled expressions and leaned her forehead against Bart's chest. How could they stand there not touching at a time like this? Bart's strong arms around her were the only thing keeping her from collapsing. "I pushed her into this. She wasn't going to go, but I insisted. And then I let four days go by before I did anything."

Bart's chin rested protectively on top of her head, increasing the weight of his words. "Stop blaming yourself. I'm the one who told you to quit calling her." She felt him swallow. "I think they're going to take Chesney with them."

That made sense. The dog had been running around wildly since Jaci and the Brennans showed up at Chance's house that afternoon. When Sheriff Blaine arrived a few minutes later, Chesney led him to the depression in the ground behind the garage.

Jaci shuddered, remembering how much it looked like an old grave.

Sheriff Blaine said it was a sinkhole that collapsed a long time ago. Although the cave was a quarter mile from the house, he'd said that its caverns might run all the way to the house and beyond.

"Here comes the sheriff." Bart gave her a kiss before she turned to face the beefy lawman. The cave entrance loomed large and dark and foreboding behind him.

"Jaci, we saw a lotta diff'rent ways they coulda gone once they got in there." Sheriff Blaine's grimy face dripped with perspiration. "Can ya think of anything that might give a clue as to which way to go?"

Jaci squeezed her eyes shut while she spoke, trying to remember every detail Kyndal had talked about. "There was a room with a column in the middle and a window-like opening. The window was high—she had to jump to get to it. The room on the other side of the window was full of crystals."

"Crystals?" The sheriff's voice was skeptical.

Jaci opened her eyes and met his gaze directly. "Crystals. Solid crystals, top to bottom."

He let out a low whistle. "Sounds like a vug."

"That's it! That's the word Chance used."

"Vugs aren't very common, so that should make this easier. Thanks." He popped his gum a couple of times, then turned back. "They'll find them."

The sincerity in those eyes pushed air deeper into Jaci's lungs than it had gone since this nightmare started with her call to the Shop-a-Lot this morning. The manager informed her Kyndal hadn't shown up for work last night or today. He was on the verge of pressing charges because Kyndal had "made off" with equipment belonging to the stores.

The next call to Chance's office didn't help. The secretary seemed unconcerned—at the time. Her distressed callback later confirmed Chance hadn't been in his office apparently for a few days.

Calls to Sheriff Blaine, to the Brennans who'd just returned from New Orleans, to Kyndal's mom who still wasn't home. Calls, calls and more calls—and her best friend might be dead or dying because she hadn't made any of them sooner.

A sob blocked the next breath Jaci tried to get into her lungs. She sent a silent prayer into the darkness, ahead of the rescue team and the dog.

"They'll find them."

Jaci turned toward the hand resting on her arm. She hadn't heard Emily Brennan approach but was relieved to see that the willowy blonde appeared to have regained her composure. The heart-wrenching hysteria when they found Chance's and Kyndal's cars in the garage had been more than Jaci could bear.

Jaci firmed her chin and nodded. "I know."

Emily's hand tightened around Jaci's arm. She stared, unblinking, and lowered her voice to a conspiratorial whisper. "God wouldn't dare take my other son from me."

Without thinking, Jaci put her free arm around Emily's shoulder and pulled her close. Emily's arms dropped to her sides, unresponsive, as though she didn't understand the meaning of a hug. Jaci held on. Even if Emily didn't need the hug, *she* did.

This is what it meant to be a mother—constant worry. Sadness that could rupture your heart beyond repair. She couldn't bear this…wasn't a strong enough person to be a mother…never would be.

Emily's posture softened, and Jaci felt the hesitant grasp of both arms around her waist. She was surprised when a third arm crossed her back. Bart hugged both of them against him. She was blessed to have such a loving husband. Did she really need more? Did she tell him that often enough?

And Kyndal. Did her best friend realize how thankful she was to have her in her life?

Over Bart's shoulder, Jaci could see Bill Brennan watching their group hug.

When his eyes met hers, he turned coldly away.

SNAP…SNAP…SNAP. The sound of Kyndal's camera should have been encouraging—and for the first couple of hours it had been. After Chance had gotten the water into her, she'd rallied—had even insisted he retrieve her bag so she could get some shots of the painted room. But now, she seemed to be drifting into a stupor, taking random shots as if her fingers were on automatic pilot.

He knelt to check the water gourd again. *Snap.* Barely a quarter-inch of water. *Snap.* A couple of tablespoons.

Gingerly carrying the bowl so as not to lose a drop, he crawled over to where Kyndal sat leaned against the wall, staring at him, her expression blank. "Here, baby. Drink this."

She opened her mouth mechanically and swallowed the few drops he dripped onto her tongue.

"I…love…you." Her rough, jagged voice sliced his heart wide-open.

"I love you, too." Her hands…so tiny and fragile. Her fingers…so cold as he kissed them.

She pushed her fingertips against his mouth. "I'm glad…we had…this time."

No! No! No! Her words had a finality about them that froze his blood. She had endured so much. They had come so far. He couldn't let it end here…like this. He wanted to cry—wanted to scream—wanted to rip this damn cave apart with his bare hands.

A wild thought formed in his brain. *I can do that.* After replacing the bowl, he pressed a long kiss on Kyndal's slack mouth then scrambled through the cranny. He would dig them out. He would not sit here and watch Kyndal die. If the ceiling came down on his head, maybe the painted cavern would keep her safe until somebody came.

With the flashlight through his belt loop, he bored his fingers frantically into the wall of dirt, grasping handful after handful and throwing them behind him. The dirt loosened and shifted, filling in the spaces he cleared.

Every time he twisted to throw the dirt, the pain in his back caught and wound its way to the front. He gasped in shock at the increasing severity, but he refused to stop.

Dirt poured into the holes his fists vacated, leaving no trace of his disturbance, nature's way of obliterating his intrusion. He let out a feral scream and pounded his fist against the unforgiving earth and the futility of his efforts.

"Chance?"

He whirled around to find Kyndal pulling herself through the gap. He rushed to her. "What is it? What is it, baby?"

"You…screamed."

He helped her turn over and lifted her onto his lap, clenching his teeth, breathing through the pain. "I didn't mean to scare you. I'm okay." He stroked her hair—her beautiful silky strands, now tangled and matted by blood and sweat and dirt. "I'm going to get us…" He paused. A noise. He listened, straining to hear even the slightest sound. There it was again! A dog's bark. Coming from the tunnel.

"Here! We're here!" Could it be Chesney? Had she broken through the electric fence? "This way! Chesney? Here, girl!"

A whine echoed down the tunnel. A shuffling. More whining. Some barking.

Chance's heart beat so hard in his ears, it muffled the sounds coming their way.

But it wasn't long before a filthy Chesney loped onto the plateau from the tunnel and launched herself at him at breakneck speed.

She went wild at the sight of him, and he feared she might collapse from overexcitement.

He praised her as he hugged her neck, trying to calm her. "Good girl, Ches. You're such a good girl."

Her tongue covered his face with slurpy dog kisses and her tail beat everything in its path—mostly Kyndal who barely seemed to notice.

His mind raced. Chesney's collar was gone. Had someone removed it or had she gotten out of it by herself? Even if she'd lost the collar, maybe he could send her for help.

He leaned Kyndal against the wall. How much longer could she hang on? His heart skipped a beat when her mouth curved into a slight smile as Chesney cleaned her face.

He stretched through the crevice far enough to grab Kyndal's backpack. Inside, he groped for the masking tape and anything that might be used as a signal. The broken water bottle? It was as good as anything. He held the bottle against Chesney's neck and wound the tape round and round until he was satisfied it wouldn't fall off easily.

He could hear Kyndal's labored breathing. The sound nearly caused his own to stop.

"Now go!" He shoved Chesney toward the opening.

She wagged her tail and licked him in response. "Go, Chesney!"

She tilted her head at the sound of her name and sat down obediently.

"Find the Frisbee. Go get the Frisbee!"

She jumped toward him, ready to play, not the least interested in leaving his side.

Okay, she's not Lassie, but maybe somebody's with her. He fumbled through his pack until he found the whistle, and he blew repeatedly with all his might. Chesney whined, running laps around him. He blew until he thought the pain in his back would break him in two—blew until he grew dizzy and faint, and lights flashed before his eyes.

After a few blinks, all disappeared but one. A dim one, but it grew brighter and larger every few seconds.

"Here!" he yelled.

"Chance?" A deep voice rumbled up the passage.

"Yes, and Kyndal! She's hurt!"

"They're here! They're alive!" The deep voice relayed its message and was answered by shouts from other voices.

It wasn't long until a giant hulk topped by a hard hat and a lamp clambered through the opening. Chance squinted as the bright light caught him full in the face, blinding him. Thankfully, it moved from him quickly and fell on Kyndal who still leaned against the wall, not seeming to comprehend what was happening.

The shadowy bulk lunged toward her.

Chance's senses revved to full awareness. This guy

was moving too fast. He could hurt her. "Be careful. Her ankle's broken, and she's badly dehydrated."

The rescuer touched her gently on the cheek. "Kyndal? Can you hear me?"

Chance watched her eyes focus and saw them soften in recognition. Something about her look identified their rescuer even before she spoke the name.

"Ranger Rick."

She took a long, labored breath and closed her eyes.

CHAPTER FIFTEEN

KYNDAL BREATHED A PRAYER of relief as she hung up the phone and sank back into the pillows. Despite his bad toupee, Charlie Short was a good person. He'd read about her and Chance's ordeal in the newspaper and called to give her a couple of days' extension to get her photos and résumé to him.

That was especially uplifting because Jaci had brought her different news. Shop-a-Lot had left her a sympathetic message that they wished her well, but they'd lost a week of revenue and had replaced her with another photographer. They had, however, forgiven the broken lamps and weren't charging her for them.

Her mom had also left a message. She and Lloyd were somewhere out in New Mexico and liked it so much they were going to stay for a while. Would Kyndal please check on the house occasionally?

Tears stung her eyes as she realized she could be dead right now, and her mom wouldn't even know.

The frustration in her chest made her want to heave something out the hospital window, but the only thing within arm's reach was her laptop. She grabbed it and flipped it open instead.

She had a portfolio to prepare.

Jaci had downloaded the photographs from the camera before bringing the laptop to the hospital. Kyndal hadn't seen them yet, and while a part of her was excited at the prospects, another part dreaded the memories that would be dredged up.

She set up the files and began going through the shots, dragging one after another into the group she would send to Charlie.

The sheer number was staggering. She never would've guessed how many shots she'd taken over the four-day span. They chronicled the journey from beginning to end, and the deeper they dragged her back, the more agonizing it was to look at them.

Not that they weren't good. They were. As a matter of fact, she knew in her heart they were amazing from the reaction she had to them.

The ones of Chance were particularly difficult to look at. The early ones showed him smiling or talking as he explained something about the cave. But there was one near the end that was so poignant she couldn't take her eyes off it even though she started to sob when it flashed onto the screen.

It was a shot of him in the ancient room, and she didn't even remember taking it. It was as though she'd been guided by instinct.

The camera caught him as he hovered over the tiny clay bowl of water, body poised in a tense crouch, hand extended and reaching but obviously afraid to grasp. The whiskers of his black beard intensified the dark circles of his eyes—eyes that bore a look of pure anguish. And all about him were the red walls with their painted ebony eyes, seeming content to watch the horrific drama play out without the least bit of preference for the outcome.

It was the best photo she'd ever taken, the kind that made the national news and won Pulitzers and solidified careers. The shot she'd been waiting for that would make her somebody.

But she couldn't use it…couldn't use any of the shots of the ancient room. She remembered too well the graffiti scrawled across the walls of the room near the entry.

Public knowledge of this room might lead to its vandalism, and she didn't want that guilt hanging over her. Chance had trusted her with his cave. She wouldn't betray that trust.

A soft knock on her door startled her. "Come in." The figure that stepped across the threshold caused a lump to form in her throat. "Rick." She stretched her hands out to him.

The ranger had been on her mind a great deal since she'd been here. He was a fabulous guy, but making love with Chance had her all mixed up. She just wasn't ready to start dating anyone yet.

He crossed the room and took her hands, giving them a gentle squeeze. "How you doing, lady?"

"I had a clean break." She pointed to the cast and the crutches leaning on the wall. "We start Crutches 101 this afternoon, and the doctor has promised I'll be out of here the day after tomorrow."

"That's good news." But as he studied her face, his wrinkled brow didn't convey the same message. "You look like you've been crying. Are you in pain?"

"Oh—" she waved her hand toward her laptop "—looking at some photos made me weepy."

His eyes locked on to the picture of Chance, and she watched his mouth press into a thin line.

She reached to close the laptop, but Rick's head got in the way as he leaned down and peered at the picture.

"Y'all must have been terrified. I've seen that same look on faces in Afghanistan." He shook his head but the movement seemed to filter down his entire frame. "Still gives me nightmares." He cleared his throat, straightened and pointed to the eyes in the background of the photo. "What's all that?"

Kyndal told him about the room with the red walls and the black eyes and the pelts on the floor. "Chance thought it might be a Native American fertility room."

Rick's eyes went wide with wonder, and he gave a low whistle. "Well, how many of your competitors are going to have anything like that? I'd say this job is yours."

Kyndal shook her head. "I'm not going to use these. Chance has had a lot of problems with vandalism, and if people knew this was there, they might try to find it and loot it." She shook her head in disgust. "Or spray paint the walls."

"Yeah, I see what you mean." Rick nodded his agreement.

"And it's not like I don't have plenty of others."

That brought a chuckle from the former marine.

Kyndal closed the laptop and set it aside as Rick pulled a chair closer to her bedside. "Have you been able to see Chance?" he asked as he sat down.

She shook her head and tried to keep the emotion out of her voice. "He's two floors up, but they won't let either of us travel that far. We've talked on the phone, though… in small spurts. Did you know he had kidney failure?"

Rick nodded. "Bart's kept me well-informed."

"Then you know he's going through dialysis."

Rick nodded again.

"He's going to be fine, but he'll have to stay a little longer than I will." Kyndal reached out and took Rick's hand. "We're alive thanks to you."

He pressed a kiss to the back of her hand. "That's what rescue teams do best."

The sweet gesture caused a pang of guilt. She had to be honest with him. "Rick…about our date—"

"Yeah," he broke in. "Um…would you mind if we cancelled that?"

She gave him a quizzical look, which he answered with a smile.

"Bart filled me in on the history you and Chance have, and I saw the way you clung to him when we loaded you into the ambulance."

Ouch! His word choice stung, reminding her of the promise she'd made. "There's nothing going on between me and Chance."

Rick snorted. "Yeah? You just keep telling yourself that until the two of you come to your senses. And, in the meantime, you and I can continue to be good friends, but there's no way in hell I'm going to get caught in the cross fire."

She looked at him directly. "Do you mean that? Can we be friends?"

"Hell-pee-roo yeah."

"Hell-pee-roo? That's a new one." She squinted in question. "What does that mean?"

"Just an expression my best friend made up." He gave a soft laugh. "It means I want to be there for you—as a friend—like Jaci and Bart." He shrugged. "And we'll be getting together more often with my night tours finishing up." He brushed a finger down her nose as he stood up. "Gotta go now, and let you get some rest. I'm going to visit Chance on my way out."

"You really are my hero," she said as he started toward the door.

He stopped at the end of the bed and shook his head. "Naw. A true hero would have gotten the girl." He winked and left her with a smile.

His words about her clinging to Chance had caused a tightening in her chest. She'd been feeling pulled toward Chance since the night they made love, and, if she wasn't careful, their chemistry would have her believing stupid things again. Like that getting this job would showcase her work and make her successful—make her somebody—make her good enough to be the kind of woman Chance needed in his life.

Crazy ideas.

She pulled her laptop onto her lap and opened Word.

When she finished typing, she sent the document as an email to Jaci along with a request: Would you print this out and bring it to me when you come to the hospital? Thanks!

She opened her bank account and stared gloomily at her dwindling savings. The hospital bills were going to take most, if not all of what she had left. Getting this job was more imperative than ever, but not because of Chance.

She opened her photo files, determined to email her portfolio to Charlie Short today.

DENISE MACOMB HAD OVERSTAYED her welcome…again.

Chance was exhausted and wanted nothing more than to settle back into the pillows and snooze the day away. He had yawned several times, but the statuesque redhead with the weird accent that irritated the shit out of him wouldn't take the hint.

"Brilliant!" Denise gasped into her phone, and Chance grimaced at the word.

Who in the hell says brilliant *around here?*

Although she grew up in Benton, Kentucky, Denise was more than proud of her college years at Oxford. Apparently, she'd practiced to rid herself of the western Kentucky accent, but the results came across as laughably phony and set Chance's teeth on edge.

He'd tried hard to like her—she was, after all, his dad's handpicked favorite. Beautiful. Successful. Well connected. She was everything Bill Brennan wanted in a daughter-in-law, and she had no qualms about showing her interest in Bill's son. Hell, she'd done everything but show up on his doorstep naked. They'd been to dinner three times, and, rather than sex, Chance had found himself fantasizing about sticking a sock in her mouth so he could eat in peace.

He closed his eyes, trying to block out Denise's phone conversation by conjuring a memory of Kyndal's nonpretentious Southern drawl.

"Is he asleep?"

Southern—but deep and male and definitely not Kyndal—the voice startled Chance out of his daydream. He opened his eyes and focused on the man standing beside his bed.

"Rick Warren."

Rick clasped his hand like a brother's. "How you doin,' guy?"

Chance gave him a weak smile. "I'm gonna make it, thanks to you."

The ranger's face pinkened at his words. "Glad I could be of service."

His visitor's presence brought an assortment of emotions to the surface of Chance's awareness. This man had saved his and Kyndal's lives so, foremost, Chance felt an overwhelming sense of gratitude. But a tiny niggle of something else was there. Resentment? Jealousy? Kyndal had shown an interest in Rick. If they started dating, as they had planned to do, she would probably be intimate with him. Maybe sometime soon.

Chance forced a yawn to release the ache in his tight jaw muscles.

But Rick Warren was a great guy—the kind of guy Kyndal deserved. Someone who would love her and take care of her…be all those things he himself couldn't be. It eased the guilt, knowing she would have Rick in her life.

"Soon then. Ta-ta."

Damn! Denise's voice instantly tightened his jaws again. *Who in the hell says* ta-ta?

Denise slid her phone into her pocket, and just as smoothly, her eyes slid over the ranger. "And who might this be?" Hand extended, she sauntered around the end of the bed, the sway of her hips exaggerated by the tight fit of her skirt.

Chance watched Warren's eyes rove over the woman in an all-too-familiar gesture.

Well, I'll be a son of a bitch. He can't do that.

Before Chance could answer, Rick had taken Denise's hand. "Rick Warren, ma'am."

"Rick's Kyndal's boyfriend," Chance interjected.

Rick shook his head. "Um, not really."

"You're the hero I've been reading about. How fascinating." Denise's voice was almost a purr, but it scraped across Chance's eardrum like a claw. She withdrew her hand, and he watched her eyes drop to Rick's left, no doubt checking for a ring.

Chance tried to shift the conversation again. "Yeah, Rick risked his life to save the woman he loves."

The ranger turned a bright red face toward Chance. "Actually, I care about Kyndal, but we're just good friends. Nothing more."

Denise laid a hand lightly on Rick's arm. "Where did you pick up that yummy Southern drawl?"

"Arkansas, ma'am."

She works to get rid of an accent, but on him it's "yummy"?

Denise's throaty laugh sounded as if she was gargling. "'Ma'am'? Ooooo!"

"If you and Kyn are just good friends, she hasn't figured that out." Chance spoke a little louder to try and get Denise's attention. She seemed to be ignoring him, yet hanging on Warren's every word. "She talked about you nonstop the whole time we were together."

Rick gave Chance a bewildered look. "So…um…when will they let you out of here?"

"A few more days." Chance pointed to Denise. "And then I'll be taking this pretty lady to a long overdue dinner."

Denise didn't acknowledge Chance had spoken. She still had both eyes on Rick, who seemed to be growing more uncomfortable by the second. "Well, I don't want to tire you out," he said, "so I'll mosey along. Just wanted to see how you were doing."

"I need to be going, too, Chance." Denise nearly vaulted across the bed for the jacket she'd left on the chair. "I'm pleased you're doing so well, and I hope to see you back in the office soon." She turned her attention back to Rick who was holding the door open, waiting for her. "I'm an attorney," she explained. "Chance and I have been involved in a case…" Blessedly, her voice faded away.

"You're losing it, Brennan," Chance muttered as he lay back against the pillows. "But one date with Kyndal and he'll be hooked."

Kyndal…with her gorgeous eyes that gave away every thought she had. He smiled, thinking about their poker games in the cave. He'd won every one. And her hair that feathered around him like elfin fingers when they made love. Her perfect body. Her passion.

No guy in his right mind would pick Denise once he'd had Kyndal.

"YOU'RE SURE YOU'RE UP TO THIS?"

Kyndal couldn't face the concern in Jaci's voice. This

wasn't something she wanted to do, but it was what she *had* to do. "I'm sure." She punched the up button, and fixed her eyes on the numbers above the elevator door.

Jaci's elevator, headed down, arrived first. "I'll be watching for you, and I'll pick you up at the door."

"I won't be long," Kyndal promised, clutching the paper in her hand even tighter.

She took some deep, calming breaths as she waited, and they worked for the few seconds it took for her elevator to arrive and the doors to open. But when she hit the button for the fifth floor, her hand started to tremble.

She hadn't fully mastered the art of crutches, and trying to hold the paper and grip the crutch at the same time slowed down her progress, but eventually she stopped at the door of room 546.

She knocked softly.

The familiar voice beckoning her to "Come in" sent her heart into a gallop.

Chance sat up in bed, looking thin and pale, but her eyes feasted on him as if they'd been starving for the sight.

"Kyn." His dark eyes glistened as he held out his hand to her.

"Hey." She shuffled over and took his hand awkwardly, but had to let go to balance on the crutches.

"So you're headed home, huh?"

"Yeah. Well, to Jaci's for a few days," she corrected herself. She cleared her throat. "You look good."

His mouth lifted at one end. "Like I told you before, don't ever play poker, babe, because you're the lousiest liar I've ever known."

"Hey." She gave a defensive shrug. "Alive is good."

He nodded his agreement. "It is good, indeed."

Although hearing him speak was comforting, Kyndal almost wished he'd been asleep when she came in. She would have loved nothing more than to sit and stare at him for hours so she would have that memory to carry with her through the years.

But she could feel emotions starting to beg to be released. It was a warning she needed to get this over with quickly.

She held out the paper. “Could I get your signature?” Chance’s dark eyes squinted in question. “It’s a release so I can sell my photographs,” she explained. “Since they were taken on your property.”

His full lips turned down as he took it and looked it over. “You didn’t need to do this.”

“I just thought it would be a good idea.” She spotted a pen lying out of his reach and handed it to him.

Chance scribbled his name on the bottom and gave the paper back to her. “So you got the job?”

“No, but Charlie wants to buy eleven of my shots.” Kyndal balanced on her good leg to ease the soreness already threatening her underarms. “This issue will have caves from all over the state taken by several photographers who are still in the running for the job. He probably won’t make his final decision until December.”

“Well, I’ll keep sending good vibes your way.”

“Thanks.” She tried to ignore the tingle his words and warm smile were causing inside her. “Well, Jaci’s waiting.” She fought to keep her voice light. “But before I go, I want to thank you for all you did.”

“Kyn.”

He paused, and she held her hand up. “Let me finish. We said a lot of things in that cave, things we wouldn’t have said if it hadn’t been for the situation we were in.” She forced a laugh, praying it sounded sincere. “I’ve heard of bedroom promises and deathbed promises, and I think we got bitten in the ass by the worst of them both.” She gave him a playful wink as she made an ungraceful, yet successful turn. "See you around, Counselor. Despite your misguided political views, you'll make a great judge."

She held her breath and made it all the way to the hall before tears escaped from the corners of her eyes.

CHANCE WATCHED HER LEAVE, torn between wanting to call her back and relief at seeing her go.

The newspaper story had linked their names together, so he'd already had to start thinking of damage control and that meant staying as far away from Kyndal as possible. Comments from well-meaning friends confirmed the scandal she'd been involved with alone would dim his political chances, but throw in her environmentalist shenanigans and she would become the dynamite that would blow his dreams to smithereens.

What he needed right now was someone with a squeaky clean reputation that he could get his named linked with for just a short time. That would clear heads of ideas about him and Kyndal.

Of all the names he'd come up with, Denise Macomb was the most promising, but his dad had already made a point of rubbing in that Denise was already referring to Rick Warren as her boyfriend in conversation since their meeting last week. Which left Kyndal alone.

He squeezed his eyes closed and tried to push thoughts of Kyndal from his mind.

Damn the chemistry between them. It made up for a whole lot of her shortcomings—made her feel so right in his arms even while he knew she was so wrong.

CHAPTER SIXTEEN

KYNDAL EASED HERSELF ONTO the chair, hoping the nausea would pass. The cushion she sat on still bore the duct tape her mom had repaired it with fifteen years before. Kyndal had sliced it by sitting on her foot while wearing in-line skates. The owl cookie jar, the chipped blue willow dishes, the wallpaper with teapots and teacups. Everything in this kitchen looked exactly the way it had for as long as she could remember. And while the familiarity was comforting, it was disconcerting, too—a reminder of how many rungs down the ladder of success she'd actually fallen.

All the way back to where she'd started.

That she'd had a fling with Chance Brennan and he was once again out of the picture seemed to magnify the fact that her upward mobility had simply curved into a closed circle.

"You okay?" Bart pulled a Dutch oven from the box and sat it on the counter.

Kyndal wiped her sleeve down her face. "Just too many changes in six weeks' time, I think. The cave, the surgery, the job, the move." She indicated the boxes strewn around the kitchen and to the living room beyond. "At least I'm hoping that's what it is and not some dreaded disease I caught from breathing bat guano."

"Well, if there's a cure for bat shit fever, I'll bet Rick knows what it is."

Kyndal laughed. Bart managed to find the humor in

everything. "Have you ever known anybody who knows so much about animals?"

"Not without their own TV show. And if he doesn't get back with those sandwiches pretty soon, I'm gonna have to hunt down the neighbor's cat."

"Ack." Kyndal grimaced at the sick joke.

"And where'd Jaci go?" He held up the Dutch oven with a questioning look, and Kyndal pointed toward the cabinet above the refrigerator.

"I don't know. She said she had an errand to run." Her friend's sudden disappearance a half hour ago was perplexing since the job here was almost done.

Bart hefted the last box onto the counter, reading the tape on the side. "DVD player. Why don't we go ahead and get this hooked up in case you want to watch a movie later?"

Kyndal followed him into the living room, noticing her limp had worsened with fatigue. She was thankful she'd gotten a walking cast before this move. Moving was tiresome—even with four people—but trying to do it on crutches would've been impossible.

"Tell me about the job. What is it that you'll be doing?" He shifted the small television off the shelf, which was nothing more than a wide board painted black atop two stacks of cinder blocks.

"I get to take Christmas pictures of pets while dressed as an elf."

She waited for the inevitable snicker, and Bart didn't disappoint. "When do you start?"

"Next Friday, the day after Thanksgiving."

"And when does the cast come off?"

"December first." She rapped her knuckles against the cast a couple of times. "Hallelujah."

Bart pulled some cords from the box and studied their

tips for a few seconds. "Have you heard anything from Chance lately?"

The mention of the name brought on another bout of queasiness. She shook her head. "Not since the hospital."

Bart placed the DVD player on the shelf and the TV on top of it. "I don't understand it. That night at Max's, he was drinking you in more than the beer. And I noticed the way you tried not to look at him. It definitely seemed like love to me." He pulled some more cords out of the box and began attaching one end of them to the TV and one end to the DVD player. The umbilical symbolism wasn't lost on Kyndal, and she vowed not to stay here in her mom's house too long. "I thought y'all would be picking out china by Christmas."

"Nope. We really have moved on."

The back door closed and Rick appeared holding sacks from Starnes Barbecue. "Your favorite, I believe."

He pitched one to Kyndal and she held it to her nose, breathing in the spicy aroma of hickory smoke and pork shoulder that never failed to make her mouth water. The nausea had passed and she was ravenous.

They all three scrambled to the table and dug into the feast Rick had brought.

Kyndal was halfway through her sandwich and the men were each on their second when Jaci returned. She disappeared into Kyndal's room before coming into the kitchen.

"Where've you been, shug?" Bart pulled her in for a kiss before she sat down.

"Needed feminine supplies." She batted her eyes at him. He groaned and abruptly let her go.

Kyndal noticed Rick blushed slightly at Jaci's comment. He'd been around them all so much lately, he felt like family. She sometimes forgot he was a relative newcomer to the group. "Jaci keeps no secrets," she warned.

"I've noticed." He gave Jaci a wink as he wadded up his sandwich wrappers and tossed them into the sack. "Okay, y'all, I need some advice. I'm going to Arkansas for Thanksgiving."

"Oh, I'll bet your mom's glad to have you home for a few days." Jaci gave his back an affectionate pat before she sat down.

The mention of mom caused the bite Kyndal had just taken to catch in her throat. Her mother wouldn't be home for Thanksgiving. She'd called last week and said she and Lloyd had gotten jobs at a motel on Route 66. He worked as the handyman and she as the maid. She sounded thrilled that the perk was a free room. The horror in her voice as Kyndal recounted the cave saga had been genuine, but apparently her daughter's near-death experience wasn't enough to bring her home.

But it had given Kyndal the go-ahead to move back to Paducah rent-free.

"So Denise and I have been dating a month. Is that long enough to invite her to Thanksgiving dinner with my parents?"

"No," Bart answered.

Jaci snarled at him and raised her eyebrows. "Yes," she said to Rick.

Kyndal shrugged. "Maybe."

Rick shook his head with a laugh. "Well, hell-pee-roo, forget I asked."

The men wolfed down the rest of the food and headed to Rusky's Sports Bar to catch the Kentucky game in high-def.

As soon as they were out of sight, Jaci ran into Kyndal's bedroom and returned holding a small sack. Her usual smile was gone, her expression serious and a bit pained.

Kyndal's stomach tightened. This wasn't like Jaci. "What's wrong?"

"Kyn, you've been sick a lot lately. You hardly touched Mom's chicken and dumplings last Sunday. You didn't eat any pecan pie." She thrust the bag into Kyndal's hand. "I don't think it's from anxiety or the surgery or bat dung flu."

Kyndal's hand shook as she pulled the box out and read it. "A pregnancy test?"

"I want you to go pee on that stick. Then I want you to come back in here and tell me the whole truth about what happened in that cave."

PREGNANT.

Kyndal stared at the word. This wasn't one of those plus or minus deals that might be iffy depending on your perspective. This home test spelled it out with no uncertainty.

"It never entered my mind." She raised her eyes to Jaci. "How did you know?"

They were sitting on her bed, which was covered in the same beige bedspread with blue hydrangeas that had covered it when they sat there ten years ago discussing how they would feel if this ever happened. She might've been this stupid at seventeen. At twenty-seven, it was unfathomable.

"You haven't been yourself since the cave. I've never known you to cry so much. You're usually so tough." Jaci gave an apologetic shrug. "At first, I thought it was like post-traumatic stress disorder, which Bart says Rick is struggling with, by the way." She paused, and then seemed to refocus her attention. "But then, the blouse you had on at Mom's was pulling across the boobs. I don't know. It just hit me."

"I thought the dryer got too hot and shrank my stuff."

Kyndal gave a little snort and wiped her hand down her face. *Pregnant.* She tried to ground her brain to the concept, but it kept bouncing thoughts around like balls in a pinball machine.

"So, I've gotta ask." Jaci clasped Kyndal's forearm firmly. "Was there more to you and Rick than you ever told me, or—"

Kyndal shook her head. "It's Chance's."

Even as she said it, with all the turmoil and upheaval those words caused, there was something calming and comforting about them, too. She wasn't sure if the tear that dropped from her cheek onto Jaci's hand was one of sorrow or fear or frustration or joy. Somehow, she was feeling all those things at once. No wonder women had morning sickness. It was enough to keep her head spinning.

"I'm on the Pill, so I thought it was safe. I didn't have them with me in the cave, and I missed those four days, but I didn't think that would make a difference. And I had a light period while I was in the hospital, so it never occurred to me..."

"You were under a lot of stress in the cave." Jaci stroked her hair. "You were vulnerable. And, hey, it was Chance."

Jaci was blaming him. That didn't seem fair. "It wasn't Chance's idea. He didn't even want to. Well, he wanted to, but he turned me down at first. I was the one who kept insisting."

"I'll bet it didn't take too much persuasion." Jaci scooted over and hugged her tightly. "The question now is what are you going to do about it? I'm here for you. Whatever you decide."

There was no decision to be made. She already knew what she would do. Abortion was out of the question. Maybe at seventeen, but she couldn't even consider that an option now. She'd stared into the face of death in the cave and had seen her desire for life reflected there. Life was precious. She remembered the high school kids who'd brought their baby girl in to Shop-a-Lot to have her picture taken. Things couldn't have been easy for them, but the baby obviously brought them joy. The child made their circumstances worth it.

And her own mother. Life had been tough. But her mom continually told Kyndal she was what gave life meaning.

It was time to find meaning to her life. She'd always known in her heart that financial success was a shallow goal. Taking photographs of what was already there was easy. There had to be more to life than that.

Creating a person? That was the highest form of spiritual calling. A goal worthy of committing her life to. The fact that it was Chance's baby gave validity to the love they'd shared. It may not have lasted forever, but what they had was real.

"I want this baby." Her voice was firm, her resolve solid. Needing Jaci to see the conviction in her eyes, she broke free of the hug and held her friend at arm's length. "I want this baby. More than anything else in this world."

Jaci wasn't a pretty crier—thankfully she didn't do it often. Kyndal watched the redness bloom quickly from the rim of Jaci's eyes, down her cheeks, and gather on the point of her chin. "When are you going to tell Chance?" she blubbered into a tissue Kyndal snatched from the bedside table.

Kyndal closed her eyes and shuddered. She'd promised him no strings attached, and now they were going to have to deal with the biggest attached string of all—an umbilical cord.

"Not until I've been to the doctor," she resolved. "I want to be absolutely positive about this before I tell him, but I'll call the doctor first thing Monday morning."

"How are you going to have time for a baby? You'll have to work. You'll need a babysitter." Jaci was fighting to lower her voice. She did that when she was trying hard to sound like a mature adult.

"I'll figure out a way." Kyndal moved over to the mirror and looked herself in the eye. "I can do this. My mother did it, and I turned out okay. I can, too."

In the reflection, she watched Jaci flop back on the bed and cross herself—adding a dramatic sigh for effect.

"I DON'T THINK THIS SYSTEM is the one you need for this job." The design engineer from the security system company folded his arms around the clipboard he'd been scribbling on and eyed the entrance to the cave again.

"Why not? What's the problem?" Chance had hoped the vandalism would be taken care of by the end of the week, but that wasn't sounding like much of a possibility.

"Well, to begin with, if we run the alarm to your house, you're likely to get yourself killed. It goes off, you come busting down here with your shotgun, somebody down here is high—maybe got a weapon—it's dark, you're outnumbered—"

"All right, all right." Chance held his hand up to stop the guy from getting any more graphic. "You've made your point. I got chased away from here one time by the former owner wielding a shotgun. Scared the crap out of me—but kids today are different." A brief memory of Kyndal's big eyes and her tight grip on his hand scampered across his mind. He let it go and forced his attention on the problem at hand.

"You hear what I'm saying then. Best to leave that to the law enforcement officials." The engineer glanced at his scribbled notes. "You'd need to call the sheriff, and if you're not at home, it wouldn't do any good. And if we set the alarm to sound at the sheriff's office, depending where the responding officer is in the county, it could take anywhere from twenty minutes to an hour to get here."

"Which wouldn't give the kids much time to do anything," Chance countered.

"Long enough—if they're smart enough to set up a look-out. This system you've ordered isn't underground cable. There will be wires—too high to reach without a ladder, but they'll be visible."

Chance could hear the cost of the system going up with each statement the engineer made. "So what do you suggest, and how much is it going to cost me?"

"We'll have to draw up a custom plan, and I'm not going to lie to you, it'll be expensive." His smile seemed to convey that the truth wasn't hurting him a bit. "Running cable underground all the way to the house will be the bulk of the cost. I hate to say this, but Thursday's Thanksgiving, and we're talking another couple of months before we can get to a project that big."

"A couple of months?"

"February, at the earliest, provided we don't get too much cold weather that'll freeze the ground. If that happens, we'll have to wait for the March thaw. Sorry, but I want to be up front with you about it."

Chance ran his hand down his face in exasperation. The cave could be ruined by then. He wanted to protect it, and there appeared to be only one way—one very costly way—of doing that. "Draw me up a design and give me an estimate. But, in the meantime, go ahead and install this one. Maybe it'll act as a deterrent for a while at least."

Cha-ching. He was standing close enough to hear the sound of the cash register ringing in the engineer's mind. No doubt it was going to cost a fortune to have this done right. But someday, when he brought his children down here to explore the cave, it would be worth whatever it cost.

The thought of kids brought the memory of making love with Kyndal to the front of his mind. Damn the woman! What would it take to be rid of her for good? The weeks since he'd seen her last had him worried that wasn't going to happen.

But sure as hell he was trying.

A BABY. SHE WAS GOING to have a baby. She was going to be a mother. A little more than seven months from now, her whole life would change.

Forever.

Jaci had finally left, and Kyndal lay in bed watching the progression of Sirius across the window. How many times, as a kid, had she wished on that star from this very spot? Adulthood…motherhood seemed so far away then. How many times, as a teenager, had she wished on it for her and Chance to be together?

Forever.

She ran her hand across her abdomen. That wish had come true now. They may not be physically together, but a part of him would be with her forever. And a part of her would love him forever, though it was a part she would keep in a secret place—the way she was sure her mom did with her feelings for Mason Rawlings.

She wouldn't be like her mom, wouldn't move from man to man trying to find someone who could fill the empty space. The baby would be all she needed.

Someday, she might meet a man who would complete the circle. But she wouldn't need him. She might love him. Might want him. Might even marry him. But she would never *need* him.

Of course, he'd have to be a fabulous father—that would be the first criterion. He'd have to be a person she could trust. Someone who would never, ever leave.

Mason Rawlings, her three stepdads, Chance. They'd taught her how *not* to trust, and she wouldn't make any mistakes this time. For the rest of her life, this child would be her number-one priority, hers to love and nurture and protect.

She grabbed the purple Grateful Dead teddy bear from the pillow and hugged it close, marveling at the ferocity of the protective instinct already present.

She would have to provide for her baby from Day One.

Getting a good job had suddenly become more important than ever.

JACI RINSED THE EMPTY ice cream bowls and placed them in the dishwasher, her head still spinning with the news. Kyndal pregnant with Chance's baby. It was like she was watching a bad soap opera and couldn't change the channel.

She filled the soap dispenser and shut the door. Why did life have to suck so much? She and Bart had tried to have a baby but lost it. Kyndal hadn't been trying, but was having one. Bart would be thrilled to be a father. Her gut told her Chance wouldn't have that reaction, but she prayed she was wrong.

If I'd cut his balls off like I wanted to the first time he hurt her, this wouldn't have happened.

She punched the button harder than necessary, and the sound of swishing water filled the kitchen.

Who was she kidding? She could blame Chance all she wanted, but she was the real blame behind all of this.

"Hey, babe," Bart called from the other room. "Would you fix me a cup of coffee?"

"Okay." She placed a pod in the coffeemaker and waited while the liquid brewed.

All of this could've been avoided if I'd kept my mouth shut.

Kyndal wouldn't have gone back to the cave with Chance…wouldn't have almost died…wouldn't be pregnant now.

Overwhelming guilt weakened her knees. She leaned on the counter for support.

What did this show her about the kind of mother she'd be? She blinked back the tears that burned her eyes.

A good mother anticipated danger, she didn't send her child into it deliberately. She thought back to her childhood and how often her mother had warned, "Jaci, don't…"

The coffee finished brewing. She took the cup and stared into it, the dark liquid reminding her of Kyndal's descriptions of the blackness in the depths of the cave. How terrified she must've been—and in pain with a broken ankle.

She stirred in some cream and watched the black change to tan.

Life's bitterness can't be taken away with a swish of something stirred in. But then she thought of Bart—the something that mellowed any bitterness that came into her life.

Despite what he kept insisting, he wanted a baby, and her head kept telling her she should want to give him one. But this ordeal with Kyndal made her doubt her capabilities more than ever.

She picked up the cup and started for the living room, pausing at the light switch. Since she was a child, she'd always hated turning a light off when she left a room—afraid something would grab her out of the dark.

She flipped the switch off with a shudder and hurried out.

I'm such a coward, she thought.

CHAPTER SEVENTEEN

CHANCE PAUSED FOR A MINUTE before he got out of the car. Never had he imagined sitting here again, in this driveway, in front of this house.

The small, green tract home hadn't changed much. The crack running through the middle of the front stoop had never been patched. The shutter to the left of Kyndal's bedroom window still hung slightly askew. The giant maple tree that shaded the entire front yard had given up its leaves, covering the area in a blanket of red and yellow just as it always had.

And Kyndal was waiting for him inside.

When she'd called yesterday and asked him to come to dinner, he'd almost said no. But somehow the word had become yes even against his better judgment.

He'd finally gone back to work and gotten his mind off the time they spent together. Hell, he'd even had a date Saturday night. A bad one that had gone nowhere and ended early, but a date just the same.

Then Kyndal called. Her voice sounded odd, and when he'd commented on it, she'd said she was fine. It was a lie—something wasn't fine. She'd moved back to Paducah and into her mother's house.

Concern had brought him here—and maybe curiosity. Did she want to rekindle their relationship, after all—want to renege on the things she'd said in the hospital?

He reached to loosen his tie and realized he wasn't wearing one.

She was the one who'd said they'd moved on, but sitting in this driveway had him doubting her words. *He* had moved on, but Kyndal was spinning her wheels.

He should've said no to dinner. Nothing good could come of it. Well, the dinner would be good, but hooking up with Kyndal again—big mistake.

Still, this was Kyndal. It would be easier for him to fly to the top of that giant maple tree than to say no to her.

He pushed the door open, snatching the bag of peanut M&M's from the passenger seat as he climbed out.

The pleasant sound of crunching leaves filled his ears, so he didn't know the door had opened until he started to knock. And then the sound of her "Hi" replaced the crunch of the leaves and the sight of her filled his eyes—a one-two punch that took his breath away.

He'd never seen her so radiant.

"You look fantastic, Kyn." He brushed his lips to hers in greeting, weighing her reaction to see if she expected something more substantial.

She stepped back away from him. "Thanks for coming."

A tantalizing aroma suffused the living room with the floral sofa and blue recliner he remembered so well. "Mmm. Lasagna."

"Your favorite. At least, it used to be."

It was then that he noticed the wary look lurking behind her green eyes and the tiniest hint of tightness around the lips he'd just kissed.

Dressed simply with her hair loose and shimmering around her shoulders and a pair of jeans with a yellow shirt covering an emerald-green camisole, she seemed to glow, and things started to fall into place in his mind.

She'd no doubt chosen the look—the colors that would

enhance her skin tone, the form-fitting jeans that showed off her curves, the hair style that captured light in its strands—for his benefit.

And, of course, there was the lasagna.

The little minx *was* set on seducing him…again.

And there was no way he could say no to Kyndal.

Might as well enjoy myself.

He held out the yellow bag he'd kept behind his back. "These are for you."

Immediately the night began to crumble before his eyes.

Instead of the snort of laughter he'd expected, her eyes filled with tears and she limped toward the kitchen at a surprisingly fast speed.

Or maybe not.

"I'm sorry, Kyn." He followed her through the arched doorway, dropping the bag on the sofa table as he passed. "It was just a joke. I didn't mean to imply that I actually thought we would…"

She jerked the oven door open and pulled out a small pan of lasagna, setting it on a trivet on the counter. Grabbing a baguette, she used it to point to the bowl sitting next to where he stood. "Would you toss the salad? Dressing's there." She waggled the baguette like a weapon, warning him to keep his distance. "Chianti's there if you want some. It's the cheap kind, but they told me it wasn't bad. Glass is there."

Okay, now she was acting really strangely. No mention of the cave or the hospital. No comments about the past and the irony of them being here together. She was rushing him into a dinner she invited him over for. If she wasn't going to seduce him—and that didn't seem to be on her agenda—what in the hell was going on? Had she had some kind of breakdown?

He opted for a glass of wine to enhance his mood before

he tossed the salad. He picked up the bottle, which hadn't been opened, and noticed she'd only set out one glass.

She read his mind. "I already have a drink."

She took a gulp of what looked like soda, slid the baguette into the oven and slammed the door.

"Look, Kyn." Chance poured some of the wine into his glass and swirled it around. "I didn't mean to make you mad."

"I'm not mad." She pushed a stray hair out of her face and leaned her hip against the oven door. "I'm just overemotional these days. Since the cave."

So maybe she *had* experienced some post-traumatic stress. "That's to be expected, don't you think?" He took a sip of the Chianti, which would've earned a minus ten rating from *Wine Spectator,* and managed not to grimace. "I've had a few days like that myself. It has to do with facing mortality, I think."

"Yeah, something like that." Kyndal turned her back to him and started tossing the salad he'd forgotten.

Strange that she'd invited him here, yet was obviously uncomfortable by his presence. He moved to the end of the counter to attempt eye contact while he continued to probe. "Does moving back here mean you got the job?"

"Not yet, but I'm still in the running."

Damn! No wonder she was depressed. "Sounds promising," he said.

She scurried past him to place the salad on the table, then came back for the stack of plates, silverware and napkins.

"I do have a job, though. Starting Friday, I'm going to be taking shots of animals with Santa at that big pet store across from the mall."

Chance's heart sank for her, and he wasn't sure which left a worse aftertaste—her news or the bad wine. He tried to force some enthusiasm into his voice. "Well, that should be…interesting."

"It'll get me through until I start at the magazine."

That was the most chipper he'd heard her since he walked in, and it coaxed a genuine smile from him. "What are you doing for Thanksgiving?" He decided to keep up the small talk figuring eventually he'd hit on whatever it was that had put this bug up her ass.

"Jaci's having me over." She concentrated on pouring some olive oil into two dipping bowls and getting them safely to the table. "You can sit here," she instructed, as if he'd forgotten the seat he'd occupied for two years in this kitchen.

Chance ignored her order and got the drinks, while she put the hot bread in a basket and brought it and the lasagna to the table.

When all was ready, he pulled out her chair and got her settled before he sat down. Raising his glass, he had to think fast to come up with something not-too-corny, yet appropriate. It came to him—the perfect toast for tonight. "To life." He clinked his glass to hers and watched her bottom lip quiver so hard she caught it between her teeth. She sat her glass down without drinking and ran her hand over her face.

"What is it, Kyndal?" He leaned forward and brushed his fingertips across her hand that sat on the table now, visibly trembling. "Tell me."

She locked her eyes with his and blew out a long breath. "I'm pregnant."

The force of the word pushed him to the back of his chair. "Pregnant?" he repeated, as if it were a foreign word he wasn't familiar with.

"Six weeks."

He did the math. "The…the cave."

She nodded.

"You told me you were on the Pill." Her pained expression made him regret his accusing tone.

"I was, but I didn't have them with me those four days. I didn't think it would matter." She shrugged. "It did."

"Hell, yes, it did." He drained his glass of wine, keeping the last bit in his mouth so he had a reason to not speak as he gave his brain time to adjust.

Oh, my God...a baby. As of that moment, his world changed forever, and she handed him the news with a pan of lasagna, a glass of wine and a freakin' shrug? He remembered how she'd waltzed into his hospital room and presented him with a release. Hell! He was the attorney! Then she'd traipsed out of his room with a nonchalant, devil-may-care, to-hell-with-the-world ta-ta...or its damn equivalent. A blasé attitude seemed to be her modus operandi these days. Was she even ready to be a mother or he, a father? His world teetered.

"I'm sorry, Chan—"

"Sorry?" He fought the rising tide of panic in his chest. "You didn't step on my toe or scratch my car. This is a baby we're talking about. *My* baby."

Kyndal lifted her chin. "It's *our* baby. And I'm not sorry about the baby. I'm sorry about telling you this way. I just found out for sure yesterday..."

"You've been to the doctor?"

She nodded. "I did a home pregnancy test Saturday and called the doctor Monday morning. They got me in right away."

"So you've known this since Saturday and didn't tell me until now?"

She gritted her teeth. "I didn't know for sure until *yesterday,* and if it turned out to be a false positive, there was no point in getting you all riled up."

"I'm not 'all riled up'!"

She quirked an infuriating eyebrow.

"How can you sit there so calmly? We're going to have a *child*." He poured another glass of wine and took a swig, his brain lurching from one extreme to the other, from excitement to anxiety…from joy to trepidation. The responsibility she'd just placed in his hands was mind-blowing. "You're going to need prenatal care, healthy food…" He looked around the kitchen wondering if she had enough to eat in the cabinets. "Doctor's appointments. Furniture. Clothes."

He tried to estimate the cost in his mind. Would he need to cancel the contractor working on the house?

"Don't worry. I'll manage."

She obviously hadn't thought this through, and her complacency irritated him. "How are you going to take care of all that and yourself and the baby? You don't even have a job to speak of. Taking Christmas shots of pets? What kind of half-assed job is that?"

Her breath stuttered. A tear slid from the corner of her eye, but she swiped it away, hurt quickly replaced by an angry glare.

"I'm sorry to be so blunt, Kyn, but you know it's the truth, and one of us has to be logical about this."

Logic was all he had to hang on to at the moment because it felt like the floor had dropped out from under him. His career in politics…his future judgeship. Everything suddenly slipped out of focus and all he could think about was the baby. Shared custody? Passing the child back and forth and somehow making it all jive with his work schedule? He didn't want to be a part-time dad. He wanted the baby in his life at all times. Being in a constant state of worry about where Kyndal and the child were and if they were safe…he couldn't stand the thought.

"There's only one way for us to be certain the baby's taken care of the way it should be." He used his closing arguments' voice. "We have to get married."

IT WASN'T SUPPOSED to be this way.

Chance's wording set off warning sirens in Kyndal's head. It was the same phrase her mom always used to rationalize Mason Rawlings's disappearance from their lives. *"Your dad and I had to get married. He just wasn't ready to settle down yet."*

Chance's admission in the cave screeched into her brain. He'd felt the same way…not ready to settle down…smothered by their relationship…unable to breathe. Trapped.

And at his house that day before they went to the cave, he'd talked about having a family *someday,* but had reacted with horror at the idea of *now.* By his own admission, he wasn't ready.

Kyndal remembered what it felt like to be trapped, constantly searching for the way out.

And there was a way out. Mason Rawlings had taken it. All of her stepdads had taken it. Even Chance had taken it years ago.

They *had* to get married? No talk of love. No talk of commitment. All he wanted was a way to get everything taken care of.

Hell, he had one foot out the door already.

"Marriage is out of the question." She kept her face and tone carefully neutral lest he think she was being overly emotional.

"Out of the question? I don't think I posed it as a question."

"Regardless of how you posed it, I don't want to marry you. I *won't* marry you. Not for the baby and certainly not for the convenience." She took a relieved sip of her drink when he showed no awareness of her slip of the tongue.

Since Saturday, all kinds of scenarios of telling him about the baby filled her dreams.

In her favorite one, Chance was ecstatic at her news. He swept her into his arms and twirled her around. He swore his love and undying devotion before dropping to his knee and proposing. She saw the conviction in his eyes when he swore he'd never, ever leave her again, and she knew he was telling the truth.

In the worst one, he turned around and walked out the door without a word or a look back.

This was somewhere in between and hadn't shown up in any of the dreams. She would have to wing it.

Chance's mouth opened, but he snapped it shut. The muscle in his jaw twitched with tension.

She composed herself and spoke again. "It's very kind of you to offer, but—"

"Kind of me?" He leaned forward, his dark eyes blazing. "Who in the hell are you? Where is the Kyndal Rawlings I know? The one in the cave who…who…"

"Go ahead and say it. The one in the cave who seduced you. She promised there would be no clinging. No strings attached." She leaned back to gain some distance from his penetrating eyes. "That's me. That's who I am. I've been taking care of myself for a long time if you haven't noticed, and I don't need you or anybody else taking care of me and my baby now."

"*Our* baby."

"Yeah, *our* baby. We'll be a team until you start feeling 'smothered.'" She punctuated the word by forming quotation marks with her fingers. "Before long, you'll be running for that judgeship or some other office. You'll feel me holding you back and stifling you. You'll have to step out for some fresh air so you can breathe and *poof!*" She blew out an exaggerated breath. "You'll be gone just like before."

"That's not fair, Kyndal. I was young then—a kid."

It was her turn to be incredulous. "It has nothing to do with age. It has to do with me! I've never been good enough for you, and my love has never been enough to hold you. You said I was your everything, which sounds like love, but you still left. If that was love, it was pretty ineffectual. And you think we can base a marriage on it?"

Chance stood up and pointed a finger in her face. "You wouldn't know love—ineffectual or not—if it jumped up and bit you in the ass!"

Kyndal rallied from her chair and swatted his finger away. "Oh, really? And *you* would? Where would you have learned that? From your dad? The man who may not have left *physically,* but withdrew emotionally from your mom at the time when she needed him most? That may even be worse."

"Seriously, Kyn? You want to talk about dads?" He leaned his face close to hers and held his chin in a thoughtful pose. "Well, you're the expert, I guess. How many have you had?" He pretended to count on his fingers. "Hmm. Let's see. Four legal ones and how many that stayed for a week or two? That string of men your mom paraded through your life has you royally screwed up!"

"Don't you dare talk to me like that, William Chance Brennan." Oh! She wanted to wipe that smart-ass smirk off his face, but she restrained herself and gave him a shove instead. "Get out." She pointed toward the door.

He met her glare with an unwavering stance and silence.

Her body trembled, shaking her words loose on a shout. "I…said…get…out!"

A shadow darkened his face. Without a word, he turned

and stalked across the room, slamming the door behind him.

Kyndal hobbled into the living room, her breath coming in ragged spurts as she watched Chance's car back out of the driveway.

Anger and hurt and frustration all bubbled to the surface at the same time, converging into hot tears that scalded her cheeks.

"This isn't the way it was supposed to be." The grief of sudden loss made her dizzy, and she reached out to steady herself against the sofa table. Her hand fell on something soft and lumpy.

A yellow bag of peanut M&M's.

In a gesture of raw emotion, she flung it across the room against the closed door. The force shattered the wrapper and sent a spray of rainbow-colored candy in all directions.

A perfect reflection of my life.

CHAPTER EIGHTEEN

CHANCE FOUGHT THE BED all night and got up at dawn on Thanksgiving morning. His mind was already racing, fueled by thoughts of the baby, telling his parents and Kyndal's refusal of his marriage offer. Might as well add some caffeine to the mix.

While the coffee brewed, Chesney came to him, wagging a sleepy tail, nosing his hand. He plopped down on the kitchen floor and gave her a hug. Accepting the invitation, she crawled into his lap. He scratched behind the Lab's ears, and she closed her eyes in unabashed pleasure.

Kyndal Rawlings was a piece of work. Most women in her situation would jump at the opportunity to marry a successful attorney from a well-to-do family who also happened to be the father of their baby. But not Kyndal. Oh, no, that would be too easy. She had to fight for everything she ever had...and this was no different.

He stopped scratching, and Chesney protested by nudging him with a cold nose until he massaged her neck.

The way he'd handled the matter last night was nothing to be proud of, either. Getting a pregnant woman that angry—a woman pregnant with *his* baby—was heartless. Maybe dangerous? He didn't know, but he wouldn't let it happen again.

There was just so much he didn't know. The thought of having a baby thrilled and terrified him at the same time—as did the thought of being married to Kyndal. He was almost relieved she'd turned him down even though it stung like hell.

Chesney laid her head back to look at him, and her brown puppy eyes seemed to soften with understanding.

He had a lot to learn. And he had to make peace with Kyndal. They couldn't bring a baby into a world where they were fighting all the time. Chesney licked his chin as her tail thumped in agreement.

He gave Ches her breakfast and grabbed a banana for himself. Although there would only be the three of them, his mom was preparing a holiday feast and he was expected to bring an appetite.

He needed to tell his parents about the baby, though he'd prefer to wait until the pregnancy was further along. Kyndal would've told Jaci, no doubt, and the redhead had earned her blabbermouth reputation. With Jaci in the know, the possibility that his parents might hear the news secondhand was too great.

It was times like this when he missed Hank the most. As kids, Hank had always been the primary focus, and Chance had gotten away with things simply because his parents didn't take the time to notice.

Not anymore. Privacy had been buried with Hank.

Today, when he broke the news of the baby, he would be at center stage, and Hank wouldn't be there to smooth things over the way he did so well when attention was drawn to one of Chance's misdeeds.

He tried to take a deep breath, but the air seemed to stop midway into his lungs. He needed to breathe lung-filling breaths that would take away this anxiety squeezing his core. Looking through his kitchen window, he decided that the yard didn't seem big enough to contain his energy today. He wanted to go to the cave.

Once he'd gotten over the initial trauma of the accident,

he'd started to go there often again to think or relax. Lured by its timelessness, he found comfort seeing with his own eyes that some things lasted forever. He could talk to Hank there, and, sometimes if he listened, he could hear Kyndal and him—the way they used to be.

And the dream of having his children to bring here had come true—or it would in less than a year. What a staggering thought.

"Let's go, girl." He shrugged into a jacket and attached the leash to Chesney's collar.

The November air was brisk. It felt good to be outside.

Chesney pulled at the leash, anxious to dash down the path and explore territory different from the yard. He unhooked her and let her run.

Putting off the electric company last week had been a mistake. The underground cable needed to be run so he could install the new security system. He had to keep the cave secure for the little Brennan on the way.

Excitement coursed through his veins. He took off at a full-speed run.

When he rounded the corner that brought the black-hole entrance into view, he stopped and took it all in.

Damn! The place was a mess. The kids had been partying again. And the security engineer had been right. The alarm must have gone off, but he wasn't home, so it did no good.

Beer cans and liquor bottles were everywhere. Empty bags of snacks and candy wrappers littered the entire area. More than he'd ever seen before. The crowds were getting bigger. He dreaded seeing the inside. A tightness in his gut forewarned trouble ahead.

That and the panties Chesney brought to him. She pranced about, so proud of the treasure she'd found, before dropping them at his feet.

They were small and a delicate pink, and they immediately took him back to the thong Kyndal had worn.

"I've never been good enough for you, and my love has never been enough to hold you."

Her words crashed down on him again. She'd read his mind. She would end up hating him before this was over.

He caught the panties on the toe of his boot and flung them into a pile of rubbish.

Sweat broke out on his forehead as he stepped cautiously through the entrance. He stopped to let his eyes adjust. At first glance, nothing more than the usual graffiti was visible. The wall with all the names. A couple more were added, but nothing as bad as he was expecting.

Chesney's excited bark drew him to the next room where the sight brought him to a standstill.

Air mattresses covered the floor nearly wall-to-wall. Condom wrappers, used condoms, liquor bottles, beer cans, toilet paper, cigarette packages—it would take hours to clear all this out. But he couldn't bear to leave it like this.

When the flashlight revealed what they had done to the wall, his breath exploded from his chest. "Son of a *bitch!* Those little bastards."

A trophy wall! A place to boast of their conquests. Some enterprising individual had actually drilled nail holes. Underwear—bras, panties, briefs, boxers—hung from the nails with names painted beneath.

To top it off, they were paired up—a bra with a guy's briefs, boxers and a thong. Some held two female or two male garbs, and some nails held more than two.

The guilt, fear and frustration he'd so carefully modulated since last night shot to the surface. He grabbed a bottle and smashed it against the wall, and then another and another, letting out a savage scream with each that sent Chesney scurrying away with her tail between her legs.

This had gone way past teenage fun. He stomped the air mattresses, delighting in the giant pops the pillows made.

This had all the trimmings of a drunken orgy. Beer cans crunched as he flattened them under his boots. Things were out of hand, and it had to stop before someone got raped. Or killed.

Buck Blaine needed to see this. He pulled out his phone to call the sheriff.

What a way to start Thanksgiving. It gave him no hope the rest of the day would be any better.

JACI PREPARED A CUP OF coffee and stepped out on the deck, needing a few minutes of calm before the hectic day started. The Thanksgiving crowd would arrive in a few hours.

A thick layer of frost covered the ground, confirmation that autumn was quickly being pushed out by winter's approach. The cup warmed her hands as she said prayers of thanks for Kyndal and her baby, Julia's speedy recovery and, as always, Bart.

A flock of honking geese circled overhead, making their approach to land on the pond. She watched them with interest and turned to catch their descent when a smear of red on the wooden deck caught her eye. Her gaze followed it to a sight that tore a strangled cry from her throat. "Oh, no!"

A mother cat, bloody, battered and panting hard, lay stretched against the railing at the corner of the deck. Two tiny kittens snuggled against her, nursing.

Jaci approached cautiously, but the cat was obviously too weak to move. Puncture wounds around her glassy eyes and hideous gashes around her throat and back suggested she'd lost a fight with a raccoon.

She purred loudly as Jaci stooped beside her. Despite the

soothing sound, Jaci was filled with dread. The mother's rasping breath had an ominous gurgle to it.

"It's okay." Jaci brushed a finger along the cat's whisker line, and the purring increased to a soft rumble. The kittens seemed unharmed, pushing with their tiny paws as they sucked. One was gray, the other black with white socks. They couldn't be over two weeks old. Their eyes weren't even open yet.

Jaci stroked the mother cat. "You're a good mom," she said quietly. "You saved your babies." *At least, two of them.* The mother seemed to understand, relaxing and closing her eyes as Jaci's mind raced. Could she get the cat somewhere in time to save her?

An animal hospital was located just off the interstate. She passed it every day on the way to work. The sign in front said it was open for emergencies twenty-four hours a day. Would that include holidays? She had to try.

"I'll be right back," she told the injured animal. "We'll get you some help."

Rushing back into the house, she abandoned her still-full cup of coffee in the kitchen sink and grabbed two of the towels that were folded and stacked in the laundry room. In the garage, she spied an old wooden crate that would make a good bed for transport. She dumped its contents onto Bart's workbench.

Taking the shortcut out the back door of the garage, she loped onto the deck, crate in hand and towels tucked under her arm, but then slowed her steps lest she frighten the injured cat.

The mother wasn't panting so hard, and at first, Jaci's heart leaped, hoping the animal's pain had eased. But her heart nosedived as she realized that not only was the cat not panting hard, she wasn't breathing at all. She lay motionless, the only movement from the jerking and tugging of the babies as they suckled.

A deep sob quivered in Jaci's chest as she sat down. No need to hurry now. What was the use? She'd still need to take the kittens to the animal hospital, but that could wait. She could allow them these few minutes…this last bit of love and comfort their mama would ever be able to provide.

She stroked the animal's head with one hand and swiped tears with the other. "You did good, sweet kitty. I'll—" She stopped, unsure how to finish the sentence. What was she going to do? She wouldn't make promises she couldn't keep—not even to a deceased cat. But she knew nothing about kittens and didn't have the foggiest idea if a shelter would take babies this young. She tried for something noncommittal. "What you did was very brave. They're beautif—" The constriction in her throat cut off her words.

The gray kitten, which was slightly bigger than the black, released the nipple, and, with a wide yawn, rooted against his mom's tummy and curled up, full and safe and calm.

Jaci swallowed away the lump. Arguing with herself would only waste valuable time. She already knew what she was going to do. She stroked the mama cat's head a final time. "It's okay," she cooed. "I'm here. I'll take good care of your babies."

The black kitten had its fill by then, also. Jaci picked them up and snuggled them under her chin, catching the faint scent of milky breath.

Even filled with towels, the crate seemed much too large for the two tiny creatures, but it would have to do for now. She placed them in their new bed and watched them squirm until they found each other, then settled down contented.

She carried the kittens inside, wondering how Bart would respond to the surprise.

The kittens he probably wouldn't mind.

But he wouldn't be too thrilled when he found out the first item on this Thanksgiving agenda was an unscheduled cat funeral.

STUART REINHOLT WAS A man about to bolt.

Kyndal studied him covertly as they passed around the pumpkin pie and apple dumplings. She couldn't put her finger on what it was about his manner. It was just a vibe she was too familiar with—a sort of sixth sense that she'd learned to recognize in men.

On the surface, he and Julia appeared to be a happy, loving couple. They'd stopped by Jaci's on their way home from Thanksgiving dinner at his mother's house, and Jaci was obviously excited to see her business partner feeling well enough to visit.

And while Kyndal was glad to see with her own eyes just how good Julia looked considering she'd been through a bilateral mastectomy last month, Stuart's presence set her nerves on edge.

"What did you think of your mom's pie today?" Julia tried to draw him into the conversation.

He shrugged without looking at her. "It was okay."

Julia turned her attention back to the group. "Hilda made a maple bourbon pecan pie that was to kill for."

The tiny interaction, which was no interaction at all, was sad to watch, and made Kyndal's stomach tighten. "I think I'll pass on the pie." She slid the plate over to Paul, Jaci's dad.

"Well, then…" Paul cut a generous wedge and placed it on his dessert plate. "I'll take Kyndal's portion, too."

Jaci's mom eyed his monstrous helping. "That's not just

Kyndal's portion. That's big enough for you, Kyndal and Sasquatch. Honestly, Paul, you're gonna keep on eatin' till one day you're just gonna bust into a thousand pieces."

"Maybe." Paul swallowed a large bite and winked at his wife. "But I know which piece you'll be scrambling to keep as a memento."

"Aaeeiiii!" Jaci wailed, cramming her fingers into her ears. "Please don't say things like that around me. Makes me want to lose my dinner. And remember, we have babies present." She nodded toward the wooden crate with the sleeping kittens who, with their every-two-hours feeding schedule had been the center of attention all day.

Paul shrugged. "They can't hear me. Their ears are still closed."

Everybody laughed and Bart slid his arm around Jaci's shoulder and kissed the side of her head.

This is the way it's supposed to be.

Even as a child, Kyndal had loved being at Jaci's house. Betty and Paul were crazy about each other, and their home had a warm, cozy atmosphere that made everyone feel welcomed. The holidays were a time of good-natured ribbing closely followed by a hug.

Kyndal discreetly patted her tummy. *Someday, precious one, we'll have a family like this.*

Last night's horrible scene with Chance flashed in her mind causing her hand to tremble. What if that wasn't true? What if she and the baby didn't ever have this? She and her mom had never had this, but she'd always dreamed it would be different when she had a child.

She passed the apple dumplings on to Paul, and for a second, her eyes locked with Stuart's before his darted away. He laughed with everybody else when Betty slapped Paul's hand away from the serving spoon, but Kyndal recognized the hollow ring in his laugh.

In that moment of brief connection, she read something in his eyes…something she remembered seeing in the eyes of so many others. How had she missed it completely nine years ago with Chance? Had she simply chosen to ignore it because she was afraid to admit the truth?

Come Christmas, she'd be surprised if Julia and Stuart were still together.

No doubt about it, Stuart Reinholt was about to bolt.

"ALEX DONOVAN AND I are going to meet about Rick Warren next week." Bill Brennan swiped a hot roll from the basket his wife held and dropped it onto his bread plate. "You ought to join us."

"How is the good senator?" Chance took a roll, also. "Thanks, Mom."

She patted his shoulder and sat the basket near him and out of his dad's reach, one of her little ways of trying to keep the elder Brennan's weight down.

"He's fine," his dad answered. "Impressed with what he's seen of Warren and about to come on board with my proposal, I think."

"That's great." Chance tried to gather some enthusiasm for the subject, but the other news he carried weighed it down. "I can't wish Rick enough good fortune. He deserves everything he gets."

"Damn straight. Saved your life. The guy's got my support forever."

"Are you feeling sick, sweetheart? You've only had one helping of candied sweet potatoes, and you hardly touched your green beans."

The worried look in his mom's eyes made Chance rethink his decision to wait until after dinner to break the news.

Maybe if he got this over with, he could at least enjoy a piece of pecan pie.

"Actually, I've got something I want to talk to both of you about, so I might as well get it over with. Kyndal's pregnant."

His mom's fork stopped halfway to her mouth. "But you're not seeing Kyndal, right? So that bothers you because…?"

"The baby's mine."

His dad's fork clattered onto his plate. "What in the hell, Chance? How could this happen?"

"Seriously, Dad? You want specifics? Kyndal's pregnant with my child."

"Oh, Chance…" His mother slumped back in her chair.

Bill Brennan wiped his mouth and threw his napkin down in his lap. "I mean, how could you let this happen?"

He'd asked himself that same thing hundreds of times since last night. Chance took a sip of wine before answering. His dad would remain combative, but he hoped to make his mom understand. "It happened in the cave. We were afraid and we let our emotions run away with us."

His dad grabbed the fork again, thrusting it to punctuate his words. "Well don't let her hornswoggle you into marriage, you hear me? That'd be kissing those dreams of yours goodbye. You can afford to pay child support. Plenty of it."

"She turned down my marriage proposal." The words stuck in his craw and burned all the way down to the pit of his stomach.

"Well, hallelujah!" His dad sawed at a piece of turkey as if it were leather. "At least one of you has some sense."

"What's sensible about a woman trying to raise a child alone when the job she has will barely allow her to take care of herself?" Chance pushed his plate away, confident he wouldn't be able to eat another bite.

His mom cleared her throat. "What's she doing now?"

Chance felt the heat rush into his face. "Well, she's moved back here into her mother's house. Tomorrow, she starts at Pet Me, working on a…um—" how could he make this sound less awful? "—a Christmas promotion."

"Oh, good God."

His dad's utterance reminded him of his own asshole comment to Kyndal about the job last night. "But there's a new tourism magazine the state's starting up, and she's hoping to get the job as its full-time photographer. That's why she went to the cave to start with—to get the shots."

His mom nodded. "Oh, yes, I'd forgotten that. Maybe you could put in a good word for her with Alex Donovan, Bill."

"With her politics? Not a chance. Besides, asking for one favor from him is plenty."

"We don't need any favors." Chance picked up his fork. Realizing he had no appetite left, he set it back down. "I'll see that Kyndal and the baby are well taken care of."

"Listen to me, son." The edge was gone momentarily from his dad's voice. "Take care of the baby, but don't let that woman get involved in your life. She can't help your career. Hell, with what she was involved in, she'll crush it. And look at her background. Her dad was a bum. Her mom's a…a…"

Chance's heated glare dared him to complete that sentence.

"Kyndal inherited bad genes from both sides. You know that better than I do."

Chance tightened his hold on the wineglass, then, thinking better, set it back on the table. "Enough said, Dad."

"This is my house. My table. I can say what I damn well want about anyone I damn well please."

"Please, you two…it's Thanksgiving." Emily Brennan stepped into her usual role, trying to smooth things out between her husband and her son. "She's due in mid-June, then?"

The question should have been obvious, but Chance hadn't thought about the due date. Come summer, he would be a father. He reached for the wineglass again, nodding to his mom as he raised the glass to his lips.

A faraway look came into her eyes as a hesitant smile bloomed. "Maybe the baby will come on Hank's birthday." Her voice caught, and in the candlelight, Chance saw a gleaming tear hanging on her lower eyelid. She scurried from her chair, grabbing up the gravy boat, which was still three-quarters full. "I'll get more gravy."

Chance cast an eye toward his dad, but the senior Brennan was more interested in his corn bread dressing than his wife. Chance bit back the comment that would show his disgust and followed his mom into the kitchen. When she sat the dish down, he reached for her and pulled her to him. Her face sank into his chest with a small sob.

"Sorry, Mom. I think I ruined dinner with my news."

She shook her head, leaving a streak of tearstains across his shirt. "No, you didn't, sweetheart. Babies are blessings…never bad news. It's your father. He shouldn't say the things he does."

Her words cut into Chance's gut and laid him open. "Oh, God, Mom. I'm becoming him. Everything he said out there about Kyndal…I've thought them all." His voice cracked, making him sound—and feel—thirteen again.

"I was afraid this would happen if you went into practice with him." The sadness in her voice nearly broke him all over again. "But you have a kind heart, Chance, and a good head on your shoulders. You can choose not to be like him."

He wasn't so sure. All those terrible things he said to

Kyndal seemed to prove that his choice had been made. "You don't think it's too deeply ingrained in me?"

"That you feel guilty tells me it's barely scraped the surface. I'm thankful." Her arms tightened around his waist as she leaned back to look him in the eye. "You've given me something else to be thankful for today, too. There's going to be a new little Brennan."

Their shared smiles brightened the moment, and Chance felt lighter than he had in years. "We don't smile together like this enough, Mom. It feels good."

"I think maybe the reconnection to Kyndal has something to do with it."

"I don't know." He squeezed her tighter and planted a kiss on the top of her head. "The woman drives me crazy, and she made it plain she doesn't want anything to do with marrying me."

His mom's eyebrows knitted. "That doesn't sound like the Kyndal I remember."

"Exactly! She's different. She can be cold and aloof and...and she seems to have lost her ambition...her drive."

His mom's hands moved up to hold his cheeks the way she had when he was a child and she had something important to tell him. He couldn't move to break eye contact. "She's a woman alone and pregnant with sudden limitations you'll never understand. She hasn't lost her drive. She's refocused it. She makes every decision now with the baby foremost in her mind. You'll do well to remember that." She gave his cheek a pat, and a wistful look came into her eyes. "Now tell me about this marriage proposal I didn't even know was in the works."

Chance leaned against the counter and studied the texture in the granite floor. "I didn't know it was in the works, either. She told me she was pregnant, and I figured it was what needed to be done, so I just sort of blurted it out.

Insisted, actually." His mom tilted her head. "Okay, demanded."

Emily Brennan gave a sarcastic snort. "How romantic. Sounds like every woman's dream proposal."

"She just makes me crazy, Mom."

"Love makes us all crazy."

Love?

Nobody had said anything about love…except Kyndal. "She said the love I felt for her when we were kids was ineffectual because I left her, anyway." He grimaced, realizing how much it sounded like he was tattling.

His mother laughed, a pleasant sound even with its scolding implication. "'Ineffectual,' huh? Well, she hasn't lost her way with words. But why did she say that?" She raised a knowing eyebrow. "And the bigger question is why did you sabotage the proposal? I mean, even a spontaneous one can be the sweet, down-on-one-knee kind every woman dreams of. What held you back?"

He hadn't seen this kind of intensity in his mom's eyes in years. There was life in them, and they were boring a hole into his soul and opening him up, just as Kyndal did. "I'm afraid." Were those actually tears blurring his vision? His normally strong voice came out as a strained whisper. "What if she's not the woman I need in my life?"

His mom's eyes softened with her smile. "The time will come, sweetheart, when you'll know with certainty who you don't need in your life and who you do. If you love her, you need her."

That word again.

A vision of them in the cave flashed through his mind—in the ancient room when he thought he was going to lose her, he'd told her he loved her. She had been the only thing keeping him going then, the only thing he needed. And now nothing was more important than the baby—and she was the only one who could give him this child. Thoughts of holding her—making love to her—pulled at his heart. He didn't only need her, he wanted her. An understanding of how much solidified in his mind and his heart.

"Oh, God, Mom, I *love* her." The words closed his throat with emotion.

"But it can't be ineffectual love." Her tender smile brought tears to his eyes again. "There has to be purpose behind it. Love isn't a word, Chance. Saying it is easy. But it takes actions to prove it."

Even though he knew it wouldn't last, for tonight, for this moment, he felt at peace.

His mom picked up the pecan pie and waved it in front of his face. "I don't think we need more gravy. But it may be time for dessert. What do you say?"

The buttery, sweet scent made his mouth water, but he couldn't truly enjoy the luscious dessert until he got the bitter taste out of his mouth. "I say, cut me a big piece. I'll be back in a minute. I have a quick call I need to make."

He stepped out the back door and punched Kyndal's number into his phone.

It rang quite a few times. When she didn't answer, the machine instructed him to leave a message.

"Kyn, it's Chance. Today's Thanksgiving and I wanted you to know how thankful I am you chose to have this baby...our baby. We'll work things out."

He stopped there, not saying the rest of what he was thankful for—the job she was pursuing was in Paducah so the baby would be near him at all times.

And so would she.

CHAPTER NINETEEN

BUSINESS WAS SLOW THE first day, and Kyndal was grateful. Lumbering around the crowded back corner of Pet Me, which had been transformed into Santa's workshop, with a cast on her foot was a daunting task. But the added benefit of being located close to the employee bathroom gave the small nook a certain ambiance.

The festive red-and-green-striped elf costume with its pointy shoes, pointy hat and pointy green velvet vest all decked out in bells jangled constantly and made her feel more like a court jester. But she convinced herself the jingles were synonymous with paychecks, which meant food, so she worked at ignoring them.

As of yesterday, however, food had become both her greatest ally and her nemesis. She began to understand the word *craving* in all its glory, being helpless to stop eating Jaci's cranberry salad until every bite was gone. But morning sickness had become a misnomer, managing to work itself into surprise attacks at any time of day.

Chance's message on her machine had triggered an attack at around eight-thirty last night although that may have just been her body's reaction to the stress of the past two days.

She did know that her heart had gone into a wild rhythm at his words, and his kind voice pricked her conscience.

She'd thought about it all night and decided he was right. They *could* make this work. Thanks to their time in the cave, she'd gained insight into Chance's character. He needed space to breathe. Allowing him to have his life separate from them was the key to keeping the father in her baby's life.

Too tired to change out of the elf suit at the store, she headed home, praying the old Jeep would make it that far.

The heater warmed quickly, and soon her muscles were loose and relaxed. They instantly balled into hard knots, though, when she turned onto her street and spotted Chance's SUV in her driveway.

He saw her coming and was waiting to open her door by the time she switched off the ignition.

"Hi." His mouth twitched, but he couldn't keep his mirth in check as his eyes roamed over the costume. "You make a damn fine-lookin' elf, Kyn." He erupted into a laugh that heated Kyndal's face and heart at the same time.

"Thanks!" She broke into a quick shimmy, jingling from her toes to her head. "I tinkle." A flash of heat sprang into his eyes at her movements, so she cut it off abruptly. "Um, the baby might not like that."

He cocked his head and raised his eyebrows suggestively. "Maybe not, but I sure did."

"What brings you here?" She pointedly changed the subject. Giving Chance space meant no sexual contact. She was more than positive sex would bring out her clingy side.

"Do you still have a freezer in the utility room?"

She nodded. "Yeah. Why?"

Chance opened the door to the cargo hold of his SUV and lifted out a large foam box. "Because I ordered a month's supply of dinners for you from Maid-to-Order."

Kyndal had heard about the delicious, but very costly cuisine the new take-out/catering service offered. A month's worth of meals had surely cost him a small fortune. "You shouldn't have done that. It's way too expens—"

"Nothing's too expensive for my baby."

A tingle ran up Kyndal's spine at his words. When she realized he meant them literally, the tingle branched out through her whole body.

"But we need to get them in the freezer." Chance tilted his head toward the house. "I didn't know what time you'd get off, so I've been sitting here awhile."

"Oh, sure!" She hurried to get the door unlocked and he followed her through the kitchen.

They chatted while unloading the box of its delicacies. Kyndal read the labels—learning about the *nutritionally balanced five-course gourmet meals,* which included bread and dessert, and filled Chance in on the details of her first day of work.

She was astounded when he went back to retrieve a second box. By the third, she was speechless.

"I don't know what to say other than thank you. I never expected anything like this." Her emotions threatened to get the best of her, and she bit her lip.

"I meant what I said last night, Kyn. I'm thankful, and married or not, I want to be a part of your and the baby's life."

The brush of his knuckle against her cheek unleashed the tears, and they streamed down her cheeks. She swiped at them, covering her embarrassment with a laugh. "Hormones have my emotions all over the place."

"Can we sit and talk a few minutes?"

She nodded and he led her to the kitchen table and helped her into a chair.

He pulled a cell phone from his pocket and slid it over in front of her. "This is for you, too." She started to protest, but he placed a finger on her lips, which cleared her brain of any thought except that his finger was on her lips. "You need to be able to get hold of me anytime, and I need the same from you." He pointed to the antiquated telephone hanging on the wall and the answering machine on the counter under it. "That just doesn't cut it."

He powered up the new cell phone. "I've taken care of a three-year contract for this, and I've already got my cell number and the office number programmed into the favorites list as well as all of Jaci's numbers and Rick's number. I also put myself in as the in-case-of-emergency number, which I know is presumptuous, but I did it, anyway."

He shrugged and grinned, and Kyndal's heart felt so full, she thought it would burst. "I don't know how I'll repay you, Chance."

He gave her hand a squeeze. "You're having my baby."

Her arms ached to hold him, but if she did, he would have to pry himself loose because she would never let him go on her own. She'd smother him until he couldn't breathe, and they'd be back to where they were nine years ago, except with a baby on the way.

No, hugging was out. She searched for another way to show her gratitude. "Would you like to stay for supper?" It came out quickly, partly because it seemed like the least she could do considering his generosity. Mostly because she didn't want him to leave.

His eyes widened in surprise. "I'd love to. I still have a lot to discuss with you about doctor's appointments—I want to be included in them. The first trimester is the critical time to guard against birth defects…"

She nodded and smiled to herself as she listened to him quoting information from the internet she'd read hundreds of times already.

He stopped for a breath and gave a sheepish smile. "We

can talk about this during supper. What'd you have in mind? Pizza?"

"Nope." She pushed out of the chair and headed for the refrigerator. "I have a pan of leftover lasagna in here begging to be eaten."

Their laughter blended, and for a split second, she saw—or imagined she saw—something that went beyond desire in his dark eyes.

She wouldn't fool herself into thinking they could have a future together, but she could rest easy knowing he'd be there for the baby.

BILL BRENNAN POKED his head in his son's office the following Monday afternoon. "Got a minute?"

"Sure." Chance leaned back and stretched his arms over his head. For two hours he'd been hunched over his desk, writing furiously. The break was welcomed—even if it had to be shared with his dad. "What's on your mind?"

"Just wanted to talk with my son for a few minutes." His dad took one of the seats in front of the desk.

His studiously casual posture caused a tightness to grow in the pit of Chance's stomach. "About…?"

"About your Thanksgiving news." His dad's lips pressed together, forming a thin line where a mouth had been. "I overreacted."

Chance shrugged. "I probably could've chosen a better time. I know it came as a shock."

"Kyndal's doing well? Feeling okay?"

Hearing Kyndal's name and a concerned tone coming from his dad's mouth was a unique experience, and it took Chance by surprise. "Fine…good. She's doing great. Well, except for the sickness."

"Glad to hear it." Bill Brennan shifted back in his chair

and crossed his legs. "Tell me more about this job she's trying to get."

Chance explained about the new magazine and how she'd sold some shots for the first issue, but was still waiting to hear about the final choice.

"And if she doesn't get it, what then? She gonna stay on at that pet store?" He spat the last two words out as if they left him with a bad taste.

"She'll have to find something else." Chance could feel this conversation heading south. "But she's confident she'll get it."

His dad grunted in reply, and then characteristically switched topics. "You been seeing anyone?"

"No." Chance didn't want to get into the subject of women. Until now, he'd refused to open the Kyndal subject up in front of his dad since Thanksgiving, but he hadn't given up hope he might be able to break through her resistance to marriage.

"Good-looking guy like you needs to be out there."

"I'm pretty busy." Chance left it there, hoping his dad would take the hint and leave.

"So Rick Warren and Denise Macomb are an item now." It wasn't a question, so Chance merely nodded in agreement. "Lucky guy Rick. Denise is a real looker."

Chance heard a bugle blasting in the back of his brain.

"Lots of beautiful women around. May be time for you to start thinking about settling down—find yourself a sharp woman with a good career and the right connections…"

"Not interested, Dad."

"I've got somebody I'd like to introduce you to."

There it was. "Still not interested."

Bill Brennan's face turned red as he pushed out of the chair. "You need to start thinking about other people sometimes." He tossed down a piece of paper with a name and phone number scribbled across it and started toward the door. Before he exited, he threw a parting punch. "Hank would've never been so self-absorbed."

Chance brushed the note into the trash.

CHAPTER TWENTY

KYNDAL CHECKED HER WATCH as she left the employees' restroom. Eleven forty-eight. Morning sickness came at midday today. If she could convince herself to throw up and get it over with, she'd be better off. Instead, she tried to talk herself out of the nausea and always ended up having to make a run for it. It hadn't happened with a customer present yet, but no doubt it would.

Mandy, the assistant photographer, didn't even try to hide her annoyance at Kyndal's perpetual "stomach bug." She had perfected the dramatic sigh accompanied by eye roll throughout the month of December, and used it now. "You really do need to see a doctor."

Kyndal had no desire to share her personal life with the snotty little twit. "I have an appointment tomorrow" was as deep as she got. She gathered up the squeaky toys from the floor, wiping off the drool from their last customer—a pretentious poodle who growled and snapped at "Santa" Howard until he plied her with doggie treats. "Where's Santa?" Kyndal moved the conversation to a less intimate topic.

"Getting more treats." Mandy's theatrics made Kyndal well aware that the sophomore photography major felt being an assistant was beneath her talent—and she hated working the weekend shift. And wiping the dog toys. And cleaning up the accidents that some of the more excitable animals left. She would've preferred to touch only the prints themselves.

A lady with a puggle in a military jacket came through the front door and headed their way, and Kyndal stifled an eye roll of her own.

Santa Howard took his place with the dog on his lap. The dog proved to be quite placid, and Kyndal became absorbed in getting the perfect shot. It came when the dog rose up to lick Santa's nose. Howard turned his head to avoid the kiss, and a quick flick on the button made it look like the puggle was whispering his Christmas wishes in Santa's ear. His "mommy" bought twenty-four copies of the pose.

As Mandy handed the woman her envelope of prints, Jaci came through the door waving magazines in each hand.

Kyndal's heart leaped. *Kentucky Wonders* was a reality at last!

"I just got these next door." Jaci thrust one toward her. "You get to see it first, so hurry up."

The cover was one of her shots! The entrance to Chance's cave—a black hole surrounded by gray limestone edged by the reds, yellows, oranges and browns of autumn trees. The shot was still breathtaking. She realized she was holding hers when she let it out in a whoosh and came out of her spell.

"I got the last seven copies," Jaci was saying. "The lady at The Book Nook said they'd been a hot item all morning. They even moved them from the periodicals to a table up by the checkout. She said people were buying them as stocking stuffers and to send to family who've moved from the area. Cool, huh?"

"Very cool." Kyndal turned the pages slowly, savoring the sight of her photographs once again showcased in a venue to be proud of. She clutched it tight against her and did a happy dance.

"Don't wrinkle it." Jaci's eyes twinkled in opposition to her stern tone. "These may be collectors' items someday."

"Probably only if our moms decide to become collectors." Kyndal shrugged. "And speaking of my mom, she called last night."

The twinkle in Jaci's eyes flickered, replaced by two-thirds concern and one-third question. "How did it go?"

"I'll tell you over lunch if you can stay." Kyndal pointed toward the back of the store where the employees had their small kitchen. "Progresso Minestrone."

Jaci nodded. "It'll have to be fast, though. The kittens are in the car with the heating pad plugged in. I don't want to run down my battery."

Kyndal had to smile at her friend's dedication to the orphaned kittens. For the past four weeks, she'd hauled them around almost everywhere she went, including work. She'd even hired a kitten-sitter on a few occasions.

"Mandy—" Kyndal followed the young woman's dour expression to the young man in a leather jacket with a boa constrictor wrapped around his neck headed their way "—I'm taking lunch now."

"You would."

"She's a little jewel," Jaci whispered as they made their way out of Santa's Pet Station.

"Yeah, I'm pretty sure her heart's made of stone."

The kitchen was empty, and Kyndal was glad for the privacy. Most of the employees ate at the fast-food places in the area. Occasionally, someone else brought lunch, but not often.

"So what did Mom think about being a grandma?" Jaci opened the can of soup as Kyndal got the bowls out of the cabinet.

"She cried." Kyndal felt her voice about to break, so she concentrated on filling the bowls and getting them into the microwave. "Telling her was more difficult than I expected. She was shocked. Even more so when I told her the father was Chance. She wants to come home, but they don't have the money to make the trip."

Jaci's eyes narrowed. "Did she ask you for money?"

"Yeah." She filled Jaci in on the specifics of what her mom and Lloyd had been doing. Rehashing the conversation took away Kyndal's appetite. She put the bowls on the table, stirring hers to cool it. "I had to turn her down." The spoonful she took seemed to solidify in her mouth, and she forced it down. "It was the first time I've ever done that, and it felt so horrible. But I had to. Things are going to be expensive, even with Chance helping out so much."

"You're preaching to the choir, Kyn. You did the right thing. She's got to stop using you. Now's a good time."

Jaci's reassurance confirmed Kyndal's feelings. She had to stop being an enabler or her mom would never learn to take responsibility.

Wow! The baby was already bringing out her strength and resourcefulness. The second spoonful went down more easily as the zesty flavor of the minestrone woke her taste buds and her appetite. Suddenly, she was ravenous. How could she throw up and then eat less than an hour later?

"You'll come to our house for Christmas, then."

Jaci's command didn't leave any room for argument—not that Kyndal would ever have dreamed of turning her down. "What would I do without you, Jaci?"

A shadow darkened her friend's face, and she dropped her eyes. "I dunno. Maybe have an uneventful life as a photographer at Shop-a-Lot?" She paused to slurp up some soup. "So, will Rick be in town for Christmas? Do you think he and Denise would want to come to our house?"

"Maybe." Rick had become one of Kyndal's favorite people. He was so darn genuine. But the jury was still out on Denise. She had such a pretentious air...and her voice grated on Kyndal's nerves.

"Has Chance been naughty? Cause this nice stuff is getting boring."

Over the past four weeks since Thanksgiving, she and Chance had found a peace that was tentative at best. A current of underlying tension was ever present, making her feel as though she was in a perpetual tango.

When old feelings started to churn to the surface—like every time he touched her—she would avoid him for a few days to let things cool down. But avoiding him was getting to be difficult. He would surprise her at work and take her to lunch. He called her every night to check on her, and sometimes came over to spend the evening. She could say no, she supposed, but she didn't want to. She practically lived for the next time she'd see him.

And that was a very bad thing.

She reached for the salt, but changed her mind. "He's going to the doctor with me tomorrow."

"I'm glad he's being so supportive." Jaci laid her spoon down, and her sad look sent a chill down Kyndal's spine.

"What is it, Jaci? What's wrong?"

Her friend's bottom lip trembled. "I shouldn't be telling this, but I know you won't say anything. Stuart left Julia last week. She told me this morning."

"Oh, how horrible." Tears sprang up in Kyndal's eyes. "How can he do that to her with what she's going through? And right at Christmas. That's just evil."

She took a drink to help a bite of cracker go down. "Isn't it odd?" She spoke more to herself than to Jaci. "In a world where everyone's supposed to be unique, there seems to be an inordinate number of men cut from the same cloth."

"You said it, sistah. But thank God there's not two of Bart." Jaci dabbed her nose. "One's all I can stand at a time."

Kyndal smiled, but Jaci must've read the doubt in her eyes.

"I know you're including Chance in that group, Kyn, but I'm not sure he belongs there anymore."

With one insightful sentence, Jaci cracked the shell Kyndal had formed around her heart, and a tiny grain of hope seeped in.

Kyndal shrugged, which took some effort considering the weight on her shoulders. "Time will tell, I guess."

"Well, just remember, some guys leave of their own accord, but some get pushed away." Jaci finished her soup. "I've got to get back to work. Julia's not having a good day." She grabbed a Sharpie pen from a basket on the table and took three of the magazines off the stack. "These are mine. I want them autographed."

Kyndal mimicked a movie-star tone. "Oh, of course, dahling!" It was amazing how much the gesture made her feel like a celebrity even though she was sitting in the back of a pet store in an elf costume. She scrawled her name with a flourish across the bottom of the first copy.

"Those are yours." Jaci pointed to the four left on the table. "Don't get soup on them. Talk to you later."

"Thanks!" Kyndal called after her. She took a magazine from the stack and studied the cover photo. A swell of pride grew in her chest. Slowly she opened the cover and read the words at the bottom of the page. "'Cover photo by Kyndal Rawlings.'" She smoothed her fingertips over them.

This magazine was a new beginning. The tiny grain of hope took root and began to sprout, allowing her to dream big. It would pave the way to the job, getting her good reputation back…success.

A means of meeting Chance on a level playing field.

A new beginning for the three of them…and, maybe, the chance of a life together.

JACI CHOSE THE SHORTCUT through the store that would take her down the aisle of cat toys. Gandalf the Gray, showing off his tomcat instincts, had already shown an affinity for the fuzzy gray mouse toys, indicating he would be either a good mouser or a catnip addict. The little female, Arwen, had a gentler nature, preferring to bat around the balls with little bells inside.

Watching the kittens play had become the new favorite pastime during breakfast, replacing her and Bart's longstanding tradition of watching the news over a second cup of coffee.

She snickered, remembering the string of expletives Bart had unleashed when he'd crunched one of the plastic balls underfoot as he headed to the bathroom in the middle of the night. She picked out a new set for Arwen and then grabbed up another pack of mice so Gandalf wouldn't feel left out.

The kittens were asleep in the box when she got to the car, and they continued to snooze all the way to Erlene Moore's house.

The young mother, whose due date was fast approaching, met her at the door, looking tired and frazzled with her two-year-old in tow. "Cody doesn't want to take a nap today." She gave a thin laugh. "But I'm ready for one."

"This won't take long." Jaci pointed to the book of window covering samples under her arm. "The soft, pleated shades have the look you want, so we just need to decide on a color."

"My woom, Mommy." Cody stretched Erlene's arm to its full length. "My woom."

"He loves his room."

"Yay!" Jaci gave a clap of approval. Incorporating the little boy's love of baseball and his dad's love of the St. Louis Cardinals had been a winning design.

"He wants to stay in there all the time." Erlene gave a tired sigh. "All reading must now be done while sitting in the stadium seats." She motioned to Jaci and allowed the little boy to lead the way, probably too tired to argue.

During an online auction, Jaci had procured two reserved stadium seats salvaged from the old Busch Stadium. She wasn't sure who was more excited by the treasure—Cody or his dad. Some school lockers painted red gave extra storage space at eye level for a two-year-old and provided an authentic locker room atmosphere.

As she looked around, a bubble of pride swelled. The room had come together quickly and painlessly, and it was perfect.

The nursery hadn't been as easy, but it was coming along. Jaci continually scoured books and magazines for fresh, new ideas because Erlene was insisting on a total redo. She didn't want Cody to think the baby was pushing him out of his space, so she wanted everything changed.

From the looks of things, the young mother's gonna be doing some pushing of her own soon. The thought brought on a fleeting moment of what-might-have-been, but Jaci worked through the pain by thinking about Kyndal. For some reason, that always helped.

It was hard to imagine her friend with a belly as swollen as Erlene's, but she'd already proudly displayed her bump one night as they sat at their laptops, gathering lists of baby-proofing ideas.

Kyndal had seemed undaunted by the task while Jaci had been dumbfounded. So many things to think about. Too many things that could go wrong.

Erlene squeezed into one of the stadium seats and started thumbing through the samples. Cody slowed down the process, constantly demanding she return to the previous page. At this rate, choosing the window shades would take all afternoon rather than the hour Jaci had allotted.

"Cody, I have some kitties in the car. Would you like to see them?" She tried to entice the child away from his mother.

The toddler nodded enthusiastically, and pulled at his mom's hand. "Kitties, Mommy. See kitties."

"Why don't you bring them in?" Erlene suggested. "Are they housebroken?"

"They're litter trained, but I carry a litter box with me because I take them to work." Jaci read the question in Erlene's expression. "The momma cat died so we're raising the babies. I'll take them in the mudroom, then come back and get Cody."

She went to the car and got the box of sleeping kittens and their supplies and set them up in the room off the garage. When she went back and fetched Cody, Erlene was tearful with gratitude.

She felt her heart squeeze a bit when she took the child's hand, but talking about Gandalf and Arwen released the tension.

Cody was surprisingly gentle with the babies, which Jaci thought was a good sign for the infant who would soon share his home. They delighted him when they woke up ready to play, chasing the balls he rolled to them, frolicking and biting each other's tails. He was especially fascinated when they scratched around in the litter box to go potty, and, of course, it reminded him that he needed to go potty, too.

Jaci and the toddler left the kittens, who were once

again ready for a catnap after their romp, and headed down the hallway toward the bathroom.

A strange sound floated from Cody's room, and he swerved away from the bathroom and headed toward it, pulling Jaci along.

Erlene still held the samples in her lap, but her head was lolled back against the wall, and her mouth hung open. The sound they'd heard was the exhausted woman's relaxed snore.

Before she could catch him, Cody pulled from Jaci's grip and ran to his mother, slapping the book from her lap, and causing her to wake with a start.

"Oh…oh, I'm so sorry." Her face flushed deep crimson.

Jaci's heart went out to her. She waved away the apology while she gathered up the sample book. "It's okay. You need whatever rest you can get."

"Mommy, kitties." Cody pulled his mother's hand, trying to pry her from her seat. "Kitties," he whined.

"The kitties are asleep right now," Jaci told him. "They're taking a nap. Is it time for your nap?"

"No!" He remained emphatic on the subject, and Erlene sighed dejectedly.

"Tell you what." Jaci inclined her head toward the hallway. "I'm going to get out of here, and maybe he'll change his mind if you both lie down on his new bed. I'll leave the samples on the dining room table. Get to them when you can, and call me when you've made a decision."

"Okay." Erlene gave a sheepish smile. "And thanks. That half-hour was the best nap I've had in a while."

Jaci laughed and blew a kiss to Cody, who suddenly remembered he needed to go potty. As he and his mother hurried toward the bathroom, Jaci gathered up the box with her sleeping babies, and let herself out.

She remembered how tired she'd been during the first

week after she'd found the kittens, having to stop whatever she was doing, which included sleeping, every two hours to bottle-feed them. Thank heavens she hadn't had to keep that up long.

How did Erlene keep going, sleep deprived to the point of exhaustion? And, with another on the way, the cycle would soon start over.

How was Kyndal going to do it? How could she handle a job and the baby, too? Even as the thought surfaced, the answer came.

Kyndal…Erlene…they would both be fine.

These women had some kind of inner strength they called upon, a mysterious element evident in most women. In the females of all species.

Mom material.

Whatever it was, when it was given out, Jaci decided she must not have been paying attention.

She'd been talking, most likely.

"NINE WEEKS MAY BE A bit soon, but maybe we'll call in a little Christmas magic." Dr. Tally held out the fetal Doppler device to Chance. "Would Dad like to do the honors?"

Chance nodded and took the microphone in one shaky hand and the speaker in the other. "Mine's beating hard enough to hear without this thing."

Kyndal lay on the table with her shirt pulled up to expose her belly, which was still almost flat with barely any indication of a bump.

Dr. Tally's hands gripped his and guided them slowly across Kyndal's midsection. They were all silent, listening for the sound that the doctor had explained would be a representation of their baby's heartbeat, not the beat itself.

Chance held his breath, straining to hear something that made sense amidst the cacophony. He saw the anticipation in Kyndal's eyes edged with fear, and he winked at her in assurance.

Her returning smile was hesitant as she chewed her lower lip. Then his attention was jerked back to his hands by an almost imperceptible tightening of Dr. Tally's.

At first, the sound was indistinguishable from its background, but soon the regularity pulled it out.

His eyes flew to Kyndal's and locked, sharing this moment of wonder. He carefully laid the speaker on the table and took her hand, pressing a kiss to her palm. She caressed his cheek in a gesture so tender it stopped his breath.

"That's what we like to hear. Strong and sassy." Dr. Tally's exuberance broke the spell, but the magic lingered.

The rest of the appointment went by in a blur of cursory questions and mundane instructions—nothing that could remotely compete with that sound of the living, beating heart he and Kyndal had created together.

As he walked her to her car, he still vibrated with excitement. "I thought I was prepared for that, but…wow."

"Chance Brennan speechless?" Kyndal elbowed him playfully. "That's a first."

He intended to throw his arm around her shoulder and give her a squeeze, but once he got his arm around her, it didn't feel like enough. He pulled her against him and captured her mouth in a kiss.

CHANCE'S LIPS SEARED every nerve in her body and pushed every thought from her brain.

She didn't care that they were standing in the middle of a downtown parking lot with gawking eyes all around.

The only thing that mattered was that the lips on hers belonged to the only man she'd ever loved. And for that moment he belonged to her.

She gave in and responded with all the passion her hormone-flooded system could produce.

The kiss lasted much too long to be proper—and ended much too soon.

Chance gave her a lopsided grin. "I thought I was prepared for that, but…wow."

Kyndal laughed, trying to quell both the rising desire and the rising panic vying for domination within her small frame. Oh, good Lord! One taste of this man had set off a craving the likes of which no pregnancy had ever known! She stuffed her hands in her coat pockets to keep from reaching for him again and stepped up her pace. He stayed right beside her all the way to her car and opened the door for her.

She slid into the seat and buckled the seat belt. "I've got to run, Counselor. Wouldn't want to piss off Santa with only three more days of work. I need them all."

A shadow crossed Chance's face and his expression sobered. "Kyn, I have a charity event Wednesday night. Would you like to go with me? I know it's short notice, and that's the night before Christmas Eve, but you've been working so hard. A party might be a nice change."

Kyndal's brain dissolved into a congealed mass of flubber. *A date?* It would be a mistake to go, but she couldn't come up with a plausible reason not to, so she stalled. "Um…I'm not sure if I'm up to it."

"I'll get you home early."

She started the engine. "Can I let you know later? After I get home?"

He nodded. "Sure."

"Okay, then. I'll call you tonight."

She pulled away, disgusted with her inconsistent reaction when it came to Chance.

The memory of his kiss had surely inspired that response.

Her brain certainly had nothing to do with it.

CHAPTER TWENTY-ONE

THE EXCITEMENT OF CHANCE'S kiss stayed with Kyndal, giving her a rosy attitude throughout the exhausting afternoon. She'd never imagined so many people would want photos of their pets with Santa—or that anyone would expect a photo with all nine dachshund puppies looking directly at the camera—but the kiss helped her believe anything might be possible.

So when Charlie Short called and asked to meet at her home after work, she kept the sinking feeling in her stomach suspended with an optimistic smile.

One look at Charlie's face confirmed her worst fear, but she invited him in and offered him a glass of tea before he broke the bad news.

"I'm sorry, Kyndal. Yours was the name I turned in as my choice, but the Tourism Bureau chose someone else."

"I see." But she didn't. Inside, she was a roiling mass of hurt, struggling to get air back into her lungs, trying to wrap her head around this surreal situation. She was his first choice, so he thought she was the best. But being best wasn't good enough? What did it take?

"…got wrestled out of my hands when politics got involved," Charlie was saying when she focused back in.

"Politics?"

"Yeah. Senator Donovan called in a favor. Just goes to prove that old saying 'It's not what you know but who you know' is true, I suppose."

And I suppose that answers my question. "Unfortunately for me," Kyndal said, not even trying to keep the anger out of her voice, "I don't know anybody."

Charlie leaned back and propped his arm on the back of the couch. "Now, that's where you got it wrong, Kyndal. You know me—" he took a sip of tea and smacked his lips dramatically "—and I've got contacts. Plenty of 'em." He pulled a business card from his coat pocket and handed it to her.

Kyndal read it, then looked back at him, confused. "A literary agent?"

"Guy and I went to high school together. He moved to New York and has done well…really well. He represents some big-name authors."

"Why would he need a photographer?"

"He doesn't. But I read the newspaper article about you and your ordeal, and I've seen your work. You have a great deal of talent. I think you need to consider writing a book about your experience and include your photos in it."

"I—I couldn't do that." Kyndal's throat constricted. Her best shots were of the ancient room, and she'd decided never to show those publicly. Although, if she had, the job probably would've been hers in spite of Senator Donovan. "I don't think I'm ready to relive that experience yet." She held the card out to Charlie, but he shook his head.

"Keep the card. You might decide to write the book someday."

She laid the card on the coffee table and forced a smile she didn't feel. "Okay, thanks."

Charlie fished around in his pocket and brought out several more cards. "Don't know how desperate you are now for a job…"

She gave a bitter laugh. "Pretty desperate." *You can't even imagine.*

He handed her another card. This one was from Dill Thurber, a hospital administrator. "Dill's in St. Louis at one of the big hospitals. He needs a pathology photographer. I mean, like yesterday. It's good work. Pays well. Has benefits."

Kyndal perked up. "You had me at 'pays well.' What's involved in being a pathology photographer?"

"Well, it wouldn't all just be pathology. He mentioned some of the job would include PR and marketing stuff—shots of new instruments, pictures of newborns..."

"That sounds fun."

"But the bulk of the work would be for pathology reports. Measuring body parts and organs that've been removed. Taking shots of them. Cataloging. Photographing autopsies. Not an easy job, but interesting if you've got the stomach for it."

Kyndal wasn't sure she did. Hers was turning over right then. "Oh, I don't know, Charlie." Her enthusiasm had started to wane.

"Well, at least call him and talk to him about it, will you? I've already told him about you, and he's interested. Said you could start as soon as you want." He shuffled the cards and looked at another. "Photographer for a cruise line?"

Cruising for a living? Beaches? "Where?"

"Alaska."

Kyndal shivered. "Not for me, but thanks."

He flipped another card to the top of his pile. "Theme park? Taking shots of the tourists as they come down the water ride?"

How low are you willing to stoop? Kyndal shook her head. "I don't think so."

"Well—" Charlie slapped his hands to his knees and pushed to his feet "—that's all I got right now."

Kyndal walked him to the door. “Thanks, Charlie.” She didn’t want to rush him out, but the devastating news had finally sunk in, and her emotions were rocketing toward the surface. “I appreciate your vote of confidence, and especially the extra help. I know you didn’t have to do that.”

Charlie’s chin buckled as he shook his head. “Sorry it didn’t work out differently, kiddo. With your talent, you should be working for *National Geographic.*” He gave a disgusted sigh that echoed Kyndal’s pain. “The little man just doesn’t stand a chance against the political machine.”

After Charlie left, Kyndal sank down on the couch, deflated. “Little man, indeed. I feel like I’ve been crushed into oblivion.” She eyed the two business cards he’d left with her. “Write a book. Wait for months to hear back. Starve in the meantime.” She tossed that one back on the coffee table. “Move to St. Louis. Photograph diseased body parts. Eat. Some choice.” She grabbed the nearest throw pillow and punched it with her fist. “It…just…isn’t…fair!” She tossed the pillow away. “But, then, life’s never been fair, has it?”

She started to pace, venting her frustration aloud because she needed to be heard, even if it was only by herself. “I was the valedictorian, but Chance got into Harvard. I had a great job with the website, but Mike made bad choices. I took the best shots, but somebody called in a favor. I’m sick of running into roadblocks every time I think I’ve turned a corner.”

She was crying now, and she wasn’t sure why. She had nothing to be ashamed of. She’d worked hard, never asked for a handout, paid her own way. So why this…humiliation?

She sighed, and her breath became ragged at the admission.

She’d dared to hope maybe *this* time, someone would

have a reason to be proud of her...proud enough to want her in his life.

How many times had she imagined Mason Rawlings pointing to her and saying, "That's my daughter"? Or Mom turning down a chance to be with a man just to be with her.

But more than anything else, she'd wanted to be Chance's equal—someone he wouldn't be embarrassed to introduce, not just as the mother of his baby, but as the woman he loved. The woman he never wanted to leave. His wife.

She'd been foolish enough to believe there might be hope for the three of them to be a family. But nothing had changed. She and Chance still lived in two different worlds. *"And when worlds collide, bad things happen."*

Her heart was breaking in two—a very bad thing.

The cell phone startled her out of her reverie. She glanced at the caller ID. *Chance.* She wasn't prepared to talk to him yet, but maybe this was better. She wouldn't have to see the pity in his eyes—or his disappointment in her. She pressed the button. "Hello?"

"Kyn? It's Chance."

"Yeah. Hi."

"You sound funny." Worry infused his voice. "Are you okay?"

"Bad news. I didn't get the job."

There was a long hesitation. "Oh, Kyn. I'm so sorry." *Pity? Check.* "I know how badly you wanted it. Hell, I wanted it for you." *And disappointment brings up the rear.* "You want company?"

"No!" Her vociferous tone brought a pang of guilt with it. "I mean, thanks, but I want to be alone to wallow in my self-pity."

"So what's the deal? I thought Charlie loved your stuff. What happened?"

"Politics." Resentment weighed heavy in her word. "Somebody with friends much higher up."

"Ah."

Was it her imagination, or was guilt hanging in the silence on the line? How many times had the Brennans used the same kind of connections? It was a world she was banned from being any part of.

"Well." The upbeat note in Chance's voice sounded disingenuous. "Maybe the charity thing Wednesday night will cheer you up. What d'ya say?"

Images of introductions at the event hurled through Kyndal's mind. *"This is Kyndal Rawlings. She's pregnant with my child." "Hi, Kyndal. What do you do...besides get pregnant?" "Well, right now, I'm an elf, but only until tomorrow. Next week, I might take a position that will let me photograph toe fungus. But who knows, if I work really hard, I might move up to fatty tumors someday. Of course, that's only if I decide to move. If I stay here, I can sponge off Chance until he decides he's had enough."*

A prophetic shiver ran up her spine. "I'm going to have to say no, Chance. It sounds too much like a date, and I don't think dating is the direction we need to take this relationship."

"Because...?"

C'mon. You know you've got to do this. She breathed through the pain. "Because we've been there."

"I see." His voice flattened. "So the kiss this afternoon? All just a big mistake?"

"No, the kiss was a spontaneous reaction to our joy. It would only become a mistake if we let it." She twisted the phone so that he couldn't hear her labored breathing.

"Enough said."

There was a long stretch of awkward silence.

"I'll see you at the next doctor's appointment, then."

Kyndal lowered the phone long enough to croak out a couple of words into the mouthpiece. "Sounds good."

"Goodbye, Kyndal. Take care of yourself and call me if you need me."

I can't let *myself need you.*

The phone went dead.

"Goodbye, Chance," she whispered. "I love you."

She let the tears flow freely then, not attempting to hold them in, needing to wash away the resentment and frustration for the blows the universe had dealt her.

She would give herself tonight to wallow.

Tomorrow she would face a new day with strength and confidence. And she would be a mother her child could be proud of.

"DAMN! DAMN! DAMN!"

Chance threw the tennis ball across his office with such force that it came hurtling back toward the lamp on his desk. He caught it just before impact, squeezing it in his hand.

Since the first day in the cave, she'd been telling him she wasn't interested in a relationship. Why couldn't he get it through his thick skull? He'd always accused Kyndal of being pigheaded—and she was—but he made her look like an amateur.

Time after time she pushed him away, and every time he came bouncing back faster than that tennis ball.

Well, no more. This time he was finished. He might be stubborn, but he wouldn't be stupid.

He would do whatever it took to be a good father to his child, but getting over Kyndal wasn't going to be easy. Being around the baby would mean being around her a lot. He would have to find some way to keep his feelings from showing and, eventually, it would surely get easier. It had to.

The picture of Hank smiled at him from its frame. Missing him hadn't gotten any easier. He'd just been able to control it.

He could do the same with Kyndal. Control it. He squeezed the ball harder.

Hell, the woman had given him an out—permission to move on and find somebody who could be a partner. Somebody whose ambition rivaled his own. Somebody who could help advance his career.

She'd done him a favor, damn it!

He threw the ball even harder, not caring if it broke something.

He should be relieved. So why did he feel like such a loser?

CHAPTER TWENTY-TWO

"WAH—WAH—WAH!" JACI faked a temper tantrum on Kyndal's bed with her perfect imitation of an infant's cry—an attempt at levity to balance the sinking feeling. Once again, her part in Kyndal's drama was stirring up feelings of guilt. If she hadn't insisted, Kyndal wouldn't have gone to the cave…wouldn't be pregnant…wouldn't be uprooting her life. "I just got you back, and here you're talking about moving again." She pointed to the royal-blue silk hanging on the doorknob. "Try that one."

Kyndal presented her backside to be unzipped. "St. Louis is only three hours away. Not much farther than Nashville was, and we survived that." She stepped out of the dress she'd been trying on and reached for the blue one. "I bought this one for the True Tennessee premier dinner. Wish I had the money back I spent on it."

"But I like having you here." Jaci made the most of her Queen of Pout whine as she slowly zipped the dress.

"I love being here, but I've got to go where I can make a living." Kyndal turned around. "How's this?"

The guilt stalled for a moment when Jaci saw how her friend looked in that dress. "Oh. My. God. Your stubbornness isn't the only thing the baby's increased."

Kyndal backed up to look in the mirror and gasped at the amount of cleavage showing above the scooped neckline. "I look like I'm about to fall out!"

"And every man at Max's will want to play catcher." They giggled like they were in high school again.

It was wonderful hearing Kyndal laugh again. With all she'd been through lately—*thanks to me*—that she could laugh at all was amazing. "Seriously." Jaci worked at making a straight face. "People like us only have ta-tas like that when we're pregnant. I say, flaunt 'em while ya got 'em."

Kyndal took another long look in the mirror. "I'll keep this one under consideration. I may not get to dress up like this again for a long time."

"Living in the city, you'll have lots of chances to dress up. I mean…uh…opportunities."

Kyndal snorted. "It's not like I'm going to fall apart if I hear his name, Jaci." She sighed. "Now, *seeing* him might be a different story."

"Aha!" Jaci's stomach tightened as her suspicion was confirmed. She scrambled to a seated position. "I knew it! You're running away."

Kyndal turned her back and sidled up to the bed. "I'm *not* running away. I just think it might be better if I wasn't worried about running into him unprepared." She made the move sound so…reasonable, as if a visitation schedule would fix everything. She picked up the black dress. "Should I try this one again?"

"No." Jaci spoke around the lump in her throat, forcing her thoughts back to the dresses. "After seeing the blue one on you, the black's frumpy, and the red's…I don't know, too red for just dinner. I vote blue." She squeezed her eyes closed, knowing she had to ask the question she was dreading. "So, when do you have to give this guy an answer?"

"By the first."

The air left her lungs. "Geez," she whispered, "that's only a week away."

Fear clouded Kyndal's eyes only briefly—and Jaci felt

it in the pit of her stomach—before she put on her brave face. "I know, I'll have to make my mind up soon. I'll have to find an apartment and a new doctor—" she paused and grinned "—and if your bottom lip protrudes any farther, we'll be able to hang an ornament on it."

Despite the quip, Jaci's heart felt as if it had shrunk by half. There hadn't been very many times in her life when she'd been at a loss for words, but this was one.

Kyndal slipped back into her jeans. "What do you think Rick's big announcement's going to be?"

Jaci jumped at the opportunity to move the conversation to something less depressing. "I dunno. Do you think they're engaged or going to get married? It's way too soon, but maybe Denise is pregnant."

"Oh, Lord, Jaci." Kyndal buttoned her shirt and started gathering up the dresses she'd scattered about the room. "You've got pregnancy on the brain."

More than you know. "Just exploring the possibilities."

Kyndal sat on the bed beside her and took a deep breath.

Uh-oh.

"Jaci, I know how difficult the miscarriage was for you. Are you upset with me for being pregnant? Ever since we found out, I feel like there's been a veil between us."

Jaci felt the end of her nose starting to bloom red as her eyes welled up. She squeezed Kyndal's hand. "I could never be upset with you about something so wonderful. I'm upset with myself. I feel like everything is my fault."

Concern shimmered in Kyn's eyes. "What do you mean?"

Jaci choked back a sob. "I'm the one who insisted you go to the cave with Chance. If I hadn't done that, you wouldn't have gotten lost in there…wouldn't be pregnant…wouldn't be moving so far away. I've made a complete mess of my best friend's life."

Kyndal pulled her into a warm, motherlike hug. "Oh, Jaci. You've never been more wrong."

"You're just trying to make me feel better." Jaci tried to speak plainly, but it came out more as a blubber.

Kyndal loosened her grip and pushed her to arm's length, forcing her to meet her gaze. "No I'm not. Please don't think of it as taking the blame for what happened. Think of it as taking credit."

Jaci grabbed a tissue and wiped her eyes. "What do you mean?"

Kyndal smiled. "Chance and I didn't make love that first night. We had a lot of air-clearing to get through. If we hadn't gotten lost, we never would've had that time together, and I wouldn't have gotten pregnant." The look in Kyndal's eyes was so earnest, it almost hurt to see it. "Jaci, I've told you this before, but you obviously haven't believed me. This baby is the most wonderful thing that's ever happened to me. It's given my life meaning…fulfilled me. Yeah, you pushed me out of my comfort zone, but beause you did, I feel like I can face anything now."

Kyndal was drawing strength from that mom-material source, but then, her best friend had always been strong—the kind of person who faced down life without blinking. Jaci knew she should take comfort from the words, but they only seemed to highlight her own shortcomings. Her tears continued to fall.

Kyndal's smile faded. "That's not all, is it? What's going on?"

Talking about her fears with a pregnant woman was a horrible thing to do. But honesty made their relationship what it was, and the need to talk to somebody besides Bart was strong. Jaci's breath caught in her chest. "I'm afraid, Kyn, of being a mother and of not being a mother. I think about all the things that can happen to a child, and I feel so…so inept." The words poured out. "I keep thinking that maybe the miscarriage was nature's way of telling me I'm not mom material."

"That's hogwash."

Hardly the sympathetic response she'd expected. "Huh?"

"Giving birth doesn't make you mom material." Kyndal's mouth pressed into a hard line. "Look at my mom."

"Good point," Jaci admitted.

"You can't drive yourself crazy with worry. Life's unpredictable." Kyndal's frown dissolved as she rubbed her tummy. "I'm living proof of that. Bad things happen and good things happen, and you face them because that's life. You don't control it. You just do the best you can with whatever resources you have."

Kyndal refused to relinquish the floor, even when Jaci tried to cut in. "I'm not done, Eight Ball. You're the one who always says things happen for a reason. Those kittens didn't show up on your deck by accident. That mother cat brought them to you. She chose you."

"Kittens are hardly babies."

"But they're a commitment, and you made it, and you've done an amazing job seeing it through. Let me tell you, there are mothers everywhere who would consider themselves blessed if their child could be cared for by someone like you."

"Are you saying we should consider adoption?" She and Bart had never discussed that option, but she knew him well enough to know he'd be open to it.

"Maybe…or maybe animal rescue. Whatever works for the two of you." Kyndal dabbed a tissue under Jaci's eyes. "I just know that I've been on the receiving end of your nurturing for years, and you're a natural."

Jaci's brain whirled with the potential. "You've given me a lot to think about."

Kyndal gave her hand a motherly pat. "You're definitely mom material, and there's a world of possibilities out there. Motherhood comes in a lot of different forms."

Jaci took a deep breath, and it felt like the first one to reach all the way to the bottom of her lungs since Kyndal and Chance had gone missing.

CHANCE WOKE UP ON THE EDGE of the couch with Chesney behind him, snoring in his ear. The blazing fireplace had made the room warmer than was comfortable. So hot he was sweating. He sat up and rubbed his tired eyes. No, it wasn't the heat. He'd been having another erotic dream about Kyndal.

He'd awakened from a similar dream around two-thirty, just as he had the night before. Unable to get back to sleep, he'd come downstairs and read until almost four. Now it was five-fifteen. He was facing one of the biggest David-and-Goliath days in his career with only eight hours of sleep in two nights.

Wharton Barge Lines was a huge corporation, which could well afford to pay Harry Holloway fair compensation rather than the paltry sum they'd first offered. Thank God, Harry had the sense to seek legal advice. The man had lost an arm when he fell between the barges. He could've lost his life.

Harry Holloway needed a hero today, but the hero he was depending on had his head stuck so far up his own ass he couldn't see the light of day. All because of a woman named Kyndal Rawlings, who kissed him with the heat of a thousand suns one minute and turned down a date with frosty nonchalance the next.

Chance roamed around the house, straightening things

that didn't need to be straightened, running a load of laundry for two towels, waiting for dawn when he could go for a jog and out-distance his thoughts for a while.

He hadn't been to the cave all week, and Chesney could use some exercise. So at first light, he called her and grabbed her leash.

The morning breeze off Kentucky Lake held the first strong acknowledgment of winter, and he found it invigorating. The jog became a run and then a race with him and Chesney neck and neck at the bend.

Evidently the colder weather had put a stop to the partying at the cave, too. The alarm hadn't sounded and he'd been home fairly early all week. By spring, the new system would be in place.

As they neared the cave, he spotted a long rope dangling from a tree, a large loop at one end, the other thrown over a sturdy limb. Someone *had* been here. The alarm hadn't worked.

When he spied the cut wires dangling from the roof, he understood. "Well, I'll be a son of a bitch!" They'd hoisted someone high enough to make short work of effectively disarming the alarm, which led him to wonder if the culprits were kids at all.

He pulled the set of keys from his pocket with the tiny flashlight attached. It wasn't much, but it would save time if he didn't have to go back to the house for a lantern. He entered the cave and did a quick scan of the walls. No additional graffiti, but they wouldn't have gone to the trouble of cutting the wires without following up with some mischief.

He groped his way around the room slowly, allowing his eyes to adjust to the darkness. Beer cans. Cigarette butts. Nothing too awful.

And then his gaze fell on the small belt, curled against the side wall. He approached it hesitantly, not wanting to believe his eyes, but the sinking feeling told him his vision was perfect. Not a belt at all. A dog collar.

He flipped the tag over and read the name. "Jet." One of the dogs buried in Old Man Turner's secret burial room. They'd found it. A few feet away lay several more of the collars and what appeared to be a journal rolled up and tied with a shoelace.

He undid the lace and smoothed the periodical under his palm, finding a red marker rolled up inside.

A magazine. He held the light close. The photo on the front was of a cave.

His cave.

Kyndal's photos.

He slowly leafed through the pages, eyeing the familiar caverns in breathtaking detail thanks to Kyndal's amazing artistic eye. The window into the vug, enticing crystals sparkling beyond it. The stalagmite teeth, eerily beautiful in their ferocity. Damn, the shots were good. Better than good. Fabulous! His wrath cooled somewhat as he became swept up in admiration for Kyndal's talent.

How in the hell did she not get that job? What would lure an editor away from someone with talent like hers?

He came to a page that had been dog-eared. A picture of the dog cemetery circled in red with a large check beside it.

They'd left this here to use again. They were going to look for everything pictured. A treasure hunt. A game of search and destroy.

And Kyndal had provided them with a map.

It wouldn't be long before they found the bats. Disturbing them during hibernation would probably kill them. The vug. The spiders. The lower level.

They'd eventually find the ancient room.

He'd known this would happen. Telling the public about the cave was an invitation to vandalism. But he'd allowed

Kyndal to take the photos and given her permission to use them against his better judgments. Kyndal had a way of getting him to do all sorts of things against his better judgment.

Kyndal Rawlings was the disturbance in his force.

His cave. His sleep. His heart. His peace of mind.

The woman seemed to have a knack for wreaking havoc in his life.

CHAPTER TWENTY-THREE

CHANCE CAME AWAY FROM THE meeting with Wharton Barge Lines feeling as if he could take on the world. They hadn't settled with Harry Holloway, but even their big shot attorneys from St. Louis had been placating when they realized he was willing to be reasonable. No ridiculously outrageous demands for hundreds of millions of dollars, but in a couple more meetings, Harry would have all he needed to see him and his family through comfortably for the rest of their lives.

Moments like this made him glad he'd decided to follow in his dad's footsteps and more certain than ever he wanted to be a judge.

But, man! What an exhausting day it had been. The lack of sleep started catching up with him as he shook Harry's hand in parting.

He checked his watch. Already after eight, and he still had to make an appearance at the Christmas Cocktails event the Women's League was hosting. He considered changing out of his suit into the sweater he'd brought, but decided against it. He was simply too tired, and he didn't plan on staying long enough to put in the effort. He would stay long enough to be seen, and then head home and hopefully get a real night's sleep—provided, of course, he could keep Kyndal from haunting his dreams.

The cocktail party was being held at the Carson Center, just a few blocks away. He chose to walk, hoping the cold night air might bring some life into his weary bones. When he drew near, he saw the parking lot was full. A good sign. He'd be able to leave early without being missed.

Stepping through the door was like stepping into a holiday world for adults. Giant martini glasses filled with red-and-green balloons stood scattered about, flanked by shorter highball glasses filled with gold balloons to represent good Kentucky bourbon. The strong aromas of pine and spices blended, giving the odd sensation of enjoying a gingerbread cookie while roaming through a pine forest.

"Chance!"

Kiki Granger, in a sparkly dress cut so low he could see all the way to Atlanta, plastered herself against him a few seconds after he walked in the door. "Haven't seen you in soooo long," she cooed. The alcohol on the platinum blonde's breath was strong enough to make him sway.

Not long enough.

He and Kiki dated for a while in high school, pre-Kyndal. He'd made the mistake of calling her when he moved back to Paducah. The damn woman's libido ran faster than a Kentucky thoroughbred. "It's good to see you, Kiki," he lied as he extricated himself from her grip and set her away from him. "Is Colten here?" Maybe reminding her she was a married woman now would sober her up a little.

"No, he's having a night out with the boys." She laid a hand on his shoulder and stepped into him again, looking at him coyly from under her ridiculously long, fake eyelashes. "But you're here." Her finger toyed with his earlobe.

"And I can't stay long." He caught her hand with his and gave it a very businesslike shake. "Merry Christmas."

He could feel her glare boring into his back as he walked away. One date with Kiki when he first moved home to Paducah had given him a clearer understanding of the term *nympho.* What in the hell had Colten Granger been thinking?

He spotted Julia Reinholt with her coat on headed toward the door. “Hey, Julia.” He caught her and gave her a quick hug. “Are you leaving so soon?”

“Yeah.” Her eyes clouded, and she gave him a tight smile. “I’m not much in the holiday spirit this year. I suppose you’ve heard…”

He squeezed her hand gently. “Yeah, I’ve heard. I’m sorry.” *And I’d like to string up Stuart’s balls along with these holiday decorations.*

She nodded, as if she’d heard his thought, pressing her lips together. “I’ll talk to you soon.”

He could tell she wanted to get away quickly, but her haunted expression compelled him to give her another hug, anyway.

“Merry Christmas, Chance,” she whispered.

“Merry Christmas to you, Julia.”

When they broke contact, she tilted her head toward the staircase. “If you’re looking for your mom and dad, they’re at the Scotch bar.” She arranged a scarf around her neck, then left him with a wave.

Of course, his dad would be at the Scotch bar. Bill Brennan loved his Scotch and had given Chance an appreciation for the drink, also. His tongue was already anticipating the smoky peat flavor.

He meandered in that direction, stopping to talk to a few people on the way, but eventually he found them just where Julia said they were, and they weren’t alone.

“Chance!” His dad’s face broke out in an uncharacteristically huge grin as he waved him over. “I want you to meet someone.”

Chance gave his mom a kiss and turned his attention to the woman leaning against the bar.

His dad made the introduction. “This beauty is Dr. Alexis Donovan, Alex Donovan’s daughter—Senator Alex Donovan.”

Damn, Dad! Could you be any more transparent?

Alexis’s cool gray eyes smiled knowingly as she extended her hand. “I’m glad to meet you, Chance. Your dad has told me so much about you.”

Chance took her hand, admiring her firm, confident grip. “It’s nice to meet you, too.”

“I think I mentioned Alexis to you. She’s an ob-gyn with the new clinic.”

“Yes, I think you did.” The mention of ob-gyn brought Kyndal to the front of Chance’s mind, not that she was ever very far from it. Immediately, he started comparing the young woman in front of him to Kyndal.

With her hair pulled back in a tight bun, it was difficult to tell too much about Alexis’s hair. Nothing as gorgeous as Kyndal’s lustrous, ebony mane, at any rate. Her face was square-ish with a nose that was too long and thin to be in correct proportion to her other features. Definitely not “a beauty” by comparison.

“…told him I would introduce her to some people,” his dad was saying when Chance caught up with the conversation.

“And I very much appreciate your doing that.” Alexis’s cool eyes scanned the crowd, and then came back to rest on Chance. She opened her mouth, but his dad jumped in before she could speak.

“What d’ya say we ditch this party and find a quieter place to enjoy a drink?” His eyes swept from Chance to Alexis and then settled on his wife. “Maybe take a stroll down to Max’s?”

Chance caught his groan before it became audible. The happy glint in his mom’s eyes made him realize it was the first time the three of them had ever been out for a drink together. And, if it meant an hour or so of discomfort with his dad trying to cram Alexis down his throat, so be it. The time together as a family would be worth it.

"That sounds good to me," he agreed, and was rewarded with a smile from his mom that warmed him to his toes.

"Me, too." Alexis put down the Scotch she had been sipping. "I much prefer a quieter setting."

They helped the ladies don their coats and stepped back out into the cold night air for the short walk to the bistro. A few flurries had started to fall, swirling in a festive dance under the lights of the parking lot as they made their way across.

"The weatherman said we may have a white Christmas."

Chance smiled at the childlike tone in his mom's voice. He gave her a hug as they walked.

"Oh, hell!" His dad stopped abruptly as they stepped onto Kentucky Avenue.

"What's wrong, Bill?" Emily Brennan's face tightened in concern.

His dad let out an exasperated breath. "I told Dick Hodges we'd talk to him about that lot in Florida before we left. Let's go get that over with." He grabbed his wife's hand and waved to Chance and Alexis. "Y'all go on. We'll meet you there when we're done."

Blindsided by my own dad! Chance gritted his teeth as he watched his parents hustle back across the parking lot.

"Wow! He's good." Alexis gave a chuckle that said she too understood what had just happened.

Chance shook his head in embarrassment. "I'm sorry. He means well."

"I have one just like him at home if that's any consolation."

They laughed together and Chance noticed the tip of

Alexis's nose growing red in the wintry air. "Max's is just down the street." He pointed the way.

"You sure?" She gave him a wary look.

"I'm sure." He looked at his watch. "They'll show up in an hour or so."

"Well, okay. As long as your arm's not hurting too much." Alexis darted across the street.

"My arm?" Chance asked as he caught up with her long stride.

She snorted. "The one that's twisted behind your back."

"Nothing good Scotch can't help."

Alexis agreed and related a short story of her own dad's matchmaking, keeping Chance entertained the rest of the way to the restaurant.

"OH, I ALMOST FORGOT." Kyndal reached into her bag and handed Rick a copy of *Kentucky Wonders Magazine,* gently folded and tied with a wide red ribbon. "This is both Merry Christmas and congratulations to the new—" she paused, raising her glass of club soda, and they all followed her lead by raising their wine glasses and repeating the long title together "—Deputy Director for the Western Kentucky Division of the Federal Department of Wildlife."

Rick blushed again, as he had every time they'd recited the title, making them all laugh again at his modesty.

He pulled the ribbon and the magazine flattened, exposing Kyndal's cover shot. Rick's low whistle of approval was music to her ears, and it was her turn to feel her face grow hot.

"Thanks so much, Kyndal. This is really special." Rick patted her arm affectionately.

Denise snuggled against his other side, and took a long look at the cover. "Is that the cave you and Chance were lost in?"

"That's it." Kyndal nodded.

"It appears quite innocuous, doesn't it?" Denise shuddered dramatically.

Rick winked at Denise. "I thought the same thing about you, sweetheart. You appeared quite innocuous, but..." His shudder, which mimicked hers perfectly, brought on another laugh.

Kyndal was having more fun than she had in a long time, and she was so glad she'd accepted the invitation to join Rick and Denise and Jaci and Bart for Rick's big announcement dinner at Max's. Even if she did feel a bit like a fifth wheel.

After all the drama that had unfolded in her life the past two months, it felt good to be dressed to the nines and laughing with people she cared about. Best of all, it felt good to relax. Today had brought her no closer to a decision about the job in St. Louis, but this evening had certainly made her question whether or not she truly wanted to leave Paducah and her good friends—and Max's blue cheese encrusted filet, which was to die for.

"So when do you think you'll get the office open?" Bart had wolfed down a thick cut pork chop while Kyndal was only on her third bite of her scrumptious entrée.

"We're aiming for the first of February," Rick answered, "but we have a lot of remodeling to do, and the weather could slow us down."

"But Rick will be overseeing the remodeling project, so he'll be moving to Paducah next month." When Denise expressed joy, her voice wasn't nearly so obnoxious, and tonight she'd been thrilled with everything.

Kyndal watched the two couples wistfully. *This is the way it's supposed to be.*

She took another bite as Jaci nudged her in the thigh, her hand hidden by the tablecloth, and Kyndal answered the nudge with a questioning look. Jaci's wide eyes darted toward the window at Kyndal's back.

Kyndal shifted back in her chair to gain the same vantage point of the street Jaci had, and instantly wished she hadn't.

Chance, eyes crinkled in laughter, hair tousled by the wind. His perfectly tailored suit and crisp white shirt enhanced his dark features. He looked as if he'd stepped directly from the pages of *GQ* magazine.

Kyndal's heart leaped to her throat at the sight of him and then plummeted to the pit of her stomach as he held the door to the bar open for a young woman and followed her inside.

Kyndal had told herself this might happen, seeing Chance with someone else. Paducah wasn't a metropolis, so the probability was high. She'd thought she was prepared—had told herself it wouldn't be pleasant, but the discomfort would pass.

It wasn't the first time she'd underestimated her reaction to Chance.

Her heart felt as though it had been ripped out and a block of ice hung in its place. The weight and the cold pressed the air out of her lungs making breathing difficult and speech impossible.

She was afraid to swallow. There was no way the bite of steak in her mouth could make it down her constricted throat, but that was the only way she could keep from bursting into tears. She slipped the bit into her napkin by means of a subtle cough. She reached for her drink to get some moisture into her suddenly dry mouth, but her hand trembled too violently to raise the glass.

This was insane. It was crazy to put herself through this, and these extreme reactions couldn't be good for the baby. She shuddered at the thought of facing Chance this way for another seven months. Who was she kidding? This was going to be her reaction for the rest of her life. Chance was going to fall in love with someone and get married. The effect he had on her was one of those things time would never heal.

Jaci's hand clutched hers, supportive and strong…and in it, Kyndal found the strength to do what needed to be done.

She cleared her throat and rapped lightly on her water glass with her spoon. "I have an announcement of my own."

"Kyn…" Jaci's voice said *don't do this* and Kyndal gave her a look that answered *I have to.*

She forced a smile as she scanned their small group. "I've been offered a job as a pathology photographer at St. Mark's Hospital in St. Louis, and I've decided to take the job."

Jaci's chin quivered and she took a gulp of wine as the others offered their congratulations.

The questions flew at her then as her friends wanted to know all the details. She concentrated on them, answering most of them to herself for the first time.

"I have friends who live in the Clayton area of the city." Denise reached across Rick to pat Kyndal's arm. "Let's contact them and solicit their help to find you a nice place to live."

Kyndal murmured her thanks, knowing she wouldn't be able to afford anything one of Denise's friends would be familiar with.

The waiter took the dinner plates and Kyndal breathed easier. Soon, she would be able to get out of there. Chance and his date were still in the bar, so maybe, if fate was kind, she wouldn't have to face her misery again.

But why would fate want to start being kind now?

"I have a very special surprise dessert," Denise announced as she signaled the maître d'. He nodded, and a minute later a waiter appeared, bearing a silver platter of Baked Alaska covered in sparklers.

The spectacle drew the attention of everyone in the restaurant and the bar, as well. When Chance stepped through the arched passageway between the two rooms just as Denise stood to give Rick a round of applause, Kyndal noticed the quaking of her whole body—the vibration of Fate laughing her ass off.

The events unfolded around her in slow motion, and she watched like a prisoner strapped to a chair, arms and legs too overcome with the weight of emotion to move. Denise waved Chance over. He stepped back in the bar to get his date. The two of them were halfway to the table before he saw Jaci or Kyndal, who were backed into the corner and shielded from view by Rick's hulking figure.

Kyndal recognized the *oh, hell* moment when it registered in Chance's eyes, and she saw the grim set of his mouth when he realized there was nothing he could do but see this through.

"This is really awkward. I'm sorry, Kyndal," Rick whispered and shot her a sympathetic look.

"I'll be okay." But the steak was already starting to rebel in her stomach.

She couldn't decide which would be worse. Having Chance so near and not making eye contact with him, or making eye contact with him and allowing her heart to be run through a shredder. She opted for somewhere in between, making contact in short bursts. Even those seemed like more than her heart could withstand. It beat at a sickeningly fast rate, and her stomach started to churn in rhythm. She sipped cold water, hoping it would help. It didn't.

"Would you like to join us for dessert?" Denise asked

when they finally reached the table. Mercifully, Chance declined. "My mom and dad are meeting us for drinks."

Kyndal chewed her lip to keep it from quivering. This was a woman Chance was proud enough to introduce to people…someone his dad wanted to join for drinks.

Chance started the introductions, and Kyndal prayed they'd go quickly. "Alexis, I'd like you to meet Bart and Jaci Thomas, Kyndal Rawlings—" he slid over her name with no problem, no hint of emotion "—Rick Warren and Denise Macomb. This is Alexis Donovan, an ob-gyn at the new clinic."

Of course she's a doctor. The knife whittling on Kyndal's insides took out a large chunk.

Rick had stood during the introduction and he extended his hand. "Glad to meet you, Alexis. Are you Senator Donovan's daughter?"

The name of her nemesis blew a raspberry Kyndal's direction, and she flinched.

"That would be me." The young woman smiled confidently.

Chance's date is the daughter of the man who kept me from getting the job.

Kyndal gasped at the sting of the final blow. She trembled under the weight of the irony, gut twisting with anger and the excruciating pain of her and Chance's worlds colliding.

She looked anywhere to keep her eyes from connecting with his. Shifting in her seat, she caught her reflection in the window. There was the look in her eyes, the one she knew so well. No doubt about it, she was a woman about to bolt.

"Your dads worked together to get me this appointment." Rick pumped Chance's and Alexis's hands enthusiastically. "I can't thank them enough."

Kyndal stood up abruptly, drawing everyone's attention. "If y'all will excuse me, I've got to run. I'm not feeling well."

She quieted everyone's questions by forcing a smile, refusing to look at Chance. "I'll be okay," she assured them.

Jaci caught her hand. "Do you want me to go home with you?"

Kyndal shook her head. "Please don't. I'll be fine."

She edged her way behind Jaci's and Bart's chairs and had almost pulled off the charade when Denise spoke up. "I'll call you with my friends' names and numbers, Kyndal. They'll be glad to help you find a place, and there are many lovely places in their area of St. Louis."

Chance's head snapped in her direction. "St. Louis?"

She hurried past him toward the door, pretending to be too involved with getting on her coat to hear him.

"Kyndal's taken a job in St. Louis." Denise's voice had reached a new high on the obnoxious scale.

Kyndal was out the door and didn't hear the footsteps behind her, but a hand caught her arm and pulled her to a stop.

"Is this true, Kyn?" Chance's dark eyes pinned her in place.

She nodded. "Yes. I'm moving to St. Louis." Her stomach rolled with a fresh wave of nausea.

"When? When did this happen?" He wasn't angry, as she'd expected. She could read the pain in his eyes, and it made everything so much worse. "Were you even going to tell me?" The pain echoed in his voice.

"Chance, please move. We'll talk later." She stepped around him and picked up her pace toward her car.

"We'll talk now, damn it!" His long strides brought him around in front of her, blocking her way. "You know how hard this will make things, and how much this baby means to me. How can you do this?"

"How can I do this?" She started to laugh and cry at the same time as emotions tumbled around inside her. "How can I *not* do this? You and the senator's daughter are having drinks with your parents."

"It's not what you're thinking, Kyndal. She's not a date. *You* were supposed to be my date. My dad just suggested we all have a drink, and Mom seemed eager, so I agreed."

"And if I had been your date, would we be having drinks with your parents?" She read the answer in his eyes. "Of course not, but she can because she's from your world. I have to make my own world—one that doesn't include being your favorite charity. *That's* why I have to leave here. Now move out of my way. I'm going to throw up." She started to walk away, but he caught her arm and swung her around to face him, holding her other arm in a firm but gentle grip.

The movement was too sudden and too much. She lost the battle for control over the nausea. Before she could warn Chance to move, her dinner came up, spewing the front of Chance's gorgeous, expensive suit.

Horrified, Kyndal became cognizant of people milling on the street and a few gawkers through Max's window. She could imagine the gasps and the collective "ewwws" making their way through the crowd. Her face was already scalding with indignation and humiliation as she wiped her mouth with a clammy hand.

Chance still held her, and she lashed out in anger and embarrassment. "I told you to let me go."

He nodded solemnly. "Yes, you did." His eyes searched hers. "Are you okay?"

"What do you think?" She jerked out of his hold, and stepped off the curb, talking over the tops of the cars until she reached her own. "I've just thrown up in front of a crowd of people, and everybody thinks I'm drunk. I've ruined your expensive suit." She groaned. "Why couldn't you have just let me go when I asked you?"

She opened the door and swung into the driver's seat, anxious to get away from the prying eyes watching the two of them. And more anxious to get away from the look in Chance's eyes.

CHAPTER TWENTY-FOUR

HE HAD TO TALK TO HER. Talk some sense into her. Moving to St. Louis was unacceptable. He had to make her see that.

Chance turned on his heels and broke into a jog down Second Street, nearly flattening his parents in his haste.

"Chance!" His dad grabbed for him, missing. "What the hell are you doing?"

Chance paused. "Gotta catch Kyndal." He wanted to explain his actions to the unspoken question in his mom's eyes, but it would have to wait.

"Where's Alexis? Damn it, Chance, if you've blown things with her so soon—"

"She's in Max's with Rick and Denise." Chance started to jog again. His dad yelled something after him, but he let it go.

He retraced the few blocks back to his office quickly and veered into the parking lot, which was empty except for his SUV.

The drive took less than ten minutes, so when he turned onto Kyndal's street he still was unsure of what to say. A job was of utmost importance to her, and he racked his brain for ideas of where he could help her get one in Paducah. He knew of nothing that could do justice to her talent, but if they put their heads together, maybe they could come up with something.

He slowed the car as he approached the house. No lights on. No car in the driveway.

Damn it! She hadn't come home.

Pulling into her driveway, he convinced himself to wait for a little while. Maybe she'd stopped to pick up something on the way. He called her cell phone which went immediately to voice mail. No surprise there.

He waited, the heater warming the car and causing his coat to reek so badly he had to crack his windows.

He tried to ignore it by turning his mind to how gorgeous Kyndal had looked tonight. A fiery blue sapphire amidst an ocean of black. If the circumstances had been different, he would've stopped in his tracks as he approached her table and drunk her in. She'd never had cleavage like that before. He smiled, realizing the baby was the cause, but then thoughts of the baby being all the way up in St. Louis pinched his heart. He got out of the car and paced, hoping the cold would clear his mind—and his nose.

When she hadn't shown up a half hour later, he started to worry.

Where in the hell was she?

Jaci's.

Bart and Jaci's house was in a new subdivision several miles away. He backed out of the driveway and started the drive to the other side of town.

KYNDAL TURNED OFF THE cell phone after declining Chance's call.

She needed to think without interruption right then, and tonight there was only one place that would afford her that kind of privacy.

She drove down through the floodwall at the foot of Broadway and pulled into a parking space on the banks of the Ohio.

She wasn't the only one who'd thought of it tonight. Paducahans loved their riverfront, and any time day or night, any season of the year, someone would be parked there just watching the river flow by. Tonight, there were people parked and people strolling—not a huge crowd, but enough to give her a safety-in-numbers security.

She let the car idle, cracked her window and put her seat back far enough to relax. The nausea had passed with the help of a cold bottle of water in her car, and although the embarrassment of throwing up on Chance still stung, she felt oddly calm about the entire situation. No, not calm exactly. Numb.

When the numbness wore off, the guilt of moving the baby away from Chance would eat at her, but in the clarity of the moment, she knew she'd made the right choice.

She was leaving Paducah for good this time. The Brennans could have their world to themselves.

They could go to their cocktail parties and dinners and charity events with society's elite, and they could all convince themselves they'd found true happiness based on their monetary worth.

And how sad it would be for them at the end when they learned the true secret of life, the secret the baby had taught her.

Worth had nothing to do with money or success.

The child inside her didn't have a penny, and yet he or she had more worth than everything else combined.

Magazine photographer or toenail fungus photographer—it didn't matter. What mattered was that she, too, was a person of worth because she carried the most important thing in the world inside her.

She was tired. Mentally and physically exhausted. Tired of believing she wasn't good enough. Tired of thinking if she'd done something differently she might be accepted. Tired of trying to please people. Tired of trying to force her way into the lives of people who didn't want her there—and tired of wondering why.

She was a good person—a little on the hardheaded side—but fine the way she was. Her goodness outweighed her flaws by far. She had a deep capacity for love, and she had within her the ability to be a fabulous daughter…daughter-in-law…wife…if she'd been given the opportunity. The people who pushed her out of their lives? It was their loss.

Especially Chance. She loved him, had always loved him, in a way no other person on earth was capable of, yet he chose to not accept that gift because her politics were different or he couldn't take her for who she truly was? How sad for him. She was worth so much more than he would ever know.

A wave of extreme fatigue washed over her. She had to get home before she fell asleep at the wheel.

And, of course, she would have to call Jaci.

Kyndal shifted her seat upright and buckled her seat belt.

Before driving off, she took one last look at the Ohio River.

Yep, it was still there.

Everything would be okay.

CHANCE WAS FRANTIC WITH WORRY. Had Kyndal had car trouble—or God forbid, a wreck?

No one was at home at Jaci and Bart's, and he couldn't imagine where else Kyndal might've gone.

He drove in circles to follow every path she might've taken as he headed back across town to her mom's house, and even called the police station to make sure no collisions had been reported.

When he turned the corner of her street and saw her car

in her driveway, his hands trembled in relief and he sent up a quick prayer of thanks.

His intention was to go in and try and talk some sense into her, but all the lights were off, and he hated to disturb her after such a traumatic night. Her stubborn ways wouldn't allow her to listen to the same old arguments.

He needed a new strategy.

And he needed a shower and a change of clothes because he still reeked of the vomit that clung to his suit.

Most of all, he needed to brush up on Missouri law concerning unwed fathers before he confronted her.

He headed back to his office where he would be able to do all three.

SITTING AT HIS DESK SOMETIME in the middle of the night, Chance came to a realization that made everything he'd been going through seem ridiculous.

Nothing else meant anything if he lost Kyndal Rawlings. Kyndal was his life.

He'd been trying to convince his brain she wasn't the woman for him when all along his heart had known she was the *only* woman for him.

He stared at the plaque on his desk, then read it aloud, his voice echoing through the quiet office. "'Ah, but a man's reach should exceed his grasp, or what's a heaven for?'"

He moved from his desk to the couch and lay down, drifting off to sleep almost instantly with the quote still on his mind.

Kyndal was within his reach. Tomorrow, if he could get her within his grasp, he would know for certain what heaven was for.

CHAPTER TWENTY-FIVE

"MR. BRENNAN?"

A soft voice and a tentative shake woke Chance with a start. His eyes flew open and focused on Alice's concerned face hovering over him.

"Mr. Brennan, Rick Warren is here to see you."

Rick wanted to discuss last night's scene? God, he hoped not. Chance ran his hand vigorously over his face and through his hair a couple of times. "Thanks, Alice. Give me five minutes, then you can send him in."

He rushed to his bathroom, splashed cold water on his face and brushed his teeth. His reflection showed a man badly in need of a shave, but that would have to wait.

When he exited the bathroom, Rick was already seated in one of the chairs by his desk. He rose and extended his hand. "Good morning, Chance."

"Morning, Rick." Chance gave a lopsided grin. "You'll have to excuse my slovenly appearance."

Rick answered with a wary smile. "Tough night, huh?"

"Yeah." Chance massaged the back of his neck as he sat down, grimacing at the muscles that felt like iron bands. "What brings you here on Christmas Eve?"

"Well, I was going to call you later, but I happened by and saw your car. First, I want to apologize for my and Denise's part in last night's fiasco. I hadn't told her about the pregnancy yet, so she had no idea—"

"Please don't apologize. It was no one's fault but my

own." Brain still sluggish with fatigue, Chance didn't want to talk about last night with anyone but Kyndal. He did a quick visual scan, searching for something—anything—he could switch the topic to. He pointed at the magazine in Rick's hand, recognizing it as Kyndal's edition of *Kentucky Wonders*. "Kyn's photos are amazing, aren't they?"

Rick nodded, his smile losing its wary edge. "You have no idea how amazing." He flipped the magazine open to a dog-eared page and pointed to one of the bat pictures. "The bats in your cave, Chance—they're *Myotis sodalis,* commonly known as Indiana bats." The excitement in his voice was palpable. "That's a highly endangered species."

Chance studied the close-up of the tiny creature flying directly into the camera and shifted in his seat as the memory of holding Kyndal assaulted his senses.

"That means the Department of Wildlife will take whatever steps are necessary to protect them."

"'Whatever steps are necessary'?" Chance didn't like the sound of that. "Are you saying they'll take my cave away from me?"

"No, nothing like that." Rick stood up as Alice brought in a tray with coffee and some Christmas cookies.

The gentlemanly action caught Chance off guard. He rose to his feet sheepishly and thanked her.

As they fixed their coffee Chance urged Rick to continue, anxious to hear more.

"The bats could die if they're disturbed during hibernation." Rick picked up where he'd left off. "The best way we've found to keep them from being disturbed is to keep everything out of the caves where they hibernate, and the best method we've found for doing that is a custom-made chain guard."

Chance still wasn't sure where this conversation was headed. "Go on."

"The guard is fitted and permanently attached to the entrance with locks at the bottom. As the owner, you'd have the key, of course. The guard can be unlocked and rolled up during the months the bats aren't hibernating, but when they start settling in, it has to stay down. It's designed of small squares so they can move through either way, but it keeps predators, and people, out."

The possibility of securing the cave brought Chance a surge of hope. "Could it stay down all the time? I've had a lot of trouble with vandalism."

"Yeah. Kyndal told me."

Chance flinched inwardly at Rick's mention of her name. Damn, he wanted to see her.

Rick seemed not to notice, caught up in the excitement of what he was saying. "Keeping it down except for when you want to go in wouldn't be a problem. As far as the vandalism, the department will deal with that. Causing harm to an endangered species carries a hefty fine and sometimes imprisonment. There'll be signs posted and cameras installed. And vandalizing one of the cameras would be a big mistake for anybody, too."

Chance's gut twisted with guilt. So Kyndal's photos—the ones he'd blamed her for publishing—were actually going to be what saved the cave. He was losing count of the number of apologies he owed her. *What an ass I've been.* He turned another page of the magazine to a photo of the crystal vug in all its splendor. *And what a woman she is.* He sighed and shook his head at the twist in fate this Christmas Eve morning had brought him. "You've given me some fabulous news, Rick."

"Well, I'm glad I could do something to make up a little bit for the horrible position I put y'all in last night." Rick shook his head, his chin buckling. "I still can't believe it was Senator Donovan who kept Kyndal from getting that job."

"What?" Chance leaned over his desk, feeling alert for the first time since Alice shook him awake.

"Yeah. I talked to Jaci this morning. Kyndal told her the whole story last night after…well, you know." Rick sipped his coffee before continuing. "Kyndal was the first choice for the magazine job, but somebody called in a favor with Donovan, and he had the job handed to somebody else."

Oh, hell…surely not. His dad and the senator had been together a lot lately securing Rick's new position. Chance laid the cookie in his hand back on his plate as his stomach gave a sickening lurch.

"I feel awful about making a big deal to his daughter about my gratitude. Hell-pee-roo. Can you imagine how that made Kyndal feel? The irony must have stung something terrible, poor kid. But she kept her poise, didn't she? Didn't say anything. Just excused herself. She's got a lot of class, that one."

His revelation pounded at Chance's brain. He grabbed the tennis ball from his desk and started to squeeze. "Yes, she does," he agreed. "More class and spunk and grit than any woman I've ever known."

"You've got it." Rick took a long drink of his coffee, and then set the cup and saucer to the side and folded his napkin. "Well, I've got Christmas shopping to finish, so I'd better get out of here."

The proper action as a host would have been to protest and act like he wanted some more friendly chat, but Chance was chomping at the bit to confront his dad. He stood, relieved to see Rick pick up his magazine and make a move toward the door. "Don't buy anything for me, Rick." He forced a jovial laugh. "You've given me a great present already."

They exchanged a heartfelt handshake. "Merry Christmas, Chance."

"Merry Christmas, Rick." Chance clapped him on the back in parting. "Give Denise a hug for me."

As soon as his friend was out the door, Chance headed straight for his dad's office, charging in without bothering to knock. "Tell me you didn't sabotage Kyndal on the magazine job." He slammed the door behind him.

Bill Brennan looked up, startled. He dropped his eyes back to the legal pad he was writing on. "I didn't sabotage Kyndal on the magazine job."

Chance placed his hands flat on the desk and leaned over so their heads were on the same level. "Look me in the eye and tell me you didn't sabotage Kyndal on the magazine job."

His dad threw down his pen, raising his eyes to meet Chance's. "Now maybe she'll leave town."

So it was true. Chance knew it but up until the admission he'd held a flicker of hope. Now he could sense the inferno behind that flicker about to explode. "Oh, she's leaving." He flared his nostrils to get more air. "She's taken a job in St. Louis."

"Good. Then it's for the best." His dad picked up the pen as if he was finished talking and started scribbling again.

"Seriously?" Chance whisked the legal pad out from under the pen and tossed it into the chair beside him. "You take a young woman who's an amazing photographer and the best qualified for the job, who happens to be pregnant with your *grandchild* and you work against her?" He modulated his volume. "You jerk a job out of her hands by calling in a favor after she risked her life to get it? And then you sit back and say 'It's for the best'? Is that really your answer?"

"You're damn straight it's my answer." His dad's voice

raised a few decibels. "It's my answer when I'm watching my only son talk himself into a mistake he'll regret the rest of his life."

Chance slammed his palm down on the pile of papers. "It's not a 'mistake.' It's a baby. *My* baby."

"It's a baby that will tie you to the wrong woman and *that's* a mistake that'll affect your career. A career I've busted my ass to build. A career I've spent hundreds of thousands to make possible with your Harvard education and this practice." Bill Brennan rose to his feet, his eyes only inches from his son's. "You think money's not important? You think all this—" he waved his arms around the room "—just happens? You think that judgeship you have your eye on will just happen?"

"I want the judgeship so people like Kyndal will get a fair shake. Right now, they don't stand a chance because people like you keep them down and they don't have the power to fight back." Chance was too angry to mince words. "The truck driver with Hank's case… Judge Salter crucified him and you sat back and let him, knowing it wasn't that poor guy's fault. Salter closed his eyes to justice because of you and your damn connections."

Hank's case had never been allowed as a topic of discussion, and this time was no different. "You're nothing without the right connections. I've always tried to tell you, it's not what you know, but who you know." His dad's eyes hardened, but for the first time, Chance could see behind them into the workings of his mind. "Kyndal…she's not what you want in your life. She's never had a pot to piss in or one to throw it out of, and she never will."

Chance broke into a sweat. He pulled the sweater over his head and hurled it at the door. "She has more ambition than both of us put together. How many teenagers do you know who would get themselves out of bed and to school if their parents weren't home to make them? Kyn did, and was valedictorian. She takes care of herself, takes any job she can just to make ends meet and works her ass off." The truth in what he was saying hit him like a fist to his gut. He spread his arms, indicating the costly office, the expensive furniture. "You've given me everything I've ever had and ever needed." He leaned forward on the desk again, and lowered his voice. "Nobody's ever given her anything—including a fair shake."

"People make their own destiny. That girl made hers when she spread her legs for you."

Chance stood to his full height and thrust a finger toward his dad's face. "Shut up, damn it!" He'd never yelled at his dad before. This was a new experience for both of them. He watched his dad's mouth close. "She's not 'that girl' and she's not 'the wrong woman.' She's the woman I love, and I won't have you talk about her like she's some kind of whore. She's carrying my baby, and I hope to make her my wife. That's right, Dad! I intend to propose to her as many times as it takes to get her to accept…and that may be a lot considering how we've hurt her."

"Be reasonable. Think about what you're saying, Hank."

The name barreled through Chance like a windstorm, sweeping away the last of his self-control. "I'm. Not. Hank!" He roared the words he'd wanted to say for ten years, punctuating them by punching his chest with his finger. "I'm *Chance.* Hank is dead, Dad. He's gone forever, and he's never coming back. I can't be him for you. I can only be me. You've got to decide once and for all if that's going to be good enough for you because I can't be both of us anymore."

Bill Brennan felt for the chair behind him and lowered himself into it as Chance continued. "And you'd better decide quickly because if you don't think you can fit my wife and baby into your scheme of things, I'll be leaving this firm to go out on my own."

Chance had to make him understand, so he laid it out as clearly as he could. "If you can't accept Kyndal, Dad, then you'll not only have lost Hank. You'll lose me, too, and you'll lose your grandchildren." He gathered up his sweater. "Now, if you'll excuse me, I'll give you some time to think about what I've just told you. I have some last-minute Christmas shopping to do, and then I'm going to try and convince the woman I love more than life itself to spend the rest of her days with me."

Bill Brennan sat silently.

Chance walked out, having had the last word with his dad for the first time ever.

WHEN HER PHONE RANG THAT morning, Jaci didn't bother to look at the call display. The business was closed for the long holiday weekend, and, surely, no one would have a decorating crisis that required attention on December 24th. She'd already spoken with Kyndal—twice—so that only left one probability.

"Hey, Mom," she answered.

"Not yet." Erlene Moore's laugh came over the line. "Still hanging in there, though."

Jaci joined her laughter. "Sorry, Erlene."

"No problem. Hey, I won't keep you long. Just a quick question."

"Sure. Whatcha need?"

"A kitten?" Erlene's voice lowered to almost a whisper. "Cody's been talking about the kittens since you were here that day, and we just decided this morning to get one for his stocking. Are yours available for adoption?"

"I...um." Jaci's heart thudded so hard she felt it in

her stomach. "I don't know. I mean…we haven't talked about it."

"I know how attached you are, but we would give it a good home. We have plenty of space. And we're all animal lovers."

Jaci's knees went weak, and she slid into the nearest chair. She should have known that this time would come. She just hadn't allowed herself to think about it.

Bart came into the kitchen. His eyes met hers and widened with concern. "What's wrong?" he mouthed.

"Can you hold a minute, Erlene? Bart just came in. Let me see what he thinks." Jaci covered the receiver with a shaking hand. "It's Erlene Moore. She wants a kitten for Cody's stocking."

Bart's eyes went even wider. "One of ours? Have you lost your mind?"

Relief flooded through her. She quickly spoke back into the phone. "We're too attached to give either of them up, Erlene. But my friend Kyndal works at Pet Me. I know they have several kittens there who need a good home."

"Okay. We'll try there. Thanks, Jaci."

She was gone before Jaci could say goodbye.

Bart moved toward her slowly, with a smile that was both wicked and sweet. "That would be like giving away our firstborn."

Jaci laughed at his words that echoed her own thoughts. She stood up to meet him, throwing her arms around his neck and pulling him close. "I don't know what I ever did to deserve you." Tears of joy warmed her cheeks, and she became aware of tiny paws with playful claws swiping at the hem of her pajama bottoms.

She reached down to scoop up Arwen just as Bart did the same with Gandalf. They bumped heads lightly and laughed at their clumsiness.

She held the little female out to him. "Merry Christmas, Mr. Thomas."

Bart took the black fur ball and offered her Gandalf the Gray, in return. "And Merry Christmas to you, too, love."

Then he kissed her, and his kiss left no doubt it was going to be a Merry Christmas, indeed.

DECEMBER 24 AND KYNDAL couldn't imagine that this many people still had shopping to do. She'd finished weeks ago, but, of course, she only had three presents to buy. The line of people waiting to get their pet's photo with Santa had been short but steady all morning, which was good because it kept her mind off the events of last night.

At the moment, she was pondering if she might've died and gone to purgatory somewhere between home and the store. The terrified look on Santa Howard's face reminded her of Michelangelo's depiction of lost souls. He definitely had that look that he might bolt, and she wouldn't blame him if he did.

Howard's white knuckles gripped the chair arm, and she sensed he was determining whether to swat or not to swat. Her skin crawled each time the horrid thing moved, inching its way slowly up Howard's arm. Why would anyone in his right mind have a freakin' tarantula for a pet? And why in the world would he want its picture with Santa Claus?

She aimed the camera, closed her eyes and fired off four shots. A quick peek showed she had the image. She let out her breath and announced, "Done." A trickle of sweat ran between her breasts.

Only Mandy seemed unfazed by the ordeal. She took the print as it came out of the printer and slid it into the Christmas card frame, attaching the receipt. "You pay for this at checkout," she instructed the tarantula's owner who was making cooing sounds toward the cage. Mandy then turned her attention to Kyndal with an annoyed sigh. "Okay, I'm outta here. I'm twenty-three minutes past break now."

The store manager's voice came over the loud speaker. "Kyndal Rawlings, please come to the manager's office. Kyndal Rawlings, come to the manager's office, please."

Mandy's growl brought a smile to Kyndal's lips. She shrugged. "Sorry." But she really wasn't. Her smile broadened when she caught herself humming "Jingle Bells" along with the music coming over the loud speakers.

The manager's office was a small glassed-in enclosure at the front of the store. She hurried that direction until the office came into view and then her steps slowed. Chance. In the office chatting with the owner. Her heart flip-flopped before bouncing into that quick rhythm it always hit when he was near.

Why was he there? If he expected her to pay for his ruined suit, she would remind him what happened was his fault. She'd warned him.

She jerked the door open and stepped into the small space, ready to field whichever ball he threw her way.

"Kyndal." His eyes looked tired as they took her in, and he was unshaven, which made his features even darker and more brooding. But he smiled that infuriatingly, gorgeous smile, and instantly her brain went fuzzy.

"I'll leave you two alone." Nancy hustled out, and her absence seemed to make the walls close in tighter.

Kyndal didn't trust the look in his eye…or the way his presence seemed to engulf her space. "What do you want, Chance?" She tapped her foot in annoyance. The tinkling bell on the tip of her toe ruined the desired effect. She watched one side of Chance's full mouth lift, so she stopped tapping and crossed her arms instead.

His expression turned serious. "I just found out Dad

worked against you on the magazine job, and I came to apologize, Kyn. I know how hard you worked, and how much you wanted that job. I'm sorry you were treated so unfairly." The contrition in his voice sounded sincere.

Kyndal remained outwardly cool, despite the mixed emotions swarming through her body. "If you want me to say it's okay, you're in for a long wait, Counselor. I *was* treated unfairly. But I'll survive." She placed her hand on the door handle. "I have clients waiting. Thanks for the apology."

"Wait!" In two strides, Chance stood beside her, his hand covering hers, holding the door closed. His familiar scent mixed with the cold from his clothes, filling the space between them and depriving her of air. She pulled her hand from the door and stepped away to gain some distance from him. "There's more I want to say. I'm sorry for the way I've treated you." His deep voice hummed with emotion. "The truth is..." He hesitated, ran his hand through his hair. "I love you, Kyndal." His words gave her a claustrophobic feeling. She breathed deeply, fighting for her share of the oxygen in the tiny space.

His eyes held hers as he went on. "I love you, but I've been afraid to love you. I've snubbed you, thinking you weren't good enough to have a part in my dreams."

A flash of anger tore through Kyndal, hearing the truth spoken so brazenly. She opened her mouth to speak, but her breath sputtered to a stop when Chance took a step toward her.

"But I know now that I don't have any dreams without you."

Sweet words, but they didn't change anything. "Your dad has enough for both of you," she assured him. "And I'm not in any of his."

His full lips pressed into a thin line. "Dad and I had a

meeting of the minds this morning. I'm never going to be the kind of man he wants me to be, thank God. I've got some changing to do, but Dad's got more if he wants to remain in my life—and in his grandchild's life."

Kyndal's heart softened at the mention of the baby. Chance must have sensed the weakness because he stepped near enough to brush a finger down her arm, leaving a tremor of emotion in its wake.

"I want us to be a family, Kyn. You, me and the baby."

Kyndal squeezed her eyes closed. She wanted to believe him, but she'd believed him before. She opened her eyes and looked at him through her blurred vision. He'd been brutally honest; she could be, too. "I'm tired of trying to be what other people want and always falling short. I can only be who I am." She tapped her chest with the tip of her finger. "I have fears, too, Chance. Fears of not fitting into your life. Fears of trusting you. And fears of driving you away." He reached out to her, but she moved out of his reach, far enough away to not be swayed his touch. "I don't know how to love without clinging," she admitted. "And when I cling—and I would if we were together—you wouldn't be able to breathe, and then you'd leave just like before. Nothing's changed, Chance. It's never going to work."

She understood Chance's feelings of suffocation then because suddenly she was in a vacuum, and all the air in the room was being sucked out. She needed air. She pushed past him, through the door, and out into the front of the store.

"Kyndal! Stop right there." His authoritative voice boomed out behind her. "We're not finished. Don't you dare take another step away from me."

She stopped and turned to face him. In fact, everyone in the store stopped and turned to face him. The lines at the cash registers went silent. The only sound was the combined voices of Alvin and the Chipmunks singing "The Christmas Song."

Chance's voice grew loud as if he *wanted* everyone to hear him. "It's true, Kyndal. I left you when I was eighteen years old. But I only left you *physically.* My heart never left. It's been with you—and only you—since the day we met. That's *clinging. Love* is clinging. Clinging together forever. Never letting go. Never leaving. And you don't have to worry about fitting into my world. You *are* my world."

Kyndal could swear she heard a collective sigh move through the crowd of onlookers.

His eyes pinned her to the spot as he closed the space between them, grasping her arms in a firm hold. The touch broke through her control, smashing her resolve into tiny pieces and scattering them about her feet.

"I've got to know, Kyndal." He leaned down to look in her eyes, his warm breath catching on her lashes. "Do you love me?"

She caught her bottom lip between her teeth, dropping her eyes from the gaze that held so much love she could hardly bear to look. Her heart swelled as his warm hands cupped her cheeks and raised her face.

"Do you love me, Kyndal?" he repeated.

She gazed into the espresso depths that had melted her heart at first glance. "You know I do," she answered. "I've never stopped loving you."

"Do you want to be with me?" He paused, and she saw him swallow. "Think about it, because I'm talking about forever."

She swallowed, too, and nodded. "That's all I've ever wanted."

He smiled, and his dark eyes flashed with emotion. "Then I have one more question."

When Chance dropped to one knee in front of her, a sob exploded from her lungs, and she started to tremble. Could this really be happening? She watched in wonder as he took a small box from his pocket and out of the box he produced a ring with a diamond that sparkled more brightly than any of the surrounding holiday lights.

She swayed, but he took her hand, and she knew then that this was Chance in the flesh—no dream, but he was about to make every dream she'd ever had a reality.

"Kyndal Elizabeth Rawlings—" his deep voice suffused her, became a part of her "—I love you and the child you're carrying with the most perfect love I've ever known, and I want to have the two of you beside me for the rest of our lives. Will you marry me?"

Kyndal's heart swelled as joy poured in and stretched it wide. This was the way it was supposed to be. This was the love that would last forever. The one that would never leave.

"Yes," she answered.

Chance stood up and she rushed into his outstretched arms. He laughed and she cried and his mouth pressed to hers in a kiss that was the stuff of dreams.

A wild cheer erupted around them as the customers broke into a spontaneous show of jubilation. And with perfect timing, the Mormon Tabernacle Choir blessed the union with a joyous "Hallelujah" booming from the speakers.

EPILOGUE

Nineteen months later

"DID SHE INDICATE HOW long the process could take?" Kyndal set the Winnie the Pooh cake on the tray and arranged the three cupcakes to look like balloons, running their strings to Pooh's hand.

Jaci poured herself a handful of peanuts from the bag. "She said the average adoption from their agency takes around two years. Could be more…could be less. In the meantime, we're going to keep trying the old way."

Kyndal gave her a wink. "There's easy access to the ancient fertility room now, if y'all want to give it a try."

Rick's hunches had turned out to be correct. The depression in the backyard was the cave-in she and Chance encountered at the end of their cave odyssey. Her husband had called in a storm shelter company, who made quick work of digging out the area, shoring up the walls with concrete, pouring a set of steps leading down to the area, and putting in a door.

Not only did they now have a large storm shelter, but easy access to the ancient room, and a second entrance to the cave, as well.

Jaci snorted. "You could rent it out nightly and make a lot of money."

Kyndal laughed. She wouldn't admit it even to her best

friend, but the room had become a favorite getaway when she and Chance had some time alone.

Jaci seemed to read her thoughts. She shook her head as she stuck one candle into the blue cupcake. "Y'all keep this up, and you're going to end up with a litter."

Chance came through the door in time to catch the end of the conversation. "A litter?" His dark eyes grew wide. "Chesney's not in heat again, is she?"

Kyndal and Jaci laughed, and Kyndal shook her head. "Chesney's still a virgin, Dad."

"Whew." His face relaxed. He moved behind Kyndal, snaking his arms around her waist and leaning down to nibble her ear.

The movement sent a pleasant tingle from her neck downward—a feeling she would never grow tired of. "Are the natives getting restless?" she asked.

"Hank and Chesney are keeping everybody entertained. Chesney's keeping Bart, Denise and Rick busy throwing the Frisbee. Mom's bouncing Hank on her knee, and Dad is plying him with Cheerios, bound and determined his first word is going to be *grandpa.*"

Kyndal pointed to the tray with the lemonade and cups. "Would you get those, Jaci?" She turned and gave Chance a quick kiss. "And if you'll take this tray, I'll grab my camera. The lighter's over there on the counter."

The small procession started down the steps leading from the back door to the patio. Emily Brennan started singing "Happy Birthday," and everybody joined in as she placed Hank in his high chair.

Kyndal's heart twinged for a moment. Her mom was missing so many things, but Kyndal wouldn't let it ruin this special day—or any more days. The woman was making her choices. She'd have to live with them.

The twinge passed quickly as Hank gave a delighted

squeal when he saw the cake and stretched out his chubby hands. With his dark hair and darker eyes, he was the spitting image of his father…and he melted Kyndal's heart.

Chance helped blow out the candle, and Hank dug into the chocolate cupcake, smearing blue icing from his forehead past his chin. His giggles filled the air, and Kyndal took shot after shot, each one cuter than the next.

When they settled down to their own pieces of cake, Chance took the camera away from her. "I want my beautiful wife chronicled at this event, too."

Bill Brennan became a different person when he was around Hank. It never ceased to amaze Kyndal how the child coaxed the gentleness out from behind that coarse exterior.

"Say 'grandpa,' Hank." Bill held out a bite of cake. "Can you do that? Can you say 'grandpa'?"

"Ggggggg," Hank answered.

"Kyndal." Rick leaned across the picnic table and tapped her hand. "We found a group of orange-foot pimplebacks yesterday that had been suffocated by zebra clams. Would you be able to take some photos for us to use? We're trying to get some additional funding for relocation."

"Oh, good God," Bill muttered under his breath. He leaned toward his grandson. "Hank, can you say 'treehugger'?"

Hank giggled. "Teehuh."

The group went silent.

Hank beat his palms on the tray, flattening chunks of cake and spraying a happy Chesney with a shower of chocolate crumbs. "Teehuh!" he shouted, obviously enjoying being once again the center of attention.

Kyndal squeezed her eyes shut and shook her head. "Please tell me my son's first word was not *tree hug.*"

A roar of laughter met her ears with her father-in-law's guffaw loudest of all.

"Oh, Lord," she groaned. "Hank didn't just inherit his dad's looks, he got his politics, too."

A warm arm circled her shoulder and pulled her in close, her mother-in-law's whisper feathering across her ear. "Don't worry, sweetheart, he's going to have your way with words."

* * * * *

COMING NEXT MONTH
from Harlequin® SuperRomance®
AVAILABLE SEPTEMBER 4, 2012

#1800 THE ROAD TO BAYOU BRIDGE
The Boys of Bayou Bridge
Liz Talley

Newly discharged from the navy, Darby Dufrene is ready to settle down. But not anywhere close to his family home in Louisiana. Then he discovers something that ties him here—and to his high school sweetheart Renny Latioles—much more than he imagined!

#1801 OUT OF BOUNDS
Going Back
Ellen Hartman

The budget from a fundraiser has been embezzled and Posy Jones tries to fix it before anyone finds out. Unfortunately, Wes Fallon has been appointed head of this charity. He's determined to prove himself and she's running out of excuses to avoid him!

#1802 PLAYING THE PART
Family in Paradise
Kimberly Van Meter

As an actress, Lindy Bell is used to drama. But she gets more than she bargains for when she butts heads with sexy single dad Gabe Weston.

#1803 THE TRUTH ABOUT TARA
Darlene Gardner

Tara Greer doesn't want to know if she was kidnapped as a child. To protect her mother—and herself—she must fight her attraction to Jack DiMarco, the man who could force her to face the truth.

#1804 THE WOMAN HE KNOWS
Margaret Watson

Darcy Gordon is on the run. If she gets complacent or tells anyone who she really is, her freedom—and even her life—will be at risk. So getting close to sexy FBI agent Patrick Devereux is a very bad idea....

#1805 SEEKING SHELTER
Angel Smits

Amy Grey lives one day at a time—no looking forward, and definitely no looking back. But when Jace Holmes rides into town on his motorcycle with surprising news, he turns the single mom's carefully constructed life on its head.